IMAGINE A GREAT WHITE LIGHT

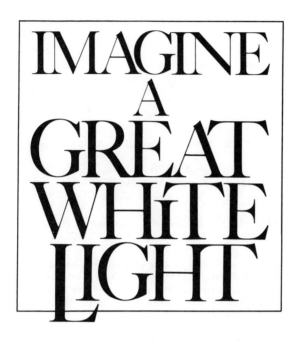

IMAGINE A GREAT WHITE LIGHT

STORIES BY SHEILA SCHWARTZ
WINNER OF THE EDITORS' BOOK AWARD

PUSHCART PRESS

Winner of the Ninth Annual Editors' Book Award

Copyright © 1991 by Sheila Schwartz
ISBN 0-916366-67-7
LC—90-063922

Sponsoring Editors: Simon Michael Bessie, James Charlton, Peter Davison, Jonathan Galassi, David Godine, Daniel Halpern, James Laughlin, Seymour Lawrence, Starling Lawrence, Robie Macauley, Joyce Carol Oates, Nan A. Talese, Faith Sale, Ted Solotaroff, Pat Strachan, Thomas Wallace. Bill Henderson, Publisher.

Nominating Editor for this book: Lynne McFall

These works are fiction and no reference is intended to real persons, places or circumstances.

The following stories have appeared in these magazines: "Double Lives" in *Atlantic Monthly*. "Mutatis Mutandis" in *Crazyhorse*. "The Blue Coat" in *MSS*. "A Tough Life" in *TriQuarterly*. "Imagine a Great White Light" in *Sequoia*. "Passover" in *MSS*.

FOR MY PARENTS: RUTH AND PHILIP SCHWARTZ

Contents

IMAGINE A GREAT WHITE LIGHT

MUTATIS MUTANDIS

(LOVE)

There was evening and there was morning the sixth day, and for what? So that she, Miriam, could walk alone to her bunk every night while the others groped and rustled in the dark, so that her only friend, Renee, could ditch her just like that for a creep named Harvey Haas, so that Chaim Picker could torment her ceaselessly, interminably, with his obscure, a priori liking?

Everyone else that summer got smoke in his eyes, got satisfaction, got do-wa-diddy-diddy-dum-diddy-do. Not her. Not mutatis (though not yet mutandis) Miriam. All she got was, "Nu, Miriam?" All she got was the correct answer every time she raised her hand. All she got was taller and taller. (Five feet ten and who knew when it would stop? Tall like a *model,* her mother always said. An attractive girl. Only thirteen years old and so shapely. Wait!)

But there was no end in sight. Too big, too smart, and on top of all this—the teacher's pet (a real *drip* in other words). It was a simple concept with a simple proof: Chaim Picker was a real drip. Chaim Picker liked her. Ergo, *she* was a real drip.

And so the proofs of *his* drippiness, clear and manifold.

For one thing, he spoke way too many languages all of which were queer. According to the others, his Hebrew was queer, his Yiddish was queer, his English was *totally* queer. (What was all that "Omnipresence" stuff, anyway?) To make things even worse, he wore the exact same thing every single day—a creepy black suit, black shoes, black yarmulkah, and tsitsit (the *epitome* of queerness). When he lectured the tsitsit swayed with him, back and forth, back and forth, Baruch HaShem Amen V'Amen! As far as anyone knew, these fringes were the only things he had ever kissed, in the morning when he put them on, and in the evening when he lay himself down to sleep.

Miriam saw him differently. He wasn't really a drip, just an "anachronism" (as she had discovered in one of her recent forays through the dictionary). For Chaim, it was clear, reminders of God and his commandments were everywhere, not only in the ceremonial fringes he wore, but in the whoosh of pine trees, in the birds flying overhead, even in his tea glass, spoon handle pointing upward like the metal finger of God, admonishing.

A bachelor, born circa 1930, he had a propensity for closed spaces and esoteric questions. Witness the inordinate amount of time spent in his tiny cabin. Witness the thick curtains on his windows, the hours spent in the library studying. Witness (they had no choice) his probing technique in class.

They groaned. Good Lord, more questions! He was going to kill them with all his questions. At every damned word he had to stop and wonder: who what where when and why, and sometimes why again. WHY does it say "in the beginning"? Hasn't everything always been here forever and eternally? So where did this "beginning" come from? And how could God precede it?

And furthermore. What is meant by "the face of the deep"? Wasn't this "face" covered by darkness? And wasn't it also empty and formless, but still visible in the "darkness"? (If it was *truly* darkness). And how could this "darkness" *and* the spirit of God move upon the waters or whatever they were at the same time and in the same place and did this imply identity? And if so then what is meant by "in the beginning"? Miriam? Good, Miriam. *Correct.* For him, nothing in the stupid book was just simply what it was. Nothing in the whole damned world.

It was true, Miriam thought. Everything had its layers, its surfaces, its unexpected depths, even the riddle he asked them every day at the start of class: "Nu, children. What is the meaning of 'peel'?" Even the answer Barry Sternberg gave for the twenty-fifth straight day, "Miriam" instead of the true meaning "elephant." (Though it might seem otherwise, Chaim explained to her one day after class, Barry really was a good boy, he meant no harm by his remarks. "He's a sick boy," Chaim had said, "a boy with many problems. He needs people to pay attention, and not just *you*. Whom do you think has been scribbling on the walls all summer long? And other pranks I am not at liberty to mention. Just try to ignore him, Mireleh. The more any of us pays attention, the more he'll keep on doing it.")

Barry popped up and took a bow.

"Sternberg," Chaim said.

"What?"

Chaim pointed to the bench.

"Who *me*?" Barry pretended to be astonished. He spread his arms wide to capture his amazement. "What did I do? What in the 'H' did I do?" he asked the class.

"Please sit down."

"Why?"

"Sternberg. You may leave or you may sit down. *Choose*." Chaim placed both palms flat on the table.

Barry pointed. "The right one," he said.

"Sternberg!"

"The left?"

"OK OK OK," Chaim told him. "That was an

interesting exercise. You have made for us a good variation on the state of innocence and on the meaning of will. But now, *we* will go on." He clasped his hands behind his back. "Nu, children?" He turned toward the class. "And vus is 'peel'?" His smile was hopeful. He waited.

"Oy!" Barry flopped back onto the bench. "Oy oy oy!" He shook his head. "These Jews. These Jews! They are *just never* SATISFIED." Then he went into his act. He made his eyes blink, made his jaws click-clack together. "Nu, Meereyum." His voice came out slow and underwater. "Why don't youuuu tell us vussss." As though drowning in precision, he sank to another octave. "Cumpute it for him, Meeeeeer-ee-yummmmmmmmm."

They burst out laughing.

"Sternberg, *leave.*"

"Shtarenbeerg, *liv!*" Barry flapped his hands. Shoo! His grin implied a cheering crowd. He made no move to leave.

"OK OK. My accent is very funny; it's very funny indeed, I agree. There's truth in everything," Chaim said. "So, therefore, one more chance, Sternberg. This is Erev Shabbat and I'm giving you the benefit. Now what is 'peel-pool'?" He bent forward and nodded as if nudging him the correct answer.

Which gathered on Barry's face into a big, knowing grin. "An elephant pool—where Miriam swims." He sprang up from the table. "Shtarenbeerg—*LIV!*"

They laughed.

*   *   *   *   *

Miriam tried to ignore them, she tried to ignore Barry as Chaim had asked her to. After class he had repeated what he'd said before. "No matter how disturbing these events seem, we must pretend we don't notice. He's a child crying just to hear the sound of his own voice, a sad boy, a very very unhappy human being." And when she hadn't been convinced ("But why does he always pick on *me?*") he had added, "Listen, Mireleh. You are my best student. It's a shame that he spoils your concentration so I'll tell you a secret—for your ears alone, fashtays-tu?" When she'd nodded, he took hold of her hand, as if to prevent her from running in horror when she heard the truth. "Barry is an orphan," he whispered. "*Both* his parents at once—a terrible misfortune. He lives with his aunt. She's been very generous, but he has never gotten used to his fate. For this reason he sees a psychiatrist. A *psychiatrist*," he repeated. "You understand what this means? It's crucial for us to set a good example."

She tried, but it was difficult. Every day Barry sat down next to her. "Sha-loom, Meereyum." Winking to the class, he sprawled himself out until he was so close she could feel his tanned arms and legs glistening against her own pale ones, rubbing sweat. Every time she moved over, he moved over too until there was no place on the bench to sit. She tried to ignore him. She remembered what Chaim had said: "It is better to be persecuted than to persecute others." She tried to believe him. She stared at her hands, and at the trees, and at the big heart carved into the wooden table. *RANDY & JOSH IN '63.*

That was the way the summer went; this was the pattern of love. Someone looked at you in services, in class, at dinner. Three times (a holy number). His friends noticed. They kidded him and giggled. *Your* friends heard about it and they told *you*. You blushed and shrugged your shoulders, not yes, not no. Sometime later (after a movie, or lunch, or Friday night dancing on the tennis courts) you heard footsteps on the path behind you, a voice which leapt to life in your ear, "Wanna take a walk?" Sometime later, the ID bracelet, a binding silver promise on your wrist. (Or was it the ID first and *then* the walk?)

That was the way it went and it happened to these people: David Stein and Leslie Gold. Yitzi Feinberg and Shira Oster. Josh Blum and Karen Bregman. Bennet Twersky and Susan Gould. The boys from Bunk 3 and the girls from Bunk 19. The kitchen help and Gladys Ticknor. Stacy Plisky and everyone. Once it almost happened to her, but it was only Norman Levine, the boy with the slide rule.

Still, even love with a slide rule was permissible in certain cases. According to the Talmud there were many faces to love—some smiling, some weeping. Love could be a wind, a deep well; it could be a tiger waiting to spring.

That was all well and good, but *this* was nothing

of the kind. According to Leo Goelman, the camp director, love was one thing, *neetzool* was another. He gave them a long lecture about it the morning that this sign was discovered painted on the library wall:

SUZY CREAMCHEESE—WHAT'S GOT INTO YOU?

Whoever had done this, Leo Goelman shouted, had no idea what love meant, not a clue. Real love was sacred. It was not something to joke about. What *this* prankster had in mind was something else— "neetzool" he reiterated. "Neetzool" meant *exploitation,* a lack of respect, a lack of individuality. "Neetzool" was what you felt like doing with anyone at all.

His interpretation discouraged no one.

Every night there was the same rush for the woods, the same giggling in the bathrooms afterwards. Every night Miriam listened to Shira and Renee whispering about what they had done (always just loud enough for her to hear, just soft enough to make her feel that she was eavesdropping).

"We went to second. What did you guys do?"

"Only first."

Everything was euphemism. First base. Second base. Making out. Popping flies. Once Shira looked at her and laughed. "You don't know what we're talking about, do you?"

When they got between the rough, white camp sheets, instead of saying their prayers, they thought of what they had done, of what they might do tomorrow. They dreamed of scratchy bark against their backs, and later, eventually, of their names carved into that bark.

Miriam saw things differently.

They would meet somewhere, in a park, in a cafe, in the rain. He would be wearing a long coat, military style, black, but not as black as his hair which was blue-black, seething with midnight. He would smoke thin cigars and know everything there was to know about poetry and film. Whatever he stared at, he would stare at intently. "Ah! A reader," he would say. "That's good. A woman who thinks." His eyes would linger on her face.

She would hand him her copy of *Steppenwolf* and he would turn the pages slowly, his unnaturally delicate fingers slipping beneath the paper. He would pause to read some comment in the margin. "Coffee somewhere?" he would murmur.

Rain would fall. Time would pass slowly. They would go on and on.

Or it might happen like this:

They'd have something in common (a love of nature or justice). Both of them, hard workers, diligent believers in a cause. People with principles! (Civil rights, maybe? disarmament?) Whatever their protest, they would run from the tear gas together, find shelter in a burned-out basement, wrap their wounds, never come out.

Or it might be like this: Before she even spoke, he would love her.

Other girls got letters from their boyfriends back home: "Are you still stuck in that dopey Bible camp? When are you coming home? I have a great tan from hanging around the club. The women adore me. Ha. Ha."

And they wrote back, a big pink kiss on the outside flap: SWAK.

Miriam got letters from her mother every day. "My darling, Miriam," or "Dearest Miriam," or "My darling, little Miriam," they began. She hoped that Miriam was having a profitable summer, that the other girls were nice, that Miriam was wearing all her nice, new outfits.

And as if that weren't enough. "P.S." she said. "You're a wonderful girl. I miss you."

Another week passed and they were still crawling through Genesis. God had made light and plenty of it shining down on every corner of the field, making the air hum, making the horizon, through the waves of heat, seem to curl up into the sky. The grove where they had dragged their benches and table was no better. It was too hot to think. It was too hot to answer. Only Chaim, in his eternal, black wool suit, was moving.

They had been over and over the Garden of Eden. Chaim had delineated it for them in graphic detail, had made them sweat blood over it. The fragrance!

The fruit trees! The making of each creature—how splendid! The perfection of the whole thing. Now they were stuck on Adam's rib (a difficult passage).

Why was it that Eve had been made from Adam's rib and not from dust, as Adam had been? God could do anything, correct? So why then from a rib?

Shelley Katz did not know.

Danny Goldfarb did not know.

Barry Sternberg did not give two hoots.

"*Think*, children."

"To make them fit?" As soon as she'd asked it she blushed. The heat of her mistake began to rise through her, to swell inside of her, to do something, at any rate, totally awful.

"Nothing would fit *you*," Barry said. "Not even *this*." He showed her with his hands.

"I didn't mean—!" But it was too late. They were too hot to answer, but not too hot to laugh. She wondered what the Talmud had to say on the subject of laughter. It could be a wind? A deep well? A tiger waiting to spring?

Chaim bent forward to block their amusement. "Don't be a clown, Sternberg. Do you never learn? Of course Miriam didn't mean this literally," he said. Then he frowned at them. "You meant it *figuratively*, didn't you, Mireleh? A metaphor? Something for something else, wasn't that your intention?"

She nodded faintly. Something else—oh sure. The road was a ribbon of moonlight. My love is a red, red rose. That was what she had meant—some other perfect fit. "I guess so," she said.

"Correct, Mireleh. That's very good." Chaim patted the table in front of him as though it were her hand. "Very good indeed." He held up his Bible, print outward, and pointed to the passage. "You see, we have here, class, a metaphor—a lesson we can read between the lines—"

"Between the what?"

"Between the LINES, Sternberg." He tapped the page. "Beneath what is said literally, children, we have a second, more important—"

"Beneath *who?*"

Chaim sighed. "Beneath what is said *literally,* a second truth, as Miriam has pointed out—what is good is often hidden."

"You can say *that* again!"

Chaim set down the book. "Please, Mireleh. Please tell us simply and QUICKLY and in what manner, *figuratively,* these two fit."

"Yeah," Barry whispered. "Give us all the figures!"

The blush crept through her, literally, figuratively, fittingly and otherwise. However she had meant it she didn't know and didn't care. All around her they were grinning. Barry was grinning; he was coursing with possibilities (loose? tight? dry? deep?). Barry nudged her with his leg. "Nu, Mireleh—so tell us already."

She tried to slide away from him and when she did, her legs lifting from the bench made a slurping sound.

"Correct!" Barry exclaimed.

"That *is* correct," Chaim said as though she had

14

answered. His eyes told her: "Bear with him. Ignore him. Be brave." As if to demonstrate how sufferance like this was achieved, he ignored Barry and the sound and their laughter. He ignored everything he could possibly ignore. He clasped his hands together and squeezed. God made Eve from Adam's rib, he told them as he started to sway, to insure a perfect match, to make a coupling of the right and left halves so that no part should be omitted, no part lacking. It was a union perfect as the Garden, a union fragrant as a citron, alive with light. "We're talking about the crown of creation—*you understand me, class?*"

Sure. They understood.

On Friday nights it was standing room only in the woods. She could hear them in there hugging and kissing, fondling and caressing, zipping and unzipping, rubbing, pushing, their desire shredding fabric. She could hear them giggling and whispering and groaning, an ocean of sound that described each touch, that rose like steam through the woods.

(THE LIBRARY)

No one knew as much about that library as she did, except perhaps the librarian himself, and even *he* didn't know it in the same way.

She knew that the wood smelled in the morning, and the dust, of years of thought—resinous. She knew that the sun lit the letters on the bindings, gold. She knew which books had pictures, which ones had tiny, unreadable print. She knew who came there, at what hour, and for what purpose.

Chaim was there every afternoon from lunchtime until dusk poring over commentaries on the Bible. He didn't lean on one elbow like the others, but held his arms stiffly at his sides and swayed back and forth over the text as though he might dive into it. Sometimes he closed his eyes. She could watch him for hours and he never noticed her. Even when he lifted his head for air, his eyes shone with a blank, unseeing light.

Often, after he'd gone, Miriam would slip into his chair. She would pick up the book which still lay open on the table awaiting his return, and she would try to read what *he* had read that afternoon. There were reams of words, some in Hebrew, some in Aramaic, all without vowels, mysterious, impossible. She could only read the very large print—the phrase, or word, that was the subject of all that commentary: IN THE BEGINNING. DARK AND UNFORMED. She sat with the dictionary and puzzled out words. She wrote down translations, verbatim, awkward, but no matter what she did, she found nothing. The words were just words. Chaim still remained a mystery.

Then, eventually, she discovered that the words didn't matter. Maybe she couldn't understand them, but she didn't have to because it was just as pleasant simply to sit in the dark and pretend, to slide her fingers over the page, (occasionally to sway a little), to skim the elusive grains of sense, silently, as though reading. She imagined that was what mystics did when they meditated. They chose some words, they shut their eyes, they rocked themselves to sleep. Every day she did this a little longer—a half hour, forty-five minutes, an hour—when she should have been playing basketball, or making lanyards, when she saw Barry coming towards her, over the hill.

As for Chaim—. One evening she hovered over the book he had left behind until it was almost dark. The librarian had gone home to his cabin. Dusk had thickened around her and she had let it, had liked it, the feeling of darkness melting into her, the way the words melted into her fingertips, and her fingertips melted into the pages, the way the pages melted back into the darkness, slowly, very slowly, and the darkness melted back into her. She was dreaming that the letters had become figures, tall and thin, in long dark cloaks, broad black hats. They had all joined hands and were dancing in a circle around her making the room quake with joy. Faster and faster they whirled until the walls fell away, the sky became a blur—stars, moon, night thrashed against the galaxy; she couldn't catch her breath.

Wood creaked.

She opened her eyes.

A dark figure was coming towards her. Tall. Twisting. A shadow that bent. Unfolded. Bent again as though searching for a path through the twilight.

"Who's there?" she whispered.

The figure stopped. "Vus?"

Not the spirit of a letter, but Chaim. She had conjured him, complete, in his long black coat, his round black hat. "Vus machst tu, Mireleh?" he inquired.

Still not seeing clearly, she blinked. The hat he wore cast shadows on his face making from his features, shapes—caves and crags. "Ah," he said softly. "You're reading. Please don't let me disturb you," as though this were the most natural thing in the world, to be sitting in the dark with a book. She glanced down. She must have fallen asleep right on top of it. The pages were all crinkled and there were spots of saliva. She thought she smelled the oil from her hair. Ashamed, she closed the cover. "I wasn't really reading," she sighed.

But he didn't answer. Instead, a white hand leapt to his beard and began stroking it, thoughtfully, gently, as though this were a demonstration of how to treat the world. Something about this puzzled her. Not the motion, but the whiteness of his hand. Her own hands were obscured by darkness, but his shone pale as though lit up from inside. She thought of miracles that she'd studied—the Hanukkah candle that burned for eight days; the bush in the desert exploding into flames. She thought it might be some strange effect from the Ner Tamid, the Eternal Light, that burned above the Ark against the wall. Or, she might have lapsed back into her dream, lulled by his silence.

"Mireleh?"

He was asking her something. One hand soared to his hat brim where it hovered as though waiting for an answer.

"What?"

"Pirkei Avot. The Ethics of the Fathers, you remember? It says there: 'On three things the world depends—on Torah, on work, and on the performance of good deeds.' Do you believe this?" He gestured. His hand swooped towards her like a dove, plummeting down.

Another magic trick? She pushed the book away. "I guess so." Why had he come back this late? Why hadn't he turned on the light? Did he come here to hide the way she did?

He did not help to make things clearer. Folding himself into the chair across from her, he said, "May I sit down for a minute?" Then the conversation began, a long conversation which made no sense, that seemed like words weaving through the darkness, occasionally surfacing, then dipping, then floating up again making strange ripples through all that had gone before.

"So how are you liking it thus far?"

"Liking what—the class?"

"The class. Anything."

"Not bad," she said.

"Ah, I see," he said sadly. His hat bobbed agreement. "At your age life is merely 'not bad.' I suppose God thinks you should be grateful for this. Well. Let's put Him aside for a moment." There was another long silence much more than just a moment, during which pause she wondered, was this really Chaim sitting across from her saying: *Let's put God aside?* She could feel him staring at her, his gaze like the hour after midnight, a mournful, naked look that made her lose her balance, made her fall slowly towards the center of the earth.

Finally, he sighed. "You know what is my favorite poem in the English language?" He recited it for her: "Sonnet number 73," he announced, as though it were a psalm. " 'Bare ruin'd choirs, where late the sweet birds sang'—that's Shakespeare. Isn't it sad?"

"I guess so." She didn't understand at all, really. Shakespeare. The Torah. Sweet birds and ruined choirs. What did he want from her?

He didn't explain. Instead, he wished her a good evening as he stood up, then drifted from the room. "You'd better go too, Mireleh. Your counselor will be worried."

But he came back again the next night. Again, he settled himself into the chair across from hers and began speaking as though no time at all had intervened. Perhaps it hadn't. Whatever was on his mind was still there, pressing him, tugging at logic, winding good sense up into a ball—that came unraveled as soon as he opened his mouth to speak: "Do you know 'Ode to a Nightingale'?" he asked her. "Do you know this one by Hopkins?" Again he recited to her, his voice trembling as though *he* were the poet falling over the edge of the world into discovery. She knew this must be another secret he was telling her; something else he believed in besides God and good deeds and the Talmud Torah, a secret she must not divulge to anyone. The verses frightened her. In bed, after lights out, she

chanted to herself all of the lines she could remember:
"All is changed, changed utterly . . ." . . . "Though
worlds of wanwood leafmeal lie . . ." . . . "I have been
half in love with easeful Death . . ." —lines that went
against what they prayed for each morning: "Blessed
art Thou O Lord, King of the Universe, who removest
sleep from mine eyes and slumber from mine eyelids,
who restorest life to mortal creatures . . ." It was as
though she'd seen Chaim wandering through a new
landscape—a shadowy glen drenched with mist, moss-
covered, hopeless.

By the third night, she was waiting for him, for
the conversation that made such confusion, that made
her grasp the arms of the chair she sat in, so solid, so
wooden. He didn't greet her this time, just picked up
the threads of their last talk and began braiding them,
rocking back and forth as though praying, as though
fevered. He spoke until the dark became as thick as a
trance, until she leaned into this, waiting, bending towards him so that their knees brushed under the table,
his—rough and woolen, hers—bare and tender, very
warm. She wanted him to say something that would
break the spell, something ordinary: "That's fine,
Mireleh," as he would have done in class, "You're a
good girl, my *best* student . . ." But he didn't say a
word, and what he didn't say gathered between them.

She tried to think of a question to ask him, a polite question to engage his interest, but the only ones
that occurred to her pertained, oddly enough, to his

legs. What were they like beneath the fabric of his trousers? Pale? Calloused? Were they as white as his hands? As smooth?

Suddenly, he leaned forward as if he had been speaking to her all this time. "And you know what they say? They say that the Torah was written by men."

"What?" She was still thinking of his legs, white as paper, the black curling hairs.

"By *men*," Chaim repeated. His words rushed through her. He was looking at her earnestly. For a minute she imagined he had heard what she was thinking, that this was the way scholars made passes, by a reference, that he would reach across the table and draw her to him; they would kiss across the table, only the outstretched Talmud between them. Then she realized he wasn't looking at her at all. He was staring the way he did when he was unable to pry himself loose from his holy books and go back into the world. "That's what they think!" he exclaimed. "Can you believe it? By men and not by God. That there isn't any absolute and, therefore, no suffering. It's as simple as that." He laughed, incredulous. "There are no *real* laws. Only *human* laws. Is that ridiculous? We should think like the others, they say. The Chinese. The Hindus. They think it's better to meditate, that it's all right to leave the suffering of this world behind, while we Jews, we *real* Jews," he shook his head, "*we* stay and suffer, throwing our souls into the fire and groaning when we are burned. And then we think we know." He slapped the table. "And then we think we have done our part!" His fist came down.

She tried to make sense of it later. For several days, she added up the evidence, subtracted what didn't fit at all, and divided by what was obscure. On the one hand, there was the lateness of the hour each time they talked; there was his prolonged stay, the personal nature of his questions, his lingering over the poems, his knees brushing hers. On the other hand, there was his unexpected leap to the Hindus, his discussion of suffering, and after his fist struck the table, his apology: "Never mind," he had told her. "It's late and I've probably driven you crazy with all this nonsense. I keep forgetting you're only thirteen. Thirteen in America is an easier age."

Than what? she wondered.

She began to dream of him at night, a dream bathed in different lights. Gold. Dark green. Over and over.

In her dream it was a Sabbath afternoon, dry as ashes, like a day held under a magnifying glass to start a fire. Everyone was resting, tired, quiescent, in their cabins, reading newspapers, or poems or love letters: "My darling, my dearest, sweetheart . . ."

Except her.

She had been walking for hours looking for something, her eyes were fixed on the road. Whatever it was she had lost it. A bracelet? An earring? She was looking for a glimmer in the road as the sun beat down against her back pasting her yellow shirt to her skin with sweat. It was hot. It was so very hot. The road was a dusty glare—empty, forlorn, forever.

Suddenly, she looked up. There were woods! From nowhere, green rushed out to welcome her. On both sides of the road, deep green, the trickling of running water, branches waving. Leaves. Meadows of thriving grass—Queen Anne's Lace and Wild Timothy.

Someone touched her arm. A tall figure dissolving into shadows in the woods. She followed though she couldn't see, could only feel the deep cool breath of the forest soothing her. She walked for hours, until the setting sun came through the trees in threads—orange, green, yellow sprays of light that dazzled her.

Against this light, she saw Chaim. In black as always, long coat, velvet yarmulkah, clasping in one hand his Bible, the special one from Israel with its silver cover beaten to the shape of tablets, a turquoise stone inset for each commandment. In his other hand, a bunch of flowers, white, which he handed to her, then kissed her cheek. A warm, moist kiss. "I like big girls," he whispered.

They lay down together.

He began to kiss her. Lips to her mouth, lips to her hair, to the hollow of her neck, to her lips again until she shivered though his lips were warm like cinnamon or cloves, and smooth as the wood of a spice box. Then stinging. Then sweet. Over and over, his lips, until his hands moved over her too, touching her and stroking her, unbuttoning clothes, sliding them over her skin as swift as angels, (she was naked; he was naked), reading her body with his fingertips, skimming her arms, her legs, her breasts, with hands that were lighter than whispers, than blessings, until light poured over both of them, into them; they were inside it. He was rocking her back and forth; she was curling herself around him.

By day what remained of her dream? He was naked; she was naked. Nakedness in all its conjugations. I was naked, she thought. *We* were naked. Had been naked. Would be. Might.

She watched him in class as he bent over his text and she didn't see his black clothes, she saw his skin, white and smooth and glowing. When he said her name, she could hardly answer. When he moved his fingers over the pages, she flinched. And when he started to sway she felt her body swaying with him; she couldn't bear to look.

(HUNGER)

Precedents for such romances: David and Abishag, Abraham and Keturah, Isaac (he was over forty) and Rebecca, Esau and Judith, Joseph and Potiphar's wife (sort of), Pablo Picasso and what was her name? his latest wife, someone slim, exquisite; at any rate—a woman to be proud of.

She imagined how it would feel to look like that, as thin and graceful as a lulav—the wand made of palm fronds and myrtle and willow that the men waved on Sukkot, the harvest festival. She pictured herself that way, and then Chaim, taking her by the hand, introducing her proudly: "This is Miriam. She's not only a great reader, she's also very lovely—don't you think?" He would bow to his own words, dazzled, faithful. In private he would touch her as he had in the dream. "I'll tell you a secret, Miriam—for your ears alone. I'll tell you all of my secrets . . ."

But it wasn't just for Chaim she had decided to do this; there were the others as well. How wonderful, she thought, to leap and twirl and float right past them, to rise above their laughter like a wisp of smoke. How wonderful never to hear Barry say again, "Here she comes—THUMP! THUMP!" She would be thin as a switch, that's what she'd be. She'd lash the world with her beauty, make them all run before her—awed, delighted.

If not, then she'd disappear.

She had already given up lunch and sometimes even dinner; it was nothing to give up the rest. The first day she didn't even feel hungry, and whenever she did she drank a cup of tea.

Strangely enough, she seemed to have more energy, not less. Instead of going to meals and activities, she took long walks around the countryside. She hiked through the woods and trekked across pastures so that she could climb to the tops of hills rough with brambles, boulders. She searched for waterfalls, a far-off rushing sound. She made her way through marshes where only algae grew or the stumps of trees pointing upward for no reason.

Each day she dared herself to go a little further.

Once it was a walk to the next camp five miles down the road. The following day she went into town, then another five miles past an abandoned church with a cemetery plot, untended, crooked crosses scattered everywhere as wayward as weeds. On Wednesday it rained and still she hiked all the way to the lake at Equinunk. Because it was pouring no one was there, so she took off her clothes and swam. That was beautiful, floating in the lake, rain washing down through the trees, rattling in the leaves, drenching her face. The sky was iron gray, a ceiling of clouds descending.

But then, everything was more beautiful, she found. No matter what she looked at it seemed clearer as though it lit up under her gaze and announced itself: I am water. A maple tree. The sky. I am stone.

When she grew tired of just walking she began another kind of journey. She watched Chaim. A man mysterious. A man apart.

His curtains were always drawn, but she found some holes in the planking that allowed her to see different parts of the room, though never very much at once. There was the floorboard view and the closet view. There was the view of the bookcase, the view between the bottles and jars in the medicine cabinet. There was a complete view of the ceiling from underneath the bunk, but this required hardships that made it not worthwhile.

She settled for glimpses.

From various angles at various times, she saw his

feet in socks, in slippers. She saw a glass of water placed on a chair next to the bed. She saw a handkerchief dropped, a handkerchief plucked up again. A bag of laundry set down in a corner. Often, a broom swept balls of lint and hair into a pile. Pantslegs! Coatsleeves! All of a sudden—his face! as he leaned over to collect the dirt into a dustpan, as beatific as though he were gathering manna in the desert.

What she hoped to discover, she couldn't say precisely, but every day she made her pilgrimage. Every day she knelt, hidden behind the walls of his cabin, trying her best to peer in.

Some days were more rewarding than others.

On Friday afternoons, for instance, he always polished his shoes so that they would be bright and new for the Sabbath. First he removed the laces, gingerly, as though they were made of silk. Then he took a whisk broom and brushed off all the loose dirt. With a nail file he scraped mud from the welt of the shoe, then poked a pin into all of the perforations. When the shoe was finally ready, he shook the bottle thoroughly, a lurching sound, heavy, like medicine being mixed, then removed the applicator and began painting—first the sides, then the tongues, then the heels. Last, he let them dry for half an hour, then rubbed them with a cloth until they shone.

Another ritual was the preparation of tea which he drank without fail, at 4:30 in the afternoon. He had a small electric kettle stationed above the bookcase, a silver spoon, a china cup.

At night, instead of turning on the overhead light, he burned candles. Miriam could barely see anything then, but the flicker of shadows was enough to intrigue her, the occasional hiss and snap of flame made her shiver.

She shivered, too, the time she spied his slender hand lift a bar of soap from the shelf in the bathroom. As he removed the wrapper her heart leapt up, for had he not closed the cabinet door just then, she would have seen his robe removed as well, would have seen him stepping into the shower.

She never actually discovered anything she hadn't already observed just by sitting on her bench in class with the others. He was meticulous. He was thoughtful. He worshipped the acts of ordinary life the same way he worshipped knowledge. Nothing new.

But here, alone and unguarded in his cabin, he was framed in mystery. From her vantage point, each hint of flesh loomed statuesque. Each gesture swelled with meaning. The smallest act became a revelation.

Her devotion turned boundless. From his morning ablutions to his nighttime prayers, she scrutinized every motion. She was his prophet. In a thick notebook she wrote down all he did, printing the words in straight, careful lines as though they were already gospel:

"At dawn, he wakes . . ."

"Late afternoon: he groans and stirs—too much study in one position? . . ."

"Evening: Walks to the window and stares into the woods . . . He sighs . . . Eventually, he lets the curtain fall . . ."

"Later: Night has come. He waits for sleep . . ."

She studied these notes daily, searching for patterns. She asked herself questions: which had more significance—the order of his actions or the spirit in which they were performed? Could she estimate that spirit? Could she guess the exact nature of the intention that informed each action?

No more than she could understand Barry, who daily grew more bold in his troublemaking. She wasn't his only victim anymore. Perhaps because the end of summer was approaching he began to expand his horizons. From simple pranks like graffiti and pool dunkings, he leapfrogged to more elaborate crimes—putting paint in the windshield washer of the camp bus, hiding all the canoe paddles the night before the big trip down the Delaware, making streamers of the underwear he pirated from the girls' bunks and draping them in the trees. He stole cake from the baker's closet—poppy seed strudel and cream puffs and chocolate eclairs, the spoils of the camp director and the rabbinical staff always kept locked up against just this kind of invasion. During Saturday morning services he let loose a collection of live crickets that rasped and whirred like a demented congregation. He ordered subscriptions to the library from Crusade for Christ, from the American Nazi Party.

Everyone assumed it was Barry. It had to be him.

Who else would have had the nerve? Miriam, herself, saw him one night at the camp junkyard breaking windows with one of the missing canoe paddles. The junkyard was a clearing in the woods at the end of a narrow, rutted road. It was the place where they piled all the ruined furniture—the mildewed mattresses and ravaged sofas, the crippled chairs and tables, as well as things like martyred pianos, mirrors that were cracked, embittered.

Over this ruined kingdom, Barry reigned, forcing homage with beatings, breaking spirits that were already broken. He pounded and whacked and hammered and when he'd shattered every window into a thousand frightened splinters, he began ranting aimlessly, "Take *that* you bastard! Take *that* you bitch!" flailing and thrashing and smiting all of the unfortunate subjects in his path.

If his behavior in class was any measure of his loss of self-control then this was to be expected. Late in the season, he and Chaim had learned a new kind of dance—contorted, ugly. It drove away all peace and quiet, all possibility of reconciliation. By that time, it was just the two of them. As though Miriam were a shade that had been lifted to reveal his true enemy, Barry no longer bothered to tease her. Chaim was the target now, a willing target who bent to receive the arrows.

Each morning Barry strolled in an hour late: "Did I miss anything? Are we still on chapter two? That dumb old stuff? Lord! Will this ever be over?"

Each morning he pushed Chaim a little bit further: "Excuse me, dear Teacher, Moreleh, Your Highness, I mean. That just doesn't make any sense to me. Is that really the translation? Are you certain this is the answer?"

"Why do we have to study this boring garbage anyway?"

"Well that's a silly law if I ever heard one!"

He would goad and bully and impugn and just as Chaim was about to lose his temper, as his face began to redden and his voice began to shake, he would pull back: "Hey. Don't get excited, man. Take it easy, will you? I'm just an ignoramus, a clown, a boy who likes to sow his nasty oats—what do you care? Look. Don't pay any attention to me. I don't mean anything, you know. Not really."

Chaim appeared determined to endure. It was as if by yielding to his anger he would prove himself a liar; he would have to admit that Barry was not a "good boy," someone to "bear with." Setting an example was all that seemed to matter. Ignoring the price, he continued to sidestep these challenges and affronts, to pretend that they were merely bursts of high spirits. Kindling.

She was walking in circles. That's all she knew. She was further than ever from understanding him, from understanding anything. Further still the night she saw this, something so strange she was not convinced afterwards that she had seen anything at all.

She had been fasting for a week, for two weeks,

more. She had been living on tea and water and water and tea. Many times she had seen things that weren't there. Flocks of birds when she bent over, swarms of ants, dark fountains spouting from the ground. She saw afterimages of what she had just seen on top of what she saw a second later—trees on top of buildings, rocks on top of heads.

At night she couldn't sleep. She closed her eyes and had visions (she couldn't think of another name for what she witnessed). Big dots. Masses of color. Parades of geometric shapes. All the parts of the body, in parts: huge eyes, knees, foreheads, ribs. She saw lines, flashes of lightning; as before—letters from all of the alphabets dancing together without shame.

Still. Even this made a certain kind of sense. What she saw in Chaim's cabin—no sense at all.

First his feet walked over to the bookcase. They walked back to the bed and paused. She heard the sound of sheets of paper being ripped from a book, from many books. This went on for several minutes during which time the feet returned to the bookcase, presumably, to remove more books. Then she saw knees, hands, a pile of paper.

A coat was thrown to the floor, then a shirt. One set of ceremonial fringes. And just when her heart began to pound, thinking she would see him at last, she saw, instead, a pair of hands strike a match, reach forward to the paper; and when it was on fire (blazing in fierce darts of color) he muttered something in Hebrew, the hands came down; she saw him lay himself down, back first, on top of the flames.

What would it have meant provided she had actually seen it? After she awoke from her faint she thought of several possibilities. He had a rare skin disease that was held in check, though not cured, by daily doses of charcoal and extreme heat. He had decided to become a Hindu mystic. He was a magician. A pyromaniac. She was crazy.

She knew she should stop fasting. She told herself that every day. She was becoming very light. Much lighter than anyone else. Invisible. A wraith. It was true. She had found the trick. She could pass right through other people and they didn't even notice her. In turn, the words they spoke passed back through her and on into the night as if through ether. What they meant no longer sank into her flesh and lay there trapped.

But it wasn't only that. It was the strength she had achieved, the concentration. It was feeling that once she gave in, once she gave up just a little bit, she gave it all up; she gave up forever, herself. It was feeling that she might see again the flames in Chaim's cabin, and, like a ledge or a bridge, some wide open space between heights where she might fall, it was daring to see those flames again, wanting to see them rise through his back.

(CHAOS)

But that was cool, wasn't it? Barry had asked the

morning they finally finished reading chapter three. Wasn't screwing on the Sabbath a double mitzvah? a double good deed? Wasn't that the law—double your pleasure, double your fun? So why did Adam and Eve get the boot? What was wrong with one little screw?

Smoke hissed from the torches. Her insides hissed with hunger. It was the evening of Tisha B'Av, a fast to commemorate the destruction of the Temple, the precedent (as Chaim called it) for all the two thousand years of suffering that came after.

They were sitting on the floor reading "Lamentations." By the waters of Babylon, remembering Zion.

He was standing, a man apart, a man mysterious, in a corner by the door, swaying as though he had been swaying for days and days and couldn't stop. The torch light swayed with him, and the congregation, sitting in the long shadows on the floor chanted: "From above he hath sent fire into my bones, and it prevaileth against them. He hath spread a net for my feet, he hath turned me back: He hath made me desolate and faint all day . . ."

Barry had disappeared. Three days ago. "Who needs your stupid class?" he had said. "Who needs your fucking Torah?" He had stalked off into the woods and they hadn't seen him since.

At first they thought he was just going in there to sulk, to make a scene. "You were right," they told Chaim. "He was really being a jerk"; and Chaim, still furious, still clutching his Bible, had called after him only faintly: "Sternberg, wait."

He hadn't appeared on the baseball field later that afternoon when they were scheduled to practice, nor had he shown up for dinner; and by the time "lights out" had rolled around, they knew he wasn't fooling. They knew they had to look for him.

But, by then, it was too dark to find anyone. The woods had filled with fog.

They were swaying together and the room was hot. They were packed together on the floor, sitting cross-legged, swaying back and forth, voices rising with the smoke. "I am the man that hath seen afflic-tion by the rod of his wrath. He hath led me and brought me into darkness, but not into light . . ."

"Fool!" At Barry's question, Chaim had banged his book down on the desk. "For *this* you suddenly come alive? For *this* you are suddenly familiar with the text? For *this* you open your foolish mouth?"

Whatever had gotten into Barry had gotten into him as well. He was more than just angry. He was a pillar of smoke, an avenging cloud. "How many times have I asked you, children, and nobody knows? How many times and no one has even bothered to ask me themselves or to look? What's wrong with you? Can't you think? All summer long I ask you questions. All summer long you sit there like death!"

But this was not the worst. He had slammed his Bible down on the desk—a vast sacrilege; in the old days, a sin almost equal to murder. When he saw what he had done, how he had crushed the pages and broken the binding he cried: "Ah, look! Look! Look what you made me do. This is what comes of 'peel-pool'!"

But he hadn't explained.

Instead he had picked up the broken book and cradled it in his hands, turning the pages gently, slowly. Then, sighing a cold, deep sigh, as though he had found an irreparable injury, he had hugged it to his chest and started swaying back and forth chanting in Hebrew, "Forgive me, forgive me, forgive me . . ."

It was the evening of Tisha B'Av, the start of the fast to commemorate the destruction, the suffering, the marching in of armies, the marching out of hope. The fast had begun at sundown, would continue until sundown, twenty-four hours. They would pray tonight and all day tomorrow sitting on the floor and fasting, praying, sighing.

Barry had disappeared. Three days ago. "Who needs your stupid class?" he had said. "Who needs your fucking Torah?" He had stalked off into the woods and they hadn't seen him since.

The next morning they had thought they'd find him crouched behind the door of the bunk waiting for the right moment to spring out at them. "Ha! Ha! Fooled you assholes. You gave me up for dead, didn't you? Well, I'll tell you the truth now. I had a superb night. On the town, of course." (Though his clothing might be crumpled, though bits of leaves might cling to his hair.) He had done this twice before, they said. Each time, they had called his aunt. Each time, they had called his psychiatrist. "It's just a manipulation," the psychiatrist said. "His version of suicide." And the aunt had said, "It's true. He runs away all the time. He hides in some safe place. He makes everyone suffer."

"But Thou hast utterly rejected us; Thou art very much wroth against us."
Now they were finished with "Lamentations." They were beginning the long litany of suffering. Leo Goelman stepped to the podium. "Two specialties we have," he said. "Suffering. Memory. Of these we have made an art."
They were lighting candles—one for each phase of history, one for each hallmark of the art. The First Temple and the Second Temple. The exile in Babylon and the exile in Persia. The Greek occupation and the Roman. The Inquisition and the Dark Ages. The pogroms and the Cossacks. Treblinka and Auschwitz and Dachau . . .

Barry had disappeared, but he couldn't have gone very far. The evidence was clear. There were signs of him everywhere. Books pulled from their shelves. Benches overturned in the classrooms. Messages on the library wall.

And Chaim had not been in his cabin, had not been there for three days. There had been no shoes on the floor, no fringes, no pale white hand reaching towards her in the cabinet. She had waited for him and waited, had hoped he might be sitting there in the dark, within the curtains, clutching a pile of paper, maybe singing softly or muttering or clasping his hands together and curling himself up in prayer.

Barry had disappeared, but there were signs of him everywhere. In the prayer books that were stolen, in the candlesticks that had fallen down, in the pages torn from books and scattered in the grass, in the things that were missing—scarves, rings, bracelets, (handed back, lost somewhere). Some even said in the weeping at night in the cabins (from the upper bunks, from the lower).

Even here there were signs. The torches burned brightly. They swayed. She was hungry.

She had waited until after dark, herself, curled up amid the pine needles, the weeds and dry sticks, hungry and thirsty, until finally, when the first damp fog of evening began to seep into her skin, she felt she couldn't wait another minute longer. She had crept up the stairs, had nudged the door open, found a room completely empty. There had been no clothes in the closet, no books on the shelves, and, except for an old brown suitcase which stood by the door, there was only a dustpan propped against one wall, the faint smell of something burnt.

Smoke rose. Shadows rose. She could feel herself

rising with them, lighter than air, so faint she felt like vapor.

Barry had disappeared. Chaim had gone after him. She had gone after Chaim.

All day long, on the hottest day of summer, she had walked. Through pine forests, through stands of maple, through shrubs matted with vines and creepers. There was no path, but she kept on going, drifting along in a cloud of hunger. Every time she moved, a trail of sound and light churned inside her, turning to heat and dust, a dry aching thirst that caked her throat, that made her lean against a tree and gasp.

But even this was not the worst, that she had walked until late afternoon, until her thirst was so great that it pushed her through the underbrush to a stream where she drank and drank and drank. Even this was not the worst, that when her thirst stopped, when the roaring stopped in her ears, she had heard weeping, had looked up and seen a man in black sprawled on the ground weeping and weeping and weeping. Nor even this. She hadn't gone to him and caressed him. She hadn't knelt and kissed him; nor had he, in his turn, kissed her, had not said "I like big girls," had not held her until the sun came through the trees in threads: orange yellow green sprays of light.

It was this—what he *did* say. "You know what is 'peel-pool,'" Mireleh? I'll tell you what it really is. Not just the dictionary definition—*casuistry,* the athletic misinterpretation of words, in a quiet room filled with dusty old books . . ."

He had made her sit down beside him. He had held her hand.

"Listen. It was many years ago, not here, but in a village far away. There was a boy just about your age. It was going to be his Bar Mitzvah. He was coming of age. He was going to know what there was to know—about the world, about himself, and his family was very happy, very excited; or they would have been excited. But this was a bad time. A bad place. There was no Torah then. It was forbidden, strictly forbidden.

"The boy's father was a rabbi, the head of a yeshiva until they closed them down. After that, he was a rabbi in secret. He had hidden the Torahs, every single one of them. The penalty for this was death. For being a Jew. They were burning all the Torahs, burning the yeshivot; they were marching us all away.

"Every day whoever wanted to, whoever was brave enough, whoever was left, would slip out of their houses, go to this secret place to pray."

"And the Bar Mitzvah?" she had asked, though she already knew the answer. "Did he have it?"

He shook his head. "When they found the Torahs they would burn them. In a heap they would pile them in the street along with other holy books, law books, whatever they found that looked sacred. They would pour kerosene on top and set them on fire, let them burn into ashes. There were some Jews who tried to rescue them. There were some who believed in Kiddush HaShem, the commandment of martyrdom for

God, for His word, a commandment outweighing all
the others, but *never* to be invoked, some said. Others,
like my father, threw themselves onto the flames."

"But did you—"

"I, Mireleh? Not I. Not then."

And that was not the worst. It was not only that,
but this: Barry never knew when to stop. "Sure," he
had said as Chaim rocked back and forth with the ruined book. "Sure, man!" He had raised his arms and
held out both hands in benediction. "We forgive
you—no problem. No fucking problem. Forgiveness,
free and complete. Don't give it another thought."

Chaim had stopped swaying. He had set the book
down on the table carefully, very accurately, had set it
down in some precise diagram that only he could see
of a Bible set down in anger. Then, as if it were also
part of the same diagram, one which told him how to
convert thought into motion, rage into sound, he had
slapped Barry across the face, had shouted: "*You* forgive *me*? *You* forgive *me*? To whom do you think
you're speaking? To some goniff? To the devil? Get
out of here you little bastard!"

*And this. Finally there was this: "Bergen Belsen,
Madanek, Theresienstadt . . ." They were still listing,
matching up the horrors with the lights. Barry still
hadn't come back. She was still hungry. In his corner,
Chaim was still swaying, back and forth, back and
forth, Baruch HaShem, Amen V'Amen.*

Behind him, the torches swayed, glowing. And for a moment, as he bent over his text, she didn't see clothes, but flesh, saw the pale skin of his back, on either side of his spine, saw letters (the ten commandments? the ten plagues?); she saw the torches burning behind all of them, saw all of them, like Barry, alone in the woods in the dark.

DOUBLE LIVES

In the morning, when Nick gets up, I pretend to be asleep. He knows I'm just pretending, but still he makes his steps light as paper, pretending not to wake me as he dresses for work at the hospital. Sometimes I think this means he loves me.

Nick used to be a cat burglar, or so he said. In the small Pennsylvania town where he was raised he practiced in the woods by stalking deer. Sometimes he crept up on smaller, slower game.

One summer he switched to houses. He learned to climb buildings without toeholds, brick homes as smooth and solid as their owners. He would slip inside a third-floor window while the family was downstairs drinking iced tea, complaining about the heat. He would walk through the bedrooms slowly, as if he

47

were invisible, as pure and light as air. He would test the mattresses, open closets, peer into drawers. He would run his hands over the velour towels in the bathroom. He never took anything.

When we first moved to our apartment, he used to climb the furniture, crossing and recrossing the room from bed to dresser to desk to sill to bed again without ever touching earth. Now he handles the room as if it were dynamite. When he dresses for the hospital, he inches open drawers, teases the clothes from their hangers. Even the pens he clips into his white coat pocket don't make a sound. When he kisses me goodbye, I hardly feel it.

This morning, after Nick leaves, I do what I always do—act as if I have somewhere to go. When he comes home this evening, I know that he will ask me, "So, how was it today? Any leads? Any interviews? *Nothing?*" I have been looking for a job ever since we moved here, eight months ago, when Nick began his residency in cardiology at Mount Sinai Hospital. But not many jobs are available for art historians, even in New York, and particularly in my field, which is Impressionism. As I have often told Nick, "Everyone and his brother can tell you why Van Gogh cut off his ear."

Nick doesn't agree. So many museums here. So many art galleries. Even gift shops. Surely somewhere. Why don't I take a course in art therapy? Get another degree.

"It's simple," I say. "I'm not an artist."

Still, for his sake as well as my own I try to wake

with a sense of purpose. I buy newspapers. I make phone calls. Every morning I wash my hair and dry it curl by curl by curl. It's very long, almost to my waist, thick, light brown, or, as Nick described it once when he was brushing it for me, the color of dried thistles. While others have cut theirs short and tough, I've had mine permed. I think this may give me an edge. At least it keeps me from rushing right out at daybreak and finding that I have another whole day to kill.

When I've finished with my hair, I find other things to do: assemble an outfit (scarf, skirt, shoes—everything down to the slip matches). I usually change my mind at least once and start all over again. Scarf, shoes, skirt . . . Sometimes I call Aunt Marge in Vineland and we talk about Uncle Joe.

Whenever he feels sad, he buys a yacht. He has no money, but that doesn't matter. He picks up the yacht in New Jersey and drops it off in Maine, sooner if he gets caught. Usually Aunt Marge receives a call from some stop along the way—Asbury Park, Coney Island. The Coast Guard has found him drifting above the Continental Shelf, his lines trawled out for treasure. Aunt Marge explains; they ship him home; he tells the doctor, who adjusts his lithium, that he had been dreaming of the ocean as it used to be.

Sometimes I want to tell Aunt Marge I think I understand Uncle Joe. I've wanted to steal things myself: someone else's face; an apartment window framing things I'll never have—white shag carpet, peace of mind. Often I roam through the Village looking into windows bright with faraway life.

Always I say to Aunt Marge: "Don't worry. He'll get better, I just know it." Then I hang up, so that I'll have time to clean up the apartment, make it tidy in case Nick returns before I do and gets the idea that I'm slacking off. This morning when I clean up I wonder what his wineglass is doing inside the medicine cabinet. Lately wineglasses have been popping up everywhere. I find them growing like translucent mushrooms under tables and chairs, in corners behind sofas. Last Saturday morning I found one in the laundry bag, mixed in with the socks and sheets. What Nick is hiding I can't tell. He always drinks in front of me, beginning with his pre-run drink when he comes home in the evening, and then all evening long—wine at dinner, beer to cover the hours in front of the TV, whiskey late at night when he thinks I've given up, that I'm asleep. It never seems to change him, this drinking. He is calm. He is pleasant. When I ask him why he needs it he just looks at me. "Need?" he says. "I don't *need* it. I'm a doctor. I know how much my blood can take."

Usually by noon I decide that I'd better get on out there and start living up to my potential. Once in a while I really do have an interview, or I go in search of a particular item I have been planning to buy (thin gold rings that will make my fingers look long and delicate; a special spice, cardamom or rosewater, essential in the preparation of exotic, painstaking dishes, the kind that I can point to and say, "See? This is how I spend my time—for *you*").

More often, however, I spend these hours sitting

in Dewey's drinking coffee and waiting to go home. I sit on one of the stools by the window facing the street and watch the crowds go by, thinking of all the people I will never meet, of all the things that I will never know. If I were going to have an affair, which one would I choose? That tall one? That fat one? Before I met Nick, I always made decisions of this kind by erotic shorthand. Soccer Legs. Hot Kisser. Pierced Ear. That's the way I remembered them. Nick was the first man who appeared whole to me, indecipherable by any code.

If I wanted an affair, it would be easy. There is always someone interested in passing the sugar, in moving over to the empty stool beside mine so that it's easier to talk. Recently, I've been talking to the same man almost every day. He teaches a night class in meteorology at CCNY. His specialty is snow. He carries around with him, in a black briefcase sectioned off with files, hundreds of snapshots of crystals. Sometimes we sort through them together and pick out the ones we like best. He favors the kind with a lot of points, like stars. I can never make up my mind. Last week he gave me a batch to take with me. "Take all of them," he said. "I have a whole blizzard at home. I'll show you sometime."

Every night after work Nick goes running. He strips off his wrinkled hospital clothes and throws them on the floor in the closet. All except the white coat, laden with instruments: stethoscope, reflex hammer, tongue depressors, an elastic tube he uses to bind

arms when he takes blood from the veins of his patients. He empties the change from his pockets, hangs
the coat on a hook. Then he stands there for a minute,
naked, in the closet, as if the rows of pants and shirts
are a forest and he is waiting, letting the quiet, vegeta-
ble air soothe his skin. Nick has a body like a dancer's,
thin and light and clever. He can stand stock still; he
can leap over the moon.

When he runs, Nick wears only a pair of white
gym shorts and a red bandanna to absorb the sweat,
though he never sweats. At the end of a run his skin
always looks the same, smooth and brown as polished
wood. His smell, too, is constant—bittersweet, a
green-tomato smell. He doesn't sweat, neither does he
freeze. Even in winter his outfit doesn't change—the
same thin shorts, the same bare chest and legs. I tell
him he must want to kill himself, that he should know
better. He says he likes the feel of the rain or snow
against his body, the bits of ash and grit that the wind
whirls up from the street. Only once has he ever made
a concession. During a blizzard last year, when the
snow covered the steps and poles and hydrants, obscured the lines of buildings and turned them into vast
white peaks, he wore the scarf I had knitted him for
Christmas.

While Nick runs, I prepare dinner. I think of
things to say while we eat. It seems odd to have to
make conversation with your husband, but after his
day, after his run, he is tired. He will answer only simple questions: More peas? Another potato? I try to

52

think of something bright to say, something that will make him look across the table at me and really *look*, the way he used to.

I don't know where Nick goes when he runs. Sometimes he is gone for hours. Sometimes he returns after a few minutes, as tired as if he had run the same distance but in another dimension, double time. I never ask where he's been. I know that running is his time to be alone, away from the demands of the hospital. Everyone needs a quiet, private corner in his life, I tell myself, something untouchable. Still, I want to know. I wonder about his skin when he returns, so smooth, so dry.

Tonight, as on other nights, I follow him. I find my car and pretend I'm going to the store to pick up some forgotten item—cheese, or sugar. But I don't, of course. Instead I drive along slowly behind Nick, watching the white of his shorts flicker through the dusk, between the streetlamps and the passersby.

Nick weaves, though he doesn't have to. The streets are almost empty, but he crisscrosses the sidewalk, leaping over boulders that aren't there. Occasionally he runs up onto the trunk of a car, hops to the roof, and from the roof, bounds to the trunk of the next car, and so on for a block or more. Behind me drivers honk their horns. I motion that I'm looking for a parking space; they can like it or go to hell.

Sooner or later, I know, he will lose me, turn into some alley, maybe cut through a park. He always does, though never by the same route. Once he escaped me at the Jazz Institute. They were having an outdoor concert; he circled the quartet twice and then disappeared through the back rows of the audience. Another time, he ran through an alley behind a leather bar, down by the docks. The neon sign said CHAIN MALE; I waited for an hour for him to re-emerge, imagining him in pieces, imagining him in ecstasy.

Tonight he runs slowly to the end of the Village and then picks up speed as he turns toward Chinatown and Little Italy. He darts into a pastry shop, one that sells cannoli—vanilla, chocolate, chocolate chip. I go by too quickly to be sure, but I think I catch him in the rearview mirror talking to a girl behind the counter, leaning forward on his arms. "One dozen, please." Is that what he's saying to her? Or simply, "Mmmmmmmmmmmm." I picture the girl, sweet and kind and not too round, as girls in pastry shops should be, all dressed in white like a nurse. That delicate way they handle the pastry, I think, must serve them well.

Of course we have no cannoli for dinner, only wine and more wine and silence. I consider telling Nick about an article I read this afternoon while I was waiting for him to come home: "Sexuality After Marriage—Does It Exist?" The article outlined eight possible areas of disagreement between spouses: what each partner wants sexually, how each partner likes to have sex initiated, the degree of sexual variety each partner prefers, appropriate roles, preferred frequency, preferred positions, enhancements, inhibitions. A sidebar in large block print listed barriers to relationships: MISTRUST. INSECURITY. PROJECTION.

I don't really believe a word of this, but I continue
to read, because they make the solution seem so simple. You sit down together one evening and go over the
list point by point, noting your faults. Guilty. Guilty.
Guilty. You write things down on separate slips of paper and compare them. THINGS WE LIKE: 1) One of
us. 2) Both of us. 3) Neither. THINGS WE HATE: 1)
Most of the time. 2) Some of the time. 3) On Sundays.
Then you trade pieces of paper and make comments,
suggestions. When you're all through, you go to it.
You find passion again. Again, that falling through
warm, dark space.

Nick pours himself more wine.

"So how was work today?"

He sighs. "You know. Angina. Infarctions. Codes.
The usual ménage of trouble."

"Ménage?" For some reason I picture goats, lions,
cavorting around our living room. I see pastry girls
with their clothes off, their skin whitened with a layer
of flour as if to keep them from sticking to the floor.
Nick glides among them, smooth-limbed, beautiful.
His body picks up a light dusting of powder.
"Chicken?" I ask him.

He shakes his head. "Thanks."

"More broccoli?"

"Don't think so."

"Where did you go on your run?"

"Nowhere."

"Nowhere?"

"You know what I mean. This street. That street.
What's the difference?"

"Just curious."

"Don't be," he says. "My life's not that interesting." He has filled his glass halfway, but when he sees me watching him, he tips the bottle again and brings the liquid to the rim. "So how did the job hunt go today? Any leads?"

"Nothing."

"Did you try?"

"Sure I tried. I knocked on the door of every museum."

"Mm-hmmm."

"And they all said, 'Go away, little Impressionist. We don't need your kind here. The world is fuzzy enough already.' "

"Oh, Sarah, Sarah, Sarah, Sarah." He lifts his glass very carefully, not spilling a drop, and then bolts the whole thing down, neat, like a shot of whiskey. "Cheers," he says.

"Cheers," I say.

Sometimes Nick makes love to me while we're sleeping; otherwise we don't. In the middle of the night I wake and we are already deeply involved, turning, moaning. I can never tell when this will happen. It has nothing to do with what I'm wearing, or what we've said to each other at dinner, or even how he looks at me before bed. Sometimes when we've gone for days without really speaking I will find him inside me, probing, reaching. I was mugged once in Times Square. A man crept up behind me, put his arms around my waist and hugged me, gently, and ran away with my purse. It was gone before I realized he wasn't someone that I knew. When Nick touches me this way, I want to scream. I want to ask him, "Who do you think you are? What do you think this means?" Then I think, well, maybe this is better than nothing. I recede back into the dark, into his arms, the mindless roll of his will.

It's been weeks since we loved even this way, though I've waited every night, my desire outstretched like wings.

Sometimes, like tonight, now, for this, for the way it used to be, I would try anything at all, all the games that once worked, all the things he once loved. I follow him from room to room trying to remind him. "Come on, Nick. We haven't done that in a long time. You used to really like that. It used to be fun, remember? I bought candles. Musk. Lemon. A John Coltrane album. Here. Listen to this."

"Sarah—"

"Wait a minute. Don't say no. Here. Lie back down again. Listen. I'll put it on real soft, like this. It'll relax you. Come on. Lie back. Put your feet in my lap. Why not? Feels nice, huh?"

"Sarah—"

"Okay. Okay. You're not in the mood for that. I understand. Too much running, huh? Enough attention to the feet, right? You need attention elsewhere—okay. Turn over. I'll rub your back—"

"Sarah—"

"No? Okay, fine. We'll just sit here. I'll tell you the story of the water lilies. Not Monet's. *Mine.* Just let me undo my hair. That's better. The water lilies, by your Sarah—"

"Sarah—"

"No! *Listen.* Far away, in the deep, dark earth, the most secret of wonders was planted, deep in the earth, in the dark wet earth where the sun never shines, where no man ever—God, that sounds silly. Here. Put your head in my lap. I'm wearing satin. I know, you see I'm wearing satin, but just feel it. Here. Give me your hand. One touch. One touch only, you always said, drove you right up the wall—"

"Sarah. Please, *please*—"

"Okay, Nick. *Okay.* I understand."

"So," I ask the man at Dewey's, "What's the forecast for today? Any snow?"

"No snow. Very clear. Unseasonably warm." He grins as he pours sugar into the coffee he has bought for me. Then cream. Then a little more cream.

"That's great," I say.

I haven't asked his name and he hasn't asked mine, but I have learned that he's divorced (five months), that he lives above a delicatessen on the Upper West Side, that he used to date his students but lately he prefers older, more womanly types. He isn't really handsome; he has a big round face, hair that is both too sparse and too fine. But he has an interesting smile, a way of leaning forward when he listens as if sheer good will could shore up a conversation. Today he tells me that he still loves his ex-wife. She used to rub his back with oil that she warmed first in an egg poacher, then mixed with drops of perfume. Sandalwood. Rose. "That student business never meant a thing," he says. "She shouldn't have taken it so personally. People should never take things like that personally." He smiles. "But what's on *your* mind?" he asks.

Nothing. Nothing is on my mind. I tell him about Uncle Joe, how he is sick again, so soon. The lithium Uncle Joe takes used to last six months or more. "Calm as the sea in September," Aunt Marge would say when I asked how he was doing. Once he had a lucid span that went for almost two years. During that time he built himself a carpenter's bench in the basement and went to work carving wooden ducks. At first he carved the usual flat-eyed, plump-bodied mallards. He painted them black, with rings of military red and green around their necks. All of them looked exactly alike, and he built long rows of shelves to show their sameness. Everyone marvelled at the precision of his work. "Isn't it wonderful?" Aunt Marge would whisper, as if saying it too loudly might curse him.

I doubt that's what did it, but sometime after his second quiet winter the birds began to change. The red and green became orange and pink. The bodies he painted purple and turquoise with big red dots all over. He carved them all out of proportion— elongated, or foreshortened—and put their heads on askew. The faces he made contorted, almost human. Pain. Anger. Fear.

Aunt Marge tried to be gentle. "They're nice, Joey," she would say, "but I liked the others better." Or (brightly), "Why don't you make some of them look happy? Like ducks on a sunny day when the tourists throw them a lot of bread." Or (pleading), "Why can't you make them look normal?" Then she would call me and cry.

Now, I tell the man, Uncle Joe is in the hospital again. This time they caught him right at the Barnegat Inlet, run aground on a low tide. The yacht he'd stolen belonged to the Du Ponts. They were going to sue for damages until they found out he was a habitually crazy man. How he'd run aground was a mystery to both Aunt Marge and me. Uncle Joe was a very good sailor, and even though the inlet was very narrow, he'd been through it many times on previous trips north.

"The Du Ponts! *Jesus*," the man says, "*Un*-real." He throws his head back as if to laugh, but he doesn't laugh. "*Un*-real," he says again. "Like this." He reaches over and touches my hair, takes locks of it between his fingers, gently, and holds it up to the light, fanning it out and letting it drop, fanning it out and letting it drop, softly onto my shoulder right here in the front window of Dewey's. "Like gold," he says. "Just like gold. Spunnnnnn." He twirls the hair between his fingers.

"Cut it out."

"Why?"

"Because."

"Because why?" He wraps a long strand of it around his wrist.

"Please."

"Okay." He lets go. "Tell me some more secrets."

When we went to visit Uncle Joe on Sunday, I tell him, Nick ran away again.

"Nick," he interrupts. "Who's that? Your puppy? Your poodle?"

"Nick's my husband." I stress the word *husband*.

"So—surprise, surprise," he says.

"The point is," I tell him, "I can't count on Nick. There we are, visiting my crazy Uncle Joe, and Nick runs off and disappears for hours, doesn't say where the hell he's going, when he's coming back or anything. It's bad enough I have to sit there and worry about Uncle Joe, who's truly crazy, but I also have to worry about the person who's supposed to be helping me through this ordeal."

"So why worry?" the man says. "Pretty women should never worry." He pats my back as if to reassure me. His hand is warm and heavy, like the hands boys had in junior high school—sweaty, eager.

"Do you really teach school?" I ask.

He laughs. "Of course I do."

I try to laugh too. "Come on. Tell me the truth. Do you really teach meteorology? Who takes meteorology in night school?"

He looks at me. "Hell, I don't know. What's the difference? What if I just happened to like snow? What then? Would you still talk to me?"

"Of course."

"Are you a snob or something?"

"I said, *of course* I would. I was just asking."

"Why?"

I try to switch the subject back to Uncle Joe. "Speaking of weather . . ." I tell him that I tried to talk to Uncle Joe about his latest caper, but his roommate, a paranoid schizophrenic named Tim, kept interrupting us. "Who *are* you?" he asked me. "Who *are* you?" he asked Uncle Joe. "I mean *really*." Tim told us all his theories, about dreams, about witches, about telepathic crime, how 95 percent of all felonies and misdemeanors, violent and otherwise, were caused by bad thoughts transmitted from one person to another by electromagnetic impulse. If people wouldn't think bad thoughts there would be no rape, murder, incest, purse-snatching, arson—especially if the weather stayed bad, because, you see, contrary to popular belief, more crimes are committed on clear days. Thoughts travel better when it's dry. Keep an eye on your barometer, he said. When I could get a word in, I asked Uncle Joe, "How is everything here?"

Uncle Joe takes a long time to answer when he's in the hospital. While I was waiting, I tell the man, I wondered where Nick had gone. Jogging maybe, with a nurse? A whole hour passed. "Uncle Joe?" I said, finally. "Uncle Joe?"

Now the man smiles at me. He puts a warm hand on my older, more womanly knee and gives it a little squeeze. "Sounds like a wild and crazy guy, your uncle. Is your whole family like that?"

I stare at my coffee.

Another little squeeze. "Come on. Tell me what you're thinking about."

"Nick," I say, but it isn't true.

Tonight while I am waiting for Nick to come to bed, I make myself think of other things: what it's like to be Uncle Joe, what it was like when Nick and I first fell in love. It began very gently, at a party at the end of August, in a garden, at night. Roses. Crickets. All that damp midnight grass. Distant blessings of noise and music and smoke drifting past the hedges. It seemed inevitable. We were patients under ether, floating through sounds and lights and colors, the whole world rippling past. We liked it that way. We drove miles to have it. To beaches. And lakes. To the mountains where Nick had grown up, the Blue Ridge and the Tuscororas. We lay down together in fields, in sand, on wet, black earth at the bottom of forests. We covered ourselves with leaves. Climbed fire towers to look out over miles and miles of orchards, dropping apples, pears, onto October hills at twilight. There was no day or night, only us.

I remember it now as something that kept us going; we had to keep going or we would die, go mad. Is that what sends Uncle Joe to the sea, I wonder? Some unanswerable desire? Each year the yachts he steals get bigger. Each year the Coast Guard intercepts him farther from his goal. His hair has turned gray with trying. His skin has roughened. In it I see the stony surface of despair. He is storm-tossed, wild, sorry.

In the other rooms Nick is busy making noise. Clinking glasses. Slamming the refrigerator door, the cabinet doors. Skittering through the stations on the radio. Five seconds of jazz. Ten seconds of flute and harpsichord. A sonata. The excruciating growl and twang of a heavy-metal riff. A chair falls over in the living room. He is drunk, I think. Drunk. Disorderly. And sick of me. I wish he would say it. Get it over with. That is my seduction tonight. Say it, Nick. Say it.

I try to imagine my life without him. Starting over in winter. I see cold, dark rooms, unused furniture, empty closets, a corner of a bed where I curl up and wait. I wonder how many strangers' hands have fallen on *his* knee, have clutched *his* hair, have dragged *him* under.

Then I hear the front door slam, a heavy oaken thud that whams right through me. I cross the room in time to see Nick in his white shorts and bandanna pass beneath our bedroom window. Snow is falling. He is running through it, trailing silence.

Without thinking I run after him, barefoot, in my nightgown. The checkered marble of the entryway is cold and smooth, the concrete pavement freezing. There is already an inch of snow. Feathery white dust sears my feet.

I try to run anyway. By the time I go back for my robe and slippers and car keys, he will be gone. I watch my prints go down into the snow, count the number of steps I take. One. Two. Three. Four. Flakes whirl into my mouth. Five. Six. Seven. Eight. One hundred. Two hundred . . . My chest burns. My lungs. Five hundred. I pretend that I am running through sand. Summer sand. Burning hot. Nick is already far away. One block, Two blocks. Turning a corner. A small white blur.

The flakes fall on my arms and hair, teasing me.

What color is frostbite? I ask myself. White? Red? Blue? I can't remember. I can feel my feet turning colors, disintegrating. The cold air twists me inside out. Nick is miles away, turning corners, disappearing.

"Hey!" Someone whoops at me from a car. "Crazy lady! Crazy lady in a nightgown! Look at that crazy lady. Hey you, lady. You know it's snowin'?"

I pretend not to hear him. Where is Nick? The streets are empty except for this car moving slowly alongside me, plowing softly through the snow, engine breathing, tires shushing, crunching. "Hey, baby. What *is* this? Halloween? A striptease? Your mama know you out here like this? You always go runnin' this way?"

I shake my head. Leave me alone. Leave me alone.

Nick is nowhere in sight. I don't know how far I've run, how many corners I've turned, where I lost him. What keeps him immune from the cold? Are we so different? Everything looks far away and tiny. The buildings. The streetlamps. Even the sky looks too small.

"Hey, baby—come on! Get in this car. You get right on in this car. Right on in here. Get warmed *up.*"

"Hey, baby."

"Hey, *girl!*"

I wave my arms at them. "Go away! Drop dead. Bug off. Shove it up your—"

"Ooooooooooo-weeeeeeee! She a *nut.*"

Someone throws a bottle from the car.

Wheels whir.

They drive off.

I continue to run, slower now, much, much slower. So many people behind so many doors. What are they doing on a night like this? How many are crying? How many are curled together, growing warmer, warmer, warm, letting the whole world spread out distant beyond the grip of their flesh, beyond that hard, eternal shaking? I watch my reflection in the cold, dark windows, shrinking and spreading, the white scarf of my nightgown waving, waving, billowing, flapping, gone. Where would Nick go on a night like this? Which way would the snow pull him? When he runs, is this what he runs for? This pounding, aching, throbbing cold? I look down and see my bare feet moving through snow. They are attached to my legs, but my legs are no longer attached to me. I watch them lifting and falling slower and slower. Prints in the snow. One thousand. Two thousand. Three thousand. I don't know what I'm counting for. I don't know what Nick wants.

I run through the strange, empty streets.

At 5:45 A.M. a light goes on in the closet. Nick is pulling things from hangers. Shirts. Pants. Neckties. A red-and-black-plaid hunting jacket. They fall softly into his hands, one after another, ripe for something.

"What's wrong?" I whisper, but he doesn't hear me. He is dragging a large leather suitcase from the back of the closet, knocking over his ski poles and boots, and then a squash racket that was propped in front of these. They clatter on the wooden floor, but he doesn't even look over to see if the noise has awakened me. Oh, Nick, Nick, Nick, I say to myself. Is this the way you go?

He is tossing shirts one after another into the bottom of the suitcase without folding them. Socks. T-shirts. His bedroom slippers.

Wait, I want to say. This is a joke, isn't it? A practice run? A fire drill? But I am afraid to say anything, afraid that if I open my mouth and scream, it will be real.

When he has finished throwing things into the suitcase, he does another strange thing. He zips it up and jams it in the back of the closet, behind the ski poles and the squash racket. Then he drapes several towels over the poles—a red one, a green, a dark-blue flowered one we used to lie on at the beach. On top of everything he hangs an old sheet. He checks to make sure nothing is showing. Not once has he looked over here to see what I am doing.

What I am doing is this. I am making myself think of other things: Uncle Joe in his chair, in his linoleum-tiled room, in a cold gray haze, saying, "We'll buy a yacht together this time. We'll sail to Oklahoma." The man's hand, how his touch rushed through me like water.

"Are you awake?" Nick says.

"I'm awake."

The air in the room is thick as an ocean. The only light is in the closet. When he turns it out, I think I feel him coming toward me through the darkness, parting waves of it to get to me, but I'm not sure. He will lift me above the waves, I think. We will feel the spray on our faces, I think, but I'm not sure. It's much too dark to tell.

A TOUGH LIFE

"Why are *we* always the ones?" my mother asked. She had posed this same question many times before on many different occasions—on vacations, at funerals, the night my Uncle Ruben arrived from jail. Often her riddle referred to my uncles. "Grabbers," she called the ten brothers, certainly more brothers than any sane person should have, especially since all of them lived right smack in our neighborhood where they could knock on our door whenever they wanted, or just barge right in like a band of outlaws and take everything that wasn't nailed down. My father encouraged them, she claimed. "You're always so happy when they call," she used to reprimand him.

She said that my father worked harder for the brothers than he did at his job. He bailed them out when they were in financial difficulty. He took them fishing when they were depressed. He helped them paint their houses and fixed their cars for free at his garage down on Hunting Park Ave. Almost as soon as he set foot in the door at night they would arrive in procession: Uncle Sammy: "I need a wrench, Joe."; Uncle Abie: "A pair of pliers—needle-nose preferably"; Uncle Herschel: "Lend me a hand with this, will you? I need this for my project."

Haughty as pontiffs all of them but my father never said no. Much more constant than providence he nurtured them through the seasons. Almost every weekend in summer they came to our house for a barbecue or a picnic or a game of softball. In winter they sat by our fire. My mother served them tea in a glass—the old-fashioned way, and blintzes bundled up in sour cream. "Would your brothers do all this for *you?*" she used to grumble. And though my father insisted it wasn't right to make estimates of things like love and family loyalty, my mother disagreed. The brothers, she said, were "ungrateful." They accepted everything as if it were their due. My father got the merest of thanks ("You did a nice job, Joe"; "That looks pretty good, Kid"). In synagogue, God got the rest. To *Him* they bowed their heads in reverence, in appreciation for services rendered without charge. "Blessed art Thou O Lord," they chanted.

"Ten brothers and now *this!*" my mother said.

That was the summer a very strange thing happened. The brothers all disappeared, every last one of

72

them, "poof!" my mother said, "like magic." Overnight, it seemed, they forgot who we were. All ten of
them were suddenly, in mysterious unison, terribly
busy, even Uncle Isidore, the unmarried brother, who
usually spent a week with us at Longport, lathered up
in Sea & Ski, reclining in the sun on a blanket while
my mother passed him cups of icy lemonade and my
father held his fishing pole in case he got a tug. "He
has no one else," my father always whispered, as if this
were a diagnosis of terminal illness, but that summer
Uncle Isidore somehow managed to survive all on his
own without us.

Likewise the rest of them. Through the entire
month of August not one of them ventured across our
threshold, nor did they phone, nor did they send any
of their offspring to borrow those indispensable items
they always forgot to return. Whenever my father
called them they already had one foot out the door or
they had made "prior arrangements" or someone had
come down with one of those awful colds of summer—they wouldn't dream of spreading the germs!

This quarantine began the day my Uncle Ruben
arrived at our house and continued almost until the
day he left. It made my mother furious. "I rest my
case," she kept saying. "Don't jump to conclusions,"
my father would answer her back. "All the evidence
isn't in yet."

I never even knew I had an Uncle Ruben until he
sat down at our dinner table one Friday night.

"Kiss your uncle 'hello'," my mother instructed.
"He's been out West."

"Doing what?" I asked. I thought Uncle Ruben might be a cowboy in a rodeo—why else go out West?—but my mother just said, "Sha!" She tore off a piece of bread and warned me not to eat it before the blessing. "For once," she commanded, "*behave.*" As if I didn't always. What else was there to do in my house? I folded my hands in my lap and tried to look serene, at one with God and the marvelous productions of His universe.

Uncle Ruben didn't seem to care. He noticed neither my good behavior nor her warning. He popped *his* bread right into his mouth, then looked at his empty hand, surprised, as though it had cheated him.

I was surprised too, that my mother didn't yell at him ("What is this—a stampede?") as she would have yelled at me. "Hannah. *You* say the blessing," she ordered quickly.

A minute later she had to prompt me again. I was wondering what made Uncle Ruben's skin such an unlikely color, as yellow as an old newspaper lining a forgotten drawer. And why was he so thin? Why wasn't he powerful and grease-stained like my father? All of the brothers were big. "Solid mahagony," their wives said. Next to them my uncle would have looked like a man viewed through the wrong end of a telescope. His face was a sliver, as stark as the grin on a jack-o'-lantern.

"Hannah! Pay attention," my mother warned, but she looked directly at my uncle. He had his elbows on the table and was eying the oven intently as if it were a safe he was trying to detonate. He stared at it shrewdly until we'd finished all the blessings and my mother brought forth the food.

Broiled chicken, carrot-and-raisin stew, potato pudding—onto the platters my mother scooped our dinner, billowing fragrant steam. Only then, as though he'd been visited by an angel, did my uncle's face light up. He grabbed his fork and fell upon his food, hunching over his plate and stabbing things. In the presence of such an eater even my mother grew silent. She gazed at Uncle Ruben as if he were a monster in a sci-fi movie who gobbles up whole cities. Instead of rebuking him though, she mouthed the words: I told you so, and frowned across the table at my father.

My father frowned back at her. He held up his hand like a traffic cop. SLOW DOWN, he signaled. TAKE IT EASY. Then, out loud, he said, as if Uncle Ruben were far away, as if maybe "out West" they didn't speak English, "You'll hurt his feelings."

"What feelings?" my mother demanded.

"Shirley!"

But at that moment she seemed to be right. Uncle Ruben hardly noticed what was being said about him. He just kept right on eating, cramming the goods in. He didn't once pause for breath. Nor did he pick his head up when all the food was gone. After he'd finished every last shred of chicken, every last bite of carrot, he tucked his chin down on his chest and fell asleep.

My mother raised her eyebrows.

My father put his finger to his lips. "Let him sleep," he whispered. "He's had a tough life."

"So who hasn't?"

"He's no good."
"He's a maniac."
"A KLEPTO-maniac."
"He's a God-knows-what-he-is."

Every time I turned a corner, she was complaining about him, upbraiding my father vehemently, flogging Uncle Ruben's name as though it were the wrong stop on the subway, the one where all the drunks and muggers got on. "Ru-ben. RU-ben!"

My father would groan. "Please, Shirley. Can't you ease up on him a bit? He's had a rough time. Why must we add to that?" Then their argument would begin again. She could NOT ease up on him. There was "the child" to think of. She had no intention of harboring a killer, a crazy man, under the same roof with me. Awful things could happen.

Personally, I agreed with my father. I didn't believe Uncle Ruben was a killer, not a real one. Ours was a world based upon exaggeration. "Oh Joe— you're *killing* me," my mother often exclaimed when my father gave her a bit of gossip. "Shirley—my heart is breaking," he used to tease her. In this style of expression words behaved oddly. "Murderer" and "thief" took on strange connotations. They could have meant practically anything—my Uncle Ruben had actually murdered someone, or he had forgotten to feed the dog one night, or he had borrowed someone's sportsjacket without asking.

Besides, Uncle Ruben was really fascinating. He

was a man with many strange customs. He used to stand on the porch for hours, leaning over the rail as if he were gazing out to sea. He would hold his thumb up, align it with his nose, and squint, at Mrs. Kleinbard's windows or at the trellis winding towards the Rosen's bedroom. Then he would pull out a little notebook and jot down some numbers, make sketches of the houses with arrows running back and forth between the rooftops.

"Is Uncle Ruben a painter?" I asked my mother.

"A painter!" She glared at the clothespin she was holding as if it had had the temerity to venture such a silly question.

I got the same dirty look when I asked if Uncle Ruben had ever been in the circus. "Where do you get these crazy ideas?"

I decided not to tell her how Uncle Ruben had shinnied up to his bedroom window the day we got locked out, nor about the afternoon he took me to the drugstore to buy a comic book. I didn't tell her how long he had patrolled the aisles peeking through the rows of shaving creams and colognes at the druggist. Nor did I mention the five bottles of cough syrup he bought.

I wondered why Uncle Ruben needed so much cough syrup, but when I asked my mother, "Is Uncle Ruben sick?" she just sighed. "Don't you worry so much about your Uncle Ruben. Let *us* take care of that."

I worried anyway. Uncle Ruben didn't seem to be sleeping well. His room was next door to mine and at night I could hear him pacing back and forth, back and forth, as though checking and rechecking its dimensions. When he grew weary of that he would climb out onto the roof to smoke, cigarettes that had a ragged, bitter smell, or he would tune in a late night ball game that crackled and blared like a thunderstorm, then dissipated into silence. I figured he stayed up the whole night. I used to hear him at dawn retreating across the roof. Once, I thought I saw him next door creeping past Mrs. Levy's hydrangea bushes; then, suddenly!—up at her bedroom window, the same stealthy shadow—flitting, hovering, looking for a way in. I turned on my bedside lamp to make sure I was really awake. When I switched it off again the figure was gone. I decided that there had been no figure. If anything, I told myself, Uncle Ruben was probably out spying on his brothers, trying to catch a glimpse of them curled up in bed.

The thing that fascinated me most about Uncle Ruben was the degree to which my mother hated him. I couldn't figure it out. Despite his odd behavior Uncle Ruben seemed harmless enough, but my mother absolutely refused to accept him. "Why can't you just give him a chance?" I heard my father say over and over again. "What has he actually done since he came here? Has he done anything wrong?"

"He certainly has!" This was her lead-in to the list, a running cypher of Uncle Ruben's sins. Uncle Ruben had squeezed the toothpaste tube too hard and it had squirted all over the sink. He'd propped his sockless feet on the marble coffee table. He had made a mess of the newspaper while reading the baseball scores. He had sneezed without benefit of a Kleenex. "In the past twenty-four hours alone," she would add.

"These hardly sound like major crimes," my father would protest, but for her these misdeeds always tallied the same way: "He's an animal—plain and simple. He should go back to that place. Let him live with his own kind."

"We *are* his own kind," my father always said.

"Since when?"

"He's my brother."

"Who else thinks so besides you?"

Face to face with Uncle Ruben she was always polite. "Would you care for another cookie, Ruben? Is this how you like your coffee? Do you have enough towels? Do you prefer this rug by your bed or beneath the vanity table?" as if she could obliterate him with kindness. Every morning she drove my uncle to the subway station though he always objected: "I'm not an old man, Shirley. There's no reason why I can't walk." He was supposed to be working downtown in a shoe factory pounding leather, stitching seams into the tough insides of boots and moccasins. Each day as we watched him shuffle up the steps, pulling himself sadly, hand over hand along the rail, my mother would observe, "You see? He doesn't really want to go but he has to. This is what comes of no schooling."

To protect me from Uncle Ruben's fate she enrolled me, on the days she worked as a dictaphone operator in a law office, in an enrichment course in "higher mathematics" at the local elementary school. "It's for *gifted* students only." She read from a pastel pamphlet that described this internment. "A WONDERFUL OPPORTUNITY!" "AN INTRODUCTION TO THE WORLD OF TOMORROW!" "COLLEGE PREP!" "This is marvelous," she added, exchanging an intimate, knowing look with the circular.

It really wasn't Uncle Ruben's fault I played hookey that summer. I was ripe for corruption, and besides, our teacher, Mr. Blank, was right out of college and had far too much faith in the inherent interest of his subject. He was skinny and wore enormous glasses with a double bridge and he spent the whole entire first day showing us how to use the light switch. "I'm going to teach you the binary system," he announced as proudly as if it were the antidote to kryptonite. "There are only two numbers in the binary system," he continued. "Can you guess what they are, boys and girls?"

"Very good," he told Jerome Levy, a handwaver from birth. "They are ZERO and ONE. Can you repeat that, class?"

"Zero and one," we chanted. "ZERO and ONE!!"

"Excellent," Mr. Blank commended us on our fifteenth try. "Now I want you to do something else for me. Think of the ZERO as the OFF position of these lights. Think of the ON position as ONE. Can you do that?" He made each of us get up and flick the light switch: ON OFF ON OFF ON OFF.

By the following Friday when Uncle Ruben handed me the note, I was yearning for deliverance. I was mournfully packing my satchel with No. 2 pencils and plenty of bubble gum when he pulled me aside.

"PLEZE EX—KOOZE HANNA GREENE FRUM SKOOL TOO-DAY. HUR STUMIK IS HURD-ING HUR."

Despite its brevity the note looked as though it had taken him all night to compose. It was smudged and tattered and worn thin by a furious eraser. I pictured him stalking back and forth in his room worrying over each mean, stubborn word. "Excuse," I imagined him muttering to himself. "E-K-S-O—. E-K-S-K?-O. E-K-X?" shaking his head in desperation, "Gosh!" Sighing. Pacing.

"ExCUSE," he began again.

A man who couldn't spell needed protection, I decided. My poor uncle, I thought—all of those comic books he'd bought and he could only stare at the pictures. When my uncle showed up at the schoolyard later that morning, shaking and sweating and beseeching, "Hannah! You've got to help me. Hannah, *please*," I felt no compunction going with him. What choice did I have—my uncle's happiness against two little numbers? He was my *uncle* after all.

Much of what I did that summer, I realized many years later, was score drugs for Uncle Ruben. What I thought I was doing was participating in some kind of underground railroad of CARE packages for the emotionally needy—cigarettes, mostly, Camels and Pall

Malls, my uncle's favorites that my mother forbade him to smoke in the house, sometimes boxes of Good & Plenty or Raisinets or Nonpareils, a deck of cards once in a metal container that said: "Guaranteed to Play."

"I've got to have something," Uncle Ruben would declare. "You know what I mean, Hannah? You know what it feels like to be a stone wall? A piece of dirty glass someone spits on?"

Not really, but I thought that Uncle Ruben's needs were modest considering the loneliness and rejection he went through every day at my house. I became Uncle Ruben's "frontrunner," his "Pony Express." I figured these names were signs of affection, that he was teasing me as my father did when he called me his "little ragamuffin."

Most often I scored for him in the park, probably because that was the closest place he could find. He would send me to bum "smokes or whatever" from a man in blue jeans and a faded T-shirt, or a woman with bleached-out hair imprisoned beneath a red, paisley scarf. When I asked if I could borrow a cigarette, please, for my uncle over there they always gave me the whole pack. "How nice," I thought, and, thrilled by success, I'd go skipping back with our booty. "Look! They gave me all of them—*the whole bunch*," and he'd nod. "Well, isn't that good luck for once? Here. Go back there and give them this—I owe them." I'd return with whatever comic book he'd been holding at the time, "Archie and Veronica", "Richie Rich," "Thor". "There's a good part on page twenty-three,"

I'd say as he'd instructed. I never embarrassed him by revealing that he couldn't read.

I thought that people were really friendly in the park, that they were friendlier, in fact, most everywhere, than at home. We met people in all kinds of places who were more generous than most of my family. At bus stops, on the library steps, in various alleys behind taprooms that were neon-lit all day, people kept giving him things. Granted, it was mostly small things, but every so often there was a bundle of shirts straight from the cleaners or a sack filled with french fries and hamburgers and lots and lots of salt. Occasionally, we were even invited to someone's apartment. Though I was glad for Uncle Ruben, this wasn't my favorite type of jaunt. I had to sit in leprous kitchens where everything was peeling—the linoleum, the plaster, the vinyl coverings on the chairs, and drink limeade out of glasses that looked as if they'd never known detergent.

"Time out for grownups," Uncle Ruben would say. "I'll be right back—five minutes," but it always took him much longer than that. Five minutes. Ten minutes. Twenty minutes. An hour. He would fall asleep in these places on ravaged couches and armchairs, in back bedrooms on wartorn mattresses, on the cold tile floors of bathrooms, his head cradled against the U-joint beneath the sink. Whenever this happened I was horribly embarrassed and concerned that Uncle Ruben was spoiling his chances to make friends. "I'm really sorry," I'd say over and over as I tried to revive him. "This happens to him a lot. You should see him at home. I think he stays up too late or something. I know it seems weird but he really likes you. I'm sure he does." Then I'd lean over him again, quickly, to get him to prove my point. "Uncle Ruben. Uncle Ruben, wake up! Your friends are waiting for you."

Oddly enough, these strangers never got angry. No matter what Uncle Ruben did they just grinned slow billowing grins like butterflies in late afternoon. "No sweat," they'd say, or "Give the poor dude a break. He'll come to in a minute." I thought they were pretty good-natured about Uncle Ruben's social inadequacies and would have thanked them, but they always disappeared soon after, down the fire escape or out a window to "cop" some fresh air.

It wasn't true what my mother claimed later. My uncle didn't drag me along on his burglaries. Nor did he try to make a drug addict out of me. Only once did I actually see him shoot up and he had me so convinced that I was watching a diabetic rescue himself from certain death that my hands tingled with awe. Imagine giving yourself a shot! is what I thought. As for thefts, I never to my knowledge saw him steal a single thing. I suppose what Uncle Ruben called "taking measurements" was crime-related. I realized after he left that we must have been scouting the area for easy and worthwhile break-ins, but what I thought we were doing, at the time, was rating the moral fiber of the neighborhood.

Who was most openhanded? Who most loving?

Who lavished attention on their children? Their houses? What proof did I have? Was it nice inside? Nice furniture? TV sets? Radios? Was the wife very pretty? Did she dress well—lots of shiny stuff?

Each house he scrutinized as thoroughly as Da Vinci exploring the mysteries of the human form. "Tell me again," he'd prod me. "How many people live here? Is the husband a good provider? *Both* of them work? All day long?"

I never knew why he needed all of this information. There could have been many reasons, I thought. He wanted to get to know people better. He wanted to know if everyone else's family behaved as strangely as his own.

All through August while my father pleaded with his brothers on the telephone: "Couldn't you drop by for just five minutes?," "Won't you have a little snack with us?," "You haven't seen Ruben in how many years? Don't you even want to say hello? Wait! Wait! Don't hang up!," Uncle Ruben and I made our excursions together. I kept telling myself that my father would be proud of me, wouldn't he? I was keeping Uncle Ruben company the way his brothers should have been. They had treated Uncle Ruben unfairly his whole life just because he was their stepbrother. I learned this one evening by hiding in the bushes and eavesdropping while my parents were drinking iced tea in the backyard. My grandmother, a former model at Wanamaker's made headstrong by her own beauty, had refused to raise another woman's child, so Uncle

Ruben had been farmed out to a series of relatives where he would stay for a month, six months, a year if he was lucky, until they couldn't afford to keep him any longer. "My brothers thought they were better than Ruben," my father said. "They acted just like my mother and no one stopped them. My father was a weak man who would never contradict her, not even for his own son."

"What's your *point?*" my mother demanded, but my father soothed her. Uncle Ruben was a sad case. He deserved a break. A home was all he'd ever wanted. Instead he got turned over to strangers when the relatives got sick of him, people who worked him hard and screamed and yelled to straighten him out. From a grocer's house to a butcher's house, to an undertaker's house, then back to the butcher's, hauling crates of chickens, sweeping sand and sawdust, heaps of ice, entrails, until the habit of moving rocked through his blood, until he grew up and disappeared. "A home," my father repeated, "was all he ever asked for."

"Well, he's not going to find it here," my mother declared.

In this context I thought of what I was doing as reparations. I felt obligated to go along with whatever it was Uncle Ruben took it into his head to do. For example, he liked to dig an awful lot. Often when we went to the park we took spades and shovels from my mother's gardening shed. Ours was a big park with thick snarls of trees and bushes and we attacked the ragged dirt of the hillsides and gullies like merciless explorers in a hostile wilderness until we had gnawed away whole shopping bags full. These we lugged home and hid in the attic under the eaves where even my mother was usually too discouraged to clean. It was wretched earth, poor and scraggly, laden with stones, with twigs and branches that looked as if they had been trapped and decomposed before they could claw their way back to air. I wondered why my uncle wanted to save such awful stuff, but when I asked him he just winked. "Isn't this fun?"

Maybe he really didn't know, I marveled, but I never questioned him further because I thought I might offend him. If this was what he enjoyed, I didn't want to ruin it by asking stupid questions. Besides, I didn't want to miss the trip to "the diner" we always took, when we'd finished digging, to drink a milkshake. Here too I never let on to Uncle Ruben that his grasp of the truth was pretty weak. This didn't taste like any milkshake I'd ever had, nor did it look like any diner I'd ever seen. There was a long wooden counter and glasses hanging upside down and rows and rows of bottles standing straight as mummies in darkened niches beside the mirror. There was only one window in there made of cloudy glass, outlined with red neon that quivered and pulsed. The tile floor stuck to your shoes when you tried to walk. "This is a bar, isn't it?" I cried every time we went in there. "We're in a bar!"—but my uncle insisted we weren't. "You can get anything you want here, Hannah—hamburgers, hot dogs, potato chips. Does that sound like a bar to you? Hey, Eileen—mix this little girl up something in the blender, O.K.? I'll bet she's starving. Order whatever else you want," he'd tell me, then he'd disappear in the back with someone named Frank, a tall man with so many gold teeth it looked like Indian corn when he grinned.

I never knew what else to ask for—french fries? a jelly donut? What did people eat along with a milk shake if they couldn't have meat? While I was debating, the waitress would come over. "Would you like to play the jukebox, honey? We have some really nice songs. Bobby Rydell. Lesley Gore. Frankie Avalon. You like those guys? Who's your favorite?" I was afraid to tell her I hadn't heard of a single one of them; she seemed so eager to be nice to me—patting my hand and showing me her charm bracelet and bringing me extra sugar in case my milkshake wasn't sweet enough. "Frankie Avalon," I always said because his name reminded me of the seashore.

When my uncle finally returned she'd announce proudly, "Hey—guess who your kid likes?" though Uncle Ruben never seemed all that interested. "Just make me a double, will you?" He'd slide down into the seat across from me as though it were made of quicksand. He'd unfold a sheet of paper and shake his head at it. "I don't know about this. I don't like the looks of this one." On the way home he'd make me promise not to tell my mother what we'd been up to. "She'd never understand, you know what I mean?"

I thought it over quite a bit. Which part didn't he want me to tell—the milkshake? The deck of cards? Taking measurements? What about the afternoon I found him crying in the attic? Wouldn't my mother have stopped hating him if she could have seen him curled up there on the floor trembling: "It hurts. . . . It hurts. . . . Goddamnit . . ."

I knew I was going to get caught sooner or later. I could feel my doom hustling up to greet me. I had never disobeyed my mother before, not in such a deliberate way. I imagined all the usual punishments, the spankings, the weeks of hard labor helping her vacuum, polishing silverware, dusting the carved mahogony legs of tables and sofas, but I knew that wasn't enough; there could never be enough punishment for liking Uncle Ruben.

But as it turned out, my mother was much more furious with Uncle Ruben than with me. When the illicit truth, via Jerome Levy, came to light, she told Uncle Ruben to pack his bags right then and there.

"I'm going," he said.

But when my father arrived home for an emergency conference he had some different ideas. "It's only an enrichment class, Shirley. I asked you not to send Hannah in the first place. She's just a little girl. Ruben's had a hard existence. He was just afraid Hannah would miss out on all the fun the way he did."

"A hard existence, my eye," my mother huffed at him, a sound like an air hose trying to force sense into a hopelessly flat tire. "That's what you always say. How many times can the same excuse be good?" And though my father protested: "It's not a pass to the movies," she ignored him. "Are *our* lives easy?" she scolded. "Work all day long like dogs and then we have to come home at night to a good-for-nothing who wants to turn our daughter into a truant. What were they doing, I'd like to know, when they weren't doing what they were supposed to be doing—*Hannah?*"

"We read a lot of comic books," I said timidly.

"Comic books." As if this weren't sufficient bad news to condemn my Uncle Ruben forever, she added, "He's stealing now too—are you aware of this, Joe? He's up to his old tricks again."

"Stealing?"

"Yes." My mother nodded grimly. "When he thinks I'm not looking. Spoons he stuffs into his pockets, and matchbooks from the kitchen. He slips his hand inside the cupboards like he's a ghost. Voila! No more matches. Cotton balls, from the bathroom cabinet when he assumed I was upstairs sewing clothes for Hannah for the fall. Why does he need cotton balls—a whole bag?"

My father tried to defend him. "What did he take we didn't already say he could have? We told him that this was his home."

"Exactly." My mother set the word down as if it were the last brick in Uncle Ruben's tomb. "This is *exactly* the point I'm trying to make." Her arms flung wide open. "Our home is his. Our home is everyone's. They're all thieves, your precious brothers. Where are they now when you need them? Why can't they give *us* something for once?"

"All right," my father said wearily. "All right, already. I give up. I'll ask them again. I'll call every single one of them right now."

And he did: Abe, Sammy, Theodore, Herschel, Benny, Morris, Sidney, Jack and Isidore. With each of them he pleaded: "Do me a favor—just this once. Just take him for a little while—a few days, a week; conditions are very bad here right now."

"No one forgives," he told my mother bitterly.

"I want him to leave," she replied.

Uncle Ruben came downstairs with his suitcase. His face was as grim as a window in an abandoned house. "I'm going now," he said to my mother. He picked up her hand and shook it. "I'm truly sorry," he told them both. "I've made a real mess and now no one wants me; I guess nothing ever changes, does it?" He hoisted his suitcase and made for the door.

I never knew what exactly my father said to change her mind. Maybe the prospect of the brothers returning, full-force, was more than she could stand. In any case the two of us were confined for the rest of the summer—I, in my room, catching up on all of the work I'd missed, and Uncle Ruben, catching up on work too, pumping gas down at the station where my father could keep an eye on him.

Neither one of us bore our punishment very well. For me, it was torment, pure and simple, to be pinned to my desk while the hazy joys of August drifted in through my window. Bicycle races. Baby-in-the-air. Tag and double dutch and hop scotch. I saw all the other kids in the neighborhood, blessedly free, glorying beneath sprinklers and climbing the limbs of maple trees and weeping willows, and running with arms outstretched to catch fireflies. Most excruciating of all was the sound of the Good Humor truck approaching, its pealing chimes summoning the faithful. They appeared clutching nickels, their voices flushed with delight. "Give me a cherry popsicle! A chocolate cone! One grape and one vanilla!"

For my uncle things were even worse. Every morning at 6 A.M. my mother pounded on his bedroom door. "Wake up, Ruben. You'd better hurry. Joe is leaving for the station. Are you ready? Joe—do you hear him stirring?" Five minutes later she would scream up the stairwell, "Nu, Ruben! Where are you? I thought we made an agreement." She badgered him unmercifully. "How would you like to do me a little favor?" she prefaced all her commands. Then she'd tell him to take out the garbage, scrub the kitchen floor for her, spread mulch on all the flowerbeds and get those newspapers out of the basement; he could take my red wagon if he needed to—it was still serviceable for work like this.

When my father tried to intercede: "Please, Shirley—he's tired. He's been helping me all day at the shop," my mother would feign surprise: "What! A big strong character like him? Ruben. Is it true you're tired?"

By the evening when the ram's horn sounded the New Year, Uncle Ruben had sworn he was leaving on at least three more occasions—once when my mother accused him of drinking the bottle of kirchwasser she'd been saving for the holidays; again, after a neighbor saw him climbing around on our roof and reported him as a prowler, and the last time after she discovered an enormous sack of dirt hidden in the eaves of our attic.

Each fight was the same: my mother yelled: "Thief!"; my father called his brothers; my uncle packed his bag.

"What does he want with all this dirt?" my mother wanted to know. She was flabbergasted when my father announced that not only was my Uncle Ruben NOT leaving, but also, he, personally, Joe Abelov, was going to make his eldest and most deserving brother a fiftieth birthday party. "Have you gone crazy?" she asked him. She threatened to leave him. She threatened to throw all of his things out on the lawn and let him fend for himself with his rotten brother. She wanted to know who was going to cook and clean and bake for this gala event? "I want you to know," she told my father, "that I consider this a direct slap in my face."

"This isn't a slap in anybody's face. This is a big birthday coming up. Ruben hasn't had a happy day in his whole life. I'm going to set things straight once and for all."

He knew he had her. It was the beginning of the Ten Days of Awe. This was a crucial time for Jews. The entire period between New Year's and the Day of Atonement was set aside for repentance. During that interval it was each person's responsibility to seek forgiveness from those whom he had wronged during the year. Then each person's fate was inscribed for the year to come. In Hebrew school our teacher told us, "The Talmud speaks of three books being opened in Heaven. One is for the completely righteous who are at once inscribed in the book of life; another is for the wholly wicked who are in the book of the condemned; the third is for the great mass of indeterminate humans whose doom is suspended during these ten days until God decides which destiny it is that he deserves."

Although my mother refused to help with the preparations, she didn't actually stand in the way of the party. She watched the proceedings with one eyebrow raised, as if my father's magnanimity were some newfangled contraption she was sure would never work. She planted her hands on her hips and frowned as he turned the kitchen into a "shambles" strewn with pots and ladles, all of the countertops snowed under by flour.

"You call that a noodle pudding?" she jeered.

"You call that a jello mold?"

Every night after work my father baked cookies and babkas and sponge cakes while she darkened his best efforts with her scolding. The night he sat for hours painting designs on construction paper she had a laughing fit until he asked her, "What's so funny? Do you enjoy seeing me struggle?"

"Now you know," she said.

"Now I know *what?*"

"What do you call those?" She pointed at the awkward shapes, like flying saucers sprouting necks.

"They're Japanese lanterns, if you don't mind. They're for the garden. I'm going to string them between the clothespoles."

"That will be impressive," she said.

As for my Uncle Ruben, he seemed completely bewildered by this turn of events. "Is this really for *me?*" he kept asking. "Are you sure you want to do this? I feel funny about it. I don't think I deserve all this fuss. No one ever made a fuss like this before."

"I'm very sure," my father always replied, but Uncle Ruben didn't seem to believe him. "Look," he told my father, "I got along fine for all these years without a party; you really don't need to do this."

"Everyone deserves a little pleasure once in his life," my father said. He kept right on going, trimming the lawns and pruning the rose bushes and the hedges. He borrowed folding tables to be adorned with pink and yellow cloths which said, over and over, in fancy script: "HAPPY BIRTHDAY! HAPPY BIRTHDAY! HAPPY BIRTHDAY!" These he lined up in the garden, one long row to imply an endless banquet, endless reveling, then he hung up the lanterns and balloons and streamers, crepe paper around the tree trunks as if to show that the whole natural world had clamored to be included. "So much trouble for nothing," my mother said. "And who is going to attend this fabulous affair?"

"Who do you think?" he said. "They *have* to come this time." He had written their invitations on the backs of the New Year's cards he'd sent them: "Please come share with us this special occasion . . . come celebrate!!"

To entertain everyone he hired a band, a guitarist and accordian player in training for weddings and Bar Mitzvahs who plodded through their opening number, "Hava Nagillah" ("Come let us rejoice") as if rejoicing were a close relative of Death.

This turned out to be the appropriate accompaniment. The brothers weren't exactly in a party mood. They came shuffling up our path like gloomy oxen staggering beneath the weight of their obligation. It was obvious they had come only to put in an appearance, (for God's sake, not for Uncle Ruben's or my father's). They arrived late, en masse, as if they thought that in a crowd their ill will would not be recognized. They came empty-handed. Not a single one brought a gift, though on *their* birthdays my father always gave them watches or handmade tables; even, one year, a color TV set to Uncle Isidore to keep him warm on winter nights.

They huddled in a disgruntled clump near the punch bowl, whispering and muttering: "A party for a criminal—what next?" They said nothing about the display of food my father had spent all morning arranging, moving the platters of cakes and salads back and forth as if the right configuration would insure a wonderful time. They didn't notice the bouquets nor the cornucopias of fruit nor the five-layer cake rising like a ski slope under a blanket of white frosting. The only thing they noticed were the lanterns. "What in the hell are those?" Uncle Sammy said.

"What in the hell *are* those?" the others joined in the refrain.

After three rounds of schnapps they grew impatient. "Well?" they inquired. "So where's the birthday boy? There's something the matter with him—he's missing his own party?"

"Of course there's something the matter with him," Uncle Isidore exclaimed. "*Armed robbery. Manslaughter.* We saw it on the six o'clock news, remember?"

"That was ten years ago," my father said. "It was an accident. A mix-up. Hannah. Go see what's keeping your uncle, would you, please?"

"Almost there," he called when I banged on his door. "Just give me five more minutes."

Oh great, I thought. I knew what five minutes could mean with Uncle Ruben. By then I'd decided that he was from a planet of denser gravity. The world he inhabited spun as slowly as a top at the end of its centrifugal rope.

"Five more minutes," I told my uncles sadly. "He's getting dressed. He's putting on the finishing touches." As proof I began to describe the new shirt and pair of slacks my father had bought him for the festivities.

But my uncles weren't interested in sportswear. "*You* said he was so anxious to see us," they accused my father. "We made a great concession coming over here. Where *is* he?"

"OK. OK." My father set down the platter of egg salad and tea matzohs he had been passing around with furious good will. "I'll go and get him."

"No! *I* will, Daddy. I promise!" I was afraid that

if my father went upstairs my uncles would take it as an opportunity to sneak away.

I ran back to Uncle Ruben's room. "Come on!" I urged him. "They'll be leaving any second now. I know them. They're getting angry." I was starting to feel a little angry myself. After all, my father had slaved over this party. He'd given up sleep for it and endured my mother's comments. This was his chance to prove to her that Uncle Ruben was worth all his efforts. "Please come out," I begged. "There's cake downstairs. They're waiting for you." But Uncle Ruben didn't answer my knocks. There was a deep silence on the other side of the door as if he were playing hide 'n seek and wouldn't come out even though I'd found him. "Uncle Ruben?"

I had to shove on the door really hard to open it. There was a heavy thud, which turned out to be his suitcase, and then I saw him, as I'd seen him dozens of times before, lying on the bed, crumpled and lifeless as a forgotten towel at the beach.

For a moment I thought he actually might be dead, or maybe I just wished he were dead rather than see my father's disappointment when he realized *he* was the only one who cared about Uncle Ruben's party, that Uncle Ruben cared so little he'd rather sleep through the whole thing. "What on earth do you think you're doing?" I asked him. "It's your birthday! My father made you this great big party. How can you do this to him?" I went over to Uncle Ruben and tried to shake him into answering me, but he wouldn't budge. His shoulder felt like it was filled with sand, as did the rest of his body, shifting and heavy, as I pulled on his arms and legs to rouse him. I tapped him on the face and tugged at his foot and yelled directly into his ear, but none of my usual efforts to revive him made any difference. I had my head pressed to his chest to see if his heart was still beating when I heard my father coming up the stairs calling, in a voice that strained to be jovial: "Ruben! Ru—ben! Are you up there? Here we come!" I heard the sad stampede behind him just as he burst through the door: "If Mohammed won't come to the mountain . . ."

He was carrying the cake all ablaze with candles that were snapping and hissing in the breeze of his fervor, and he was so busy herding the brothers he didn't have time to assess the situation. "It's OK!" he called back over his shoulder. "He's in here. Let's surprise him! Let's sing a good chorus of 'Happy Birthday.' It goes like this," he prompted them, turning towards the bedraggled group on the steps and squaring his shoulders bravely. "Happy birthday to you. . . . Happy birthday to you. . . . Happy birthday, dear ROOOO-ben. . . . Happy birthday to you. . . ." He sang it all the way through before they joined him in whispers fit for intensive care. "Come on," he berated them. "If you're going to sing then why don't you at least sing in the human register?" It wasn't until he'd cajoled them through it twice, wincing at each plodding chorus, that he finally lost his momentum, turned around, and gave Uncle Ruben a closer look.

Uncle Ruben really did leave that time, first to the

hospital to recover from his overdose, then to a facility for drug addicts where my father paid his bills until Uncle Ruben got tired of being rehabilitated and ran away.

He didn't disappear completely, though. A trail of crimes, both great and small, unwound, unending, behind him—reports of unsolved break-ins, jewelry missing, money—several cases of cough syrup, the druggist, jumping onto the bandwagon of accusation, claimed. And he returned to us when he died, coming to the bad end my mother had predicted for him. "Here he is again," she said one day, as if he were a letter with the wrong address that kept turning up in our mailbox. We buried him, just the three of us, in a plain, pine coffin that opened only from the neck up. "When they found him he still had the needle stuck in his veins," my mother said in eulogy. "That figures." "I was right about your Uncle Ruben," became her way of clinching an argument.

I wondered about that. I thought about Uncle Ruben for years, trying to figure out if he really had to act the way he did, if he had "just cause" as my father had argued all along. I thought about him a lot the summer I was nineteen. Another strange summer, I was living in Boston then. My mother was dying of a tumor and I had run away. I couldn't stand to watch her dwindle into the ravaged sheets. I couldn't stand to watch my father worry over her, and serve, in the whole-hearted manner in which only *he* could serve. He used to make notes of everything she ate, the hourly fluctuations of her temperature, how often she sighed, putting an asterisk next to any groan that was particularly loud, as though this were a sign that she was regaining her strength. Late at night he'd sit in the kitchen reviewing this data, sifting for evidence that she might get well. He knew this wasn't possible but he worked and reworked his equations as if it were simply his own stupidity that prevented her complete recovery.

By the time I ran away that summer I'd run away so many times it had become a habit. I'd run away to rock concerts, to the sea shore, to "happenings" it took three days to hitchhike to. I got used to my father's voice trudging through the receivers of different pay phones: "Come home, Sweetheart. *Please.* We miss you. We're worried about you. Forget all this nonsense, will you? Why do you have to act this way? Your mother is very disappointed."

In Boston it was the same. He called me every night to entreat me: "Come home, darling. Your mother needs you. She really wants to see you. She's sorry for what she did—whatever it was."

"It's not her fault."

"Then why don't you come home?"

"I don't know. I just can't."

I thought I was in love that summer; that was my excuse to myself. A man I'd met said he was in love with me. I'm in love, I told myself. Love should be perfect—wasn't that true? Then I'd cry into the receiver until the man I thought I loved would grab the phone away and berate my father. "Listen—she doesn't want to talk to you every ten minutes. Don't you get it?"

The man I thought I loved played pool for a living. He was fifteen years older than I was and wore nothing but black leather pants and a black vest, and every night when he stalked off to the bars where he made his money, I thought I'd never see him again. There was no reason for him to love me. I wasn't wealthy or very pretty or especially vivacious. I wasn't particularly naive.

So, while I wondered what the man I thought I loved saw in me, I would go to the refrigerator, open a bottle of beer and hold it to my lips as though this were a movie and I wasn't Hannah, but someone different, a girl named Jill or Liza, a girl all glistening on a hot summer's day. Too soon, my father would call back to implore me: "She's afraid! She's afraid!" I would refuse again to come home, this time because he expected it. "I'm sorry, Daddy. I can't." Then I'd hang up and look out the window and wonder why I'd just hurt him.

"You'll come home now, won't you?" he said, when she finally died, as if it were just a little tiff we'd all had, something minor and reversible—a date that went on past curfew, a cigarette ash tapped onto the carpet.

"How could you?" Uncle Isidore asked me after the funeral. (He'd been helping throughout my mother's illness, doing the marketing, washing clothes, buying the fresh irises and roses my father insisted be kept in a vase on her night table). "You deserted your father," he said at every opportune moment, each time we said the prayer for the dead, or as we sat drinking tea in the evenings, eating the cakes and noodle puddings my aunts had baked for the week of mourning. "You deserted your father in his hour of need."

My father seemed to agree with him.

"Isidore's been my mainstay," he told everyone, "through all of this."

"And Hannah?"

"Hannah." He smiled with fond memory—his postcard daughter, always bright and glossy. "Yes, of course, Hannah. Hannah is always a help to me no matter what."

Maybe he believed it. I thought of that birthday party he threw for Uncle Ruben, what a disaster that turned out to be, how he always said afterwards, "That wasn't so bad, now was it? At least we got the whole family together," how, despite everything that happened, he kept on insisting, "It wasn't Ruben's fault. He had a tough life. Life can be too tough for some people—don't you see?"

THE BLUE COAT

She barely glanced at him when he first appeared, not much different from the others, just bigger and taller. He wore a blue down coat though the hall was hot with fluorescent light and steam from radiators. As she walked to the fountain she could smell the sadness of the students—a dark odor seeping from every classroom.

He came towards her dragging his feet—stopped in front of her and asked what time it was.

Smiling, she looked at her watch. "You're not late yet," she said. "It's just about seven." She waited for a 'thank you', but he said nothing. "Well, see you later." She started to turn away, but suddenly he leaned forward.

"Do—you have—class here?"

For a moment she thought he only mouthed the words and the sounds followed after—garbled—as though played at the wrong speed. She nodded and smiled, "Yes, I do," looking at him more closely. A round face, eyes buried in puffy cheeks. Dark grey eyes with no pupils, like ball bearings. She couldn't tell how old he was. Sixteen. Possibly seventeen. There was just the faintest shadow on his white skin. He towered over her—a big kid, clutching an algebra textbook. Where his blue coat had a rip below the shoulder, white fluff was spilling out.

"Wha—what class—do you ha-have—here?" He dredged the words up and examined them one by one. "What class?"

"I teach." She gazed down the hall at the cluster of students waiting in her doorway. "English." Ray Coleman sauntered into the classroom, his yellow jacket an announcement of sun on sand. He winked at her. "Look," she shifted her books, "I have to go." But he bent forward so that his blue bulk bobbed towards her, bringing a scent of damp leaves.

"I live—in En-dee-cott." He pronounced the words as though deciphering something in his first grade reader. "Do you—like—the movies?"

She smiled slightly, but he didn't smile back. His eyes were fixed on the wall behind her. He leaned forward again. "Are you busy Friday night do you want to go to the movies—" The words tumbled out.

She looked at his face—impassive, eyes staring straight ahead as though someone else had spoken. "I'm sorry. I'm really very busy." She stepped around him. "Thanks just the same," and hurried away not looking back, afraid that if she did he might follow her.

When she entered the classroom, the faces were all waiting for her, eyes on the blackboard.

"Hi. Sorry I'm late." She stopped at her desk, smiling vaguely, and set down her bag to search for her notes. Ray Coleman sat in the front row, slouched down in his seat, one big brown boot resting on her desk. "Please," she said, and he removed it—winking. He took out a pen and began drawing on the cover of his notebook in dark blue ink—a figure composed of shadows—tapping his boots against each other, softly.

She found her notes and laid them before her on the desk. "What do we mean by an image?"

No one had any answer. They stared stupidly at notebooks, the floor, the darkened windows, not wanting to give up the silent inches which protected them. They made her think of the boy she had left standing there in the hall, puzzled and suddenly alone.

"It is something formed from a sensoo-wal response," a girl in back finally answered. She was dressed as Georges Sand—black suit and thin, black tie. Her hair reddish and frizzy. Skin like egg white.

"That's right," she nodded, light glinting against her glasses so that for a second she saw only brightness—then a dark figure—then Ray's yellow jacket. The faces behind him looked flat and pale. What were they thinking? Were they thinking anything? she wondered. They looked just like a row of faces painted on the wall. She lectured on, barely listening to her own words.

Someone in the back of the room dozed. She glanced at the clock—five more minutes. "It's important," she stressed, "in any description, to remember the five senses. These form the basis of the selections you make in writing your paragraph."

Ray whispered some remark to her which she didn't understand. She nodded and smiled, watching as he outlined a white face above the dark blue bulk of the figure. "Without these concrete images, you give the reader nothing to attach himself to. Can a reader attach himself to a thought like this?" She paused and looked down at her notes—"You are the not-me." That wasn't right. She trembled. What did that mean? "You are the not-me." She stared at the words until they became squiggles crawling over the white page.

The room was silent. They were all waiting for her, blank faces raised for her next words, even Ray, eyebrows lifted, watching her. He had finished his drawing—a big blue shape like a helium balloon puffed up and ready to take off. "We'll talk about this more next time." She fumbled with her notes, stuffing them back into her bag.

They crowded around her desk.

"Will you be in your office tomorrow?"

"I need help with this other paper—it's due on Monday!"

"Could you explain that last part again?"

She said yes to all of them, even the girl with the frizzy hair who dropped a notebook on her desk: "Look—my poems."

"Of course." She nodded and smiled. "I'm glad you asked me."

Outside, the moon shone pale and silent. Not a soul on the mall; just the leaves rustling as if she had disturbed them. It was silent too in the Hall of Languages. The cold marble echoed her footsteps as she searched for the staircase to her office. She thought she would pass right through the middle corridor, up the back steps, exactly as she always did, and there she would be; but the hall was dark tonight so she turned left and then right and found that she was in a part of the building she didn't know, with halls that curved back to the same unfamiliar place. It was like being on a mountain road, proceeding blindly, not knowing what would come up next around the bend. She came to an auditorium with glass walls, but the rows of seats, the lectern, and whatever else might be in there were all concealed by floor-length drapes. She came around this twice. The second time, she felt her body go icy, and then sweat seeped under the arms of her black jersey. Her chest felt constricted, the breastbone laced up like an ice skate.

Far down the hall, too far away for her to make out clearly, someone was standing perfectly still. She waded towards the soda machine digging in her purse for a quarter, stuck it in the slot and listened to it fall with a dull thud. Ding! the light went on, but when she pressed again—an empty click.

Her hands were icy cold as she dug in the velvet pouch of her bag for another quarter. Just as it fell through the slot, she saw a large blue mass moving slowly towards her. He was coming through the bright tube of the hallway, his dark head bent forward eagerly. For a second, he stopped and scanned the air, then nodded and started forward again, one foot in front of the other. She jumped back from the machine—no escape! His blue bulk lumbered towards her. Movies? A drowning voice set the words adrift.

"I can't go with you!" she cried. "What do you want?"

But it wasn't him! Her heart quivered like a spatter of raindrops. "Hi," she said, trying to smile, but her mouth was also quivering. The man stared straight ahead as he passed. Had she actually spoken? Her finger pressed the button on the soda machine. Bang! The can dropped down. She felt it—cold wet metal in her grip. Whhhssh! The air rushed out and brown foam flowed over her hand.

She found her office. No one was there either. She stood looking at the door, afraid to open it, as if he might be standing there in the dark, waiting. She flipped on the light.

The room sprang up like the first frame of a film leaping onto an empty screen. Everything was composed and still. Books on the desk. Green blotters. A sweater draped on the back of a chair. On the blackboard a quotation:

"You are the not-me." Martin Buber.

She stared. Had she written that too? Maybe she had glanced at it before class and then remembered it in her notes. "You are the not-me." What did he mean by that? She shivered. All she wanted to do was get home to her own room, her own bed and chair, and turn on all the lamps. She swung her bike around— snapped off the light.

Outside, the moon shone round and perfect like another street lamp gazing on all the buildings. Under its cold light they were hard, silent. She looked down at the black amosite beneath her feet. That too was solid, she thought, but when she got on her bike, she wasn't sure; all she could feel were the wheels going over pebbles, like a boat bumping along through the waves. The buildings floated by. Red brick. Perfect lines. Metal pipes emerging from rooftops. They were ugly, but they would last—how many years? Much longer than she would. Or that boy. She could have talked to him more. It wouldn't have hurt her. He was only a kid. She could see him wandering the halls, asking his eternal questions. "Wha-what is your name? Do you like—movies?" Getting only a shake of the head in answer. A puzzled look. She could have talked to him more. But then his face loomed before her— that strange puffy white, those blank eyes.

As she turned onto the highway, cars whooshed by and she wondered if she were visible, or if one of them would suddenly decide to stop, to pull over to the shoulder and at the last minute, see her—pedalling slowly, strenuously, pushing up and down against the gravity of Jupiter. Too late.

Often, on the same road she had passed over the squashed remains of animals—also too late, when she looked up from the river and the trees, from thinking dreamily: What a beautiful autumn this is! watching the reflections in the water swell and disappear and suddenly bloom again. She would look down at the tufts of white fur sticking in the red matter and shudder as the wheels ran over it.

She approached the shopping plaza and slowed her bike as a car whipped in front of her, inches away, and roared into the parking lot. Another car turned and then another. A whole line of them followed. They were heading across the dark lot towards the bright glare of the supermarket, heading towards the aisles of fruits and vegetables, the long rows of cans, the puffy loaves of bread in their shiny plastic. As they swept into the lot, they paused for a second and then turned, bearing towards the garish yellow lights.

On the river road there was only darkness—the moon swallowed once more by the clouds. Occasionally, she saw the shapes of trees in the water as a car approached. The branches ahead would suddenly come clear, perfectly clear; as the lights passed along the guardrail, they loomed before her. She could decipher each brown leaf hanging from each stiff twig. Then the car would whiz by, tearing light from her back, leaving her fishing in the dark—peering at the blue remainder printed on the road. A car would come from the opposite direction—paralyze her with its spotlights: a flash of lightning—daylight!—and she saw the trees—the medial strip—the broken glass gleaming beneath the wheels of her bike. She pedalled along going bump and bump and bump over the stones and the glass and, sometimes, over something less resistant.

A car went by her—very close; so close she could feel the hot breath of exhaust on her neck. Ahead of her, a green sign lit up—½ MILE TO ROCK ROAD. She saw, before her shadow moved across it, her black cape whipping around her shoulders. She continued, her legs moving up and down—up and down up and down—making the wheels turn—click, click, click. The bike hovered in the darkness that crouched around her like sleep. Leaves swept across her hair and arms as she pushed on the pedals faster and faster, peering down the dim road with all her might. Nothing. Absolutely nothing. Her feet moved up and down in the dark.

Then she felt light on her back again, beaming down on her, growing brighter and brighter. The highway, the trees, the clouded sky began to rise before her like a stage when the floodlights come on, rising before the viewer who has been sitting in the pitch black, heart pounding, squinting into the solid air; the person next to him, horribly silent, as though the blackness has locked them apart—he wonders: will I ever see again? wonders: will I wake up alive? And then there are lights—just beginning. At first, he feels them, still not sure if he isn't perhaps seeing an echo of his wishes beginning to color the dark. And he looks to his neighbor for a minute. There is an arm. There is a leg.

In the tree before her something was hanging.

Dark. Big. What? Hanging from the branch. Bobbing up and down, nodding stupidly. It revolved slowly in the wind—holding out huge arms to her, showing her all its sad bulk. She swerved her bike out onto the highway as it brushed her shoulder—a blue coat! a blue coat!

IMAGINE A GREAT WHITE LIGHT

Morning—barely. A tide of blue sky washing through trees. Leaves the color of new pennies. Air crisp; not biting. A beautiful autumn day. A perfect autumn day, except that none of us knows the answer to this simple question: why are we here? nor to this one: what is the meaning of life? nor even to this little query, the one that comes hurtling through the receiver each morning as soon as I pick up the phone: "Dear God! Why did he have to die?"

Actually, that's an easy one. "He didn't have to die, Frances. He killed himself. Call me later."

She refers, of course, to Jeffrey, my former husband, her former son. It is a question she has reiterated often in the past few months—at the funeral parlor, graveside; and now, since I finally persuaded her to move back to her own house in another part of the city, it comes every morning courtesy Ma Bell: *Why?* Sometimes it is a whole series of questions: why why why why why? Sometimes she is subtler, the question implicit in the hour of her call, in her desperation over the waterstains on her coffee table, in her need to give me that recipe for strudel, the one that Jeffrey liked so much. Sometimes the real question hides behind another. "Why," she asks, "is the sun still so lovely?"

When she's not asking why, she's begging me to come live with her. "You rattle around in that great big old house," she says, "I rattle around in mine. If we have to eat our hearts out every night, why do it alone?" As further incentive she offers me a complete program of R&R—good healthy food, a nice room with brand new carpeting, the SONY portable she doesn't use anymore since she bought her color set (so lifelike!), day trips to factory outlets, and beyond. "We'll keep each other company," she says. "We'll be just like two girls again. Please, Annie."

"I don't want to be a girl again," I say, though this is far from true. I'm thirty-eight and I'd like to halve that, but I won't tell her. I know how she operates. Any excuse to drag me under, she'll try it—health, common sense, remember when? even what Jeffrey would have wanted, though this is moot. A case in point: the night a few weeks after the funeral when she tried to lure me back to our locked bedroom, to king-sized emptiness. "We've got to face this sometime," she said, and insisted we both sleep there. She theorized that we could change the meaning of that bed by making it the scene of in-law slumber, that two women in shapeless nightgowns would blur the original associations—silk, flannel, the salty warmth of leg over leg over leg. I tried to suggest that it wasn't exactly the same thing we were facing, but she wouldn't take no for an answer in the way that only Frances won't take no. "When my Alex first died, my sister Mary slept with me every night until I stopped crying. Just try it."

But when she opened the door, the room rushed towards us like an ocean—storm-tossed sheets, a towel stranded on the dresser, my nightgown, in the shape of our last passion, washed up at our feet.

We stepped back.

Now I sleep down the hall in a single bed with a brown coverlet and a guest room smell and she calls me every morning to harass me from afar. I've developed a system to keep her at bay—two no's for every yes, no more than five phone calls in any twenty-four hour period unless it's Mother's Day. Every Friday night we eat dinner at her house, watch the news, sometimes a movie or concert on educational TV. On Sunday nights she calls to rehash "60 Minutes". Every Jewish holiday we spend à deux. Twice a week I wake at five-thirty, drive ten miles into the city so that we can attend early morning services at the synagogue near her home, the Orthodox, which we both like because when we stand to say kaddish we are hidden by the curtain which separates the sexes. No one can see us cry.

Who has suffered more? Tough to say, though it is a source of constant speculation. "Such a scandal!" Frances says. On the one hand, according to Frances, I am the victim of a senseless suicide, the one left empty-handed after a "perfectly wonderful!" twenty-year marriage, though childless, (a terrible shame but thank God! for if there had been children just think how the poor children would feel), a marriage that had everything to live for—two cars, a nice clean house in the suburbs, vacations twice a year on cruise ships and foreign beaches. All these I have enjoyed, the fruits of the labor of a devoted husband, a doctor with a good practice, who should have known better—he was a boy who was well-brought up and loved by all-whose professional status did not stop him from bringing his mother every week on his way home from the hospital, a raisin challah from her favorite bakery.

And on the other hand there is Frances who doesn't want to complain She's had her life and who wants to listen to an ugly old woman anyway? But just in case—she is a person with little left besides herself. Five years ago she lost her husband, two years ago, both breasts, this year, her only son. She wins hands down.

This morning after I have hung up on her, I remember another obligation. I have promised to drive her to the hospital in town. She's just had her six-month checkup. It's time to receive the results of her liver and bone scans. The double mastectomy (one radical, one simple, two suspicious-looking nodes) removed her disease but not the doubt. The doctors keep a close watch for shadows. Should they find any, she will need more treatment. Chemotherapy is the probable course, the doctor said. A series of injections. Hair loss, nausea, lowered resistance.

For days I have racked my brain for an excuse not to go with her. It isn't a simple generic fear of hospitals, of the smell of pain or disinfectant, but a more specific fear. This is the same hospital where Jeffrey was a surgeon, the same hospital where he was brought in and the motions of revival were gone through, where he was then pronounced dead.

The last time I was there, two weeks ago, the morning Frances had the tests done, I was trapped in the ladies' room for over an hour. I had retreated to apply more lipstick, but when I looked into the mirror I saw a face drained of blood, a stranger's eyes, someone else's grim mouth. The more I stared, the more the face receded from my understanding, and it was not until I heard my name pronounced over the P.A. system, "Ann Goodman. Ann *Good*man!" that I believed again in my own existence. I found Frances at the main desk in the arms of one of the secretaries, weeping. "I came out and you were gone," she said. "Missing."

This morning, she calls me back to ask, as she did then, in a voice that has dredged up every tear it can remember, "Ann darling, how can you be so cruel?"

Instead of getting dressed as I know I should, I put on my robe and slippers, go outside and sit in the van. With the sunroof thrown open I stare up at the patch of sky and think, "I could be here. I could be anywhere." This is the way that Jeffrey once taught me to meditate. "Imagine a great, white light," he said. "Bring whatever is dark and binding into the light until it is absorbed, it disappears. Last of all, bring yourself."

We bought the van in those meditation days, 1969, the seventh year of our marriage, the summer Jeffrey finished medical school. We painted it purple and called it "Born Under a Bad Sign"—back then, a term of respect. Jeffrey could have started his residency that same year and remained exempt from the draft; instead, we travelled all around the country, through Mexico and Canada and back and forth across the States as though the map were some fate we had to evade. The Rockies, the Everglades, the high, empty plains in Wyoming; we pulled in wherever Jeffrey thought he could find an "adventure." While I waited in the van or a motel or somewhere, he went body-surfing after dark, slept in ghost towns under the full moon, hiked the desert with only the sun, no compass, his instinct for water. Sometimes he would complicate the issue by eating LSD or psychedelic mushrooms. At the foot of a mountain he climbed in December without crampons or ice axe, he signed his name in the trailhead book: "The Lone Dodger", and I, in what I saw at the time as an act of love, didn't notify the park guard, though he was gone for two days and for two days snow fell.

We ended our trip in a motel room in Key West one Sunday afternoon. In a bar humid with jazz, sun, tourists, we met a couple, Al and his wife or girlfriend (we never knew) Sandy. We all agreed with Jeffrey that we were sick of the dazzling sky and water, of the gentle breezes blowing through the palms, and especially sick of the Casablanca gloom of that particular bar. We found a motel, the Blue Pelican, with no checkout time, and brought in supplies—rum, beer, a bucket of clams, a bag of dope homegrown in a bathroom in Brooklyn. Then we turned on the radio and everything else, full blast.

When the room took on new dimensions, we played geography. Above the desk was a painting of quays—that was France. Beneath the air conditioner, of course, was Siberia, Sweden if you preferred. The plastic ferns were the Amazon, the clutter of suitcases—Kennedy Airport, the bed—Shangri-la. Early in the morning when I had to leave Shangri-la to find the bathroom, I rescued Jeffrey from a wicked burn on a beach along the Costa del Sol. He had drenched himself with Coppertone and was lying on the floor, his body glowing under the infrared lamp. When I snapped off the light, he woke up. "Have a heart," he said. "I was just getting warm." Then he pulled me down beside him. "Here. Help me." And I did, until we both shimmered red in the dark.

Jeffrey never did get drafted. We never went on another trip in the van, though sometimes, after a long shift at the hospital, when he couldn't stand the intimacy of sound or smell in our apartment building, we would drive out into the country somewhere and spend the night, in a field, on an abandoned logging road.

When the neighborhood became unsafe for vans, we moved here. Even after the engine seized up, Jeffrey wouldn't part with it, but parked it in the backyard where it grazed our suburban lawn. He planted flowers around it, a peach tree on one end, an apple tree at the other. At night, in summer, he used to sit out there with the sunroof open and drink beer. Sometimes he ran an extension cord from the kitchen so that he could watch TV.

A few days before his death, Jeffrey called a towtruck. "You can't hang on forever," he told me. But by the time they came he had changed his mind, said he had some plans for it, maybe put in a new engine, fiberglass against the rust, replace the tires. Since his death I've sat in here many times and wondered what sort of trip he'd had in mind, why he then gave it up. Had he really intended to go somewhere? or was he just pretending, as I do, it's 1969 again: we're somewhere—Colorado, Wyoming, a beach in Mexico: the sun has just come up and we're plotting our course.

"I almost took the subway," Frances says as I walk her to the car. "Where were you?" Instead of explaining why I am late, I tell her she looks nice and she nods—words of an errant daughter-in-law. She is dressed, as she always is once the high holidays have passed, in her Moscow nights get-up. No matter that today it is Indian summer, well over eighty degrees, that the sun turns the sidewalks white as sand; she is wearing high boots, fedora, a long-suffering mink coat. This matches her perfume. Everytime she sighs, a rose-scented fountain of grief wells up, and she sighs with every step she takes, as if it's the inaccuracy of my guiding hand that has caused all her sorrow. In this neighborhood the pavements are uneven. The steps crumble downward forgetting what it is they're supposed to do. She falters, trips.

"I can't stand it," she announces as soon as we get in the car. Her eyes are pools of sorrow, but I refuse to take the bait, to ask her what? what is it, Frances, you can't stand? It could be anything from her electric bill to the black faces and open doorways and loud dancing radios that have invaded her neighborhood. More likely it is some manifestation of Jeffrey—my lack of this or that, my stubborn refusal to move in with her and be sensible.

I am, and always have been, a grave disappointment to her, not at all the wife she had planned for her son. What she'd had in mind was a wind-chime woman: someone small, dark-haired and in the background, a former pre-school teacher perhaps, someone capable of looking quietly joyous even doing laundry in the dead heat of summer. Instead, she got me— large, red-haired and sarcastic. Before dropping out of college to marry Jeffrey, I majored in geology. I am loud and do not listen to reason. Worst of all, I never smell trouble until it's too late.

She repeats my cue. "I just can't stand it." She groans.

"Are you hot?" I ask. "I'll roll down the window."

"Hot. Schmot."

"How about some music?"

"No."

I glance at her and see one hand braced against the dashboard as if it's the mounting crest of a wave. The other hand grips the armrest. "Am I going too fast?"

Her fedora bobs sadly from side to side. "What does an old woman like me know about fast?"

Suddenly she begins to cry soft, choked tears. "Now, Frances," I say.

But this is only a prelude. She opens her hands and lets her grief fall into her palms, wet, furious. I have heard crying like this all my life, the bitterness of centuries bursting forth on all occasions: at weddings, at funerals, at the memory of slabs of pumpernickel once eaten with butter and garlic. For Frances, crying is a form of sensual pleasure. "What's wrong?" I have often asked. "My God, what's wrong?" only to pry forth admissions such as these: "The schnapps. It was this kind that my father used to drink." Or: "My sister, Beatrice, had a blouse like that." Or: "I was thinking of the junkman." I have seen her cry over tablecloths, buttons, a column of adding machine figures found unexpectedly in a drawer. But since Jeffrey's death, it is always the same answer. I don't even have to ask.

So, I think, here it comes again—the big pitch. This is the perfect moment. We're late. The traffic is bumper-to-bumper. We're heading towards the hospital where her fate, still unknown to us, has already become someone else's smile, or frown. We are both alone. If she is sick again, if they find shadows, how will I say no? We will slip into the undertow together, like two girls again, helpless.

We engage in a familiar battle of wills. She won't stop crying until I ask her what's wrong; I won't ask her what's wrong until she stops crying.

In the parking lot, however, she changes her mind. For the third time she announces, "I can't stand it. I just can't stand it."

I can't either—her crying, and besides her crying, a certain dizzy, empty whirling in my chest now that we are here. "Frances, please. It's 11:30. If you can't stand it, could you please not stand it while we're walking?"

No. She is adamant. She folds her arms across her chest and I see that she is not getting out of this car until she tells me. "You just have to sit in that waiting room until you scream, anyway," she says. Then she begins to recount the dream she had (this very morning), a dream in which Jeffrey (her only son, her sweetheart, her dollbaby), appeared to her like Banquo's ghost, wrapped in a torn shroud, covered with dirt, bleeding from all his wounds. As proof she touches my arm, as if the damp, cold feel of her hand is a message he wished to convey. "It was a sign," she says, "an omen."

"Everything is an omen."

She shakes her head. "Ann darling, I know an omen when I see one."

I get out of the car, walk around to her side.

129

"Frances," I say firmly as I open her door, "it wasn't Jeffrey. Jeffrey took sleeping pills, remember? Now come on. Let's get this show on the road."

She begins to cry again. "I should know what my own son looks like."

To top it all off, beside the main entrance to the hospital a wheel chair is parked; in it, a slab of woman (one arm, one leg) is propped, a bowl of buttons in her lap. As people go by she shakes the buttons, then puts them down and shakes the tin cup, then the buttons again, and I wonder could she possibly, so unfortunately, be mute as well? My own horizons recently expanded, I think, of course, why not? until I hear her say softly, "Buy a button? Buy yourself a bit of luck?" Not a very good place to beg, the few coins in her lap jingle lightly. As they pass, people twist away from her, drawn in by the vortex of the hospital. They shade their eyes. It's true, I think. Looking at her is like looking into the sun, and who would want to try her brand of fortune? We pass by slowly. Frances, still wrapped in a mist of tears, clutches my arm. "My God. What is that?" she asks accusingly, as if it is *I* who have unveiled this horror.

The woman lifts her head and stares at us. In her eyes, the residue of years of shame and anger, of comments such as this, both voiced and silent. She can't even get up and fight, so she moves her chair, her only hand on the wheel gripping white, then pulling, pulling until she has turned away.

"Come on," I whisper, but Frances continues to stare. She might be considering a display in a museum, looking for the card underneath to explain it all: "Human Suffering. A.D. 1981. North America."

It is here that she decides to break down completely, to turn into a raging fur-capped mountain. "God ought to be ashamed," she wails. "He ought to be ashamed." She clings to my arm, swaying back and forth, buffeted by her own grief. As if her cries are an alarm that has gone off, a knot of people begins to form: what's wrong? what's wrong? From the corner of my eye I see the flutter of a white hand, then the glint of turning metal. "For God's sake, Frances—will you shut up?" I start to drag her, still clinging to me, towards the door. "She's a woman just like you—can't you see?"

When she lets go of my arm, I realize that I have said a terrible thing. Her face has crumpled like a leaf. It is tear-streaked. In this light, a weave of wrinkles. "Oh," she gasps. "Oh." As the automatic doors swing open, she folds her arms across her chest once more, huddles down into her coat as if bracing against all the forces that would strip her naked. "A mother has no business outliving her son," she declares grimly. She enters the building alone.

In the waiting room of the department of oncology there is no sound or movement but the flutter of sidelong glances. How long? they wonder. How long? More than that one there? the pale one with the stiffened wig? Less than that one? still robust, sun-tanned even from some long-deserved, finally accepted trip to Florida. They gaze at their fading futures in the gloomy technicolor of magazines.

Awed silence.

Frances is nowhere in sight.

"Mrs. Goodman," I say to the receptionist. "Where is she?"

She smiles briefly, a ritual smile—regret, understanding. "In therapy," she says. "The doctor's with her now."

"Therapy?"

"She'll be at least an hour or two. Usually after they give the injection the patient feels some discomfort. The doctors like them to rest for awhile. You might want to go down to the cafeteria and have lunch." She offers me a pamphlet from her desk, "Chemotherapy—A New Beginning?" "Here," she says, "why don't you glance through this?"

"No, no," I say. I refuse the yellow folder, decide to try again. Perhaps she didn't hear me correctly. Perhaps she is thinking of someone else. "Frances *Good*man," I tell her. I repeat it slowly. "Fran-ces Good-man."

She nods carefully. "That's right," she says. "She's just gone in."

"Are you sure?"

When I was very small, four or five, I got lost once on the beach in Atlantic City. In the distance I saw an elephant rising up out of the sand and I wandered off to see if it was real. As I walked, a haze of seaspray and late afternoon sun swallowed first the legs, then the belly, finally the head and trunk. When I turned back to find our blanket I saw only a litter of faces, of colors, nothing that I recognized. The lifeboat I remembered nearby, had multiplied into many lifeboats spaced all along the beach. The woman with the black transistor radio was one of a hundred women with black transistors. Not even the ocean was constant. The waves had changed shape. The sand was cold.

All afternoon, I wander through the hospital looking for a familiar spot, some place safe to sit. It all seems strange to me—a replica of a hospital, a replica of my life. I could be here, I think. I could be anywhere.

In an empty stairwell, on a cold iron step, I sit down and wonder why she didn't tell me. To spare me? To surprise me? Everything that has happened this morning now appears in a different light. She was frightened, I think, frightened.

CHILD ABUSE

Because no matter what I did you were always there before me. That's how I remember you from years before—racing past me to claim him, throwing yourself against his body as though you were leaping a vast, inhuman canyon to safety. And how I remember him sometimes—draping his arm across your shoulders, with a calmness like sky, gathering you in. "That's my little girl," he sighed. "That's my little sweetheart."

You two were always a pair. Even Mother said so. "Just look at them," she'd whisper as if you were a couple of rare birds we had startled into flight, the kind she always promised we might see on the nature hikes we took to compensate—for the time you spent with him, for the way he doted on you. "We can have a nice time too," Mother assured me. Together we plodded through the scraggly woods that cowered along the railroad tracks near our apartment. "The forest" she called it, as if this exaggeration could hide the fact that you alone had gone with Father that day.

He had some very important errands to do; that's what Mother said, things he couldn't do by himself, but *you* told me about the trips to sporting goods stores and coffee shops, about wading in the white, rushing water of the Wissahickon, or sometimes, when the weather was inclement, slipping off to the movies, to the Sunday matinees where he bought you popcorn and cherry soda and Nonpareils. More than once he took you afterwards to Lenny's taproom, right under the El. Each time a train went by the glasses rattled, some old drunk in the corner shouted, *What, June? What?,* the dark air swarmed with shadows that swayed and shivered, then drifted out over the unused dance floor, and the jukebox blinked, blinked, blinked again, then started to play your song, the one about the girl named Ronnie who breaks her boyfriend's heart: "Ronnie . . . Ronnie . . . *Why* did you go?"

Maybe Mother had no idea. She just said he needed your help—that's why you were always with him. It was true that often, on Saturdays, he took you to work at the gas station. He let you sit at his desk and fiddle with the adding machine while he fixed engines and pumped gas. When you got bored playing accountant you stood outside by him as he raised the car hoods. You put your hands alongside his and aped the way he braced with his knees and lifted skyward as if he could lift the clouds and the sun as well. When the hood was open he showed you how to check the oil, how to turn the stick towards the light, gently, as if it were a thermometer. You wiped windshields and then he wiped where you had missed. The boys who worked for him used to tease you: *Hey, Beautiful . . . Hey, Gorgeous . . .* , as you stood up straight and basked in it. You knew who you were. It never surprised you when he skipped work for you either. He took you someplace to cheer you up because you were in one of your "moods" staring out the window for hours without speaking or sitting on the fire escape clutching your notebook, the one marked: "Personal— Keep Out or Drop Dead." You wrote with the real fountain pen you made him buy for you, secret messages to yourself, too secret even for your own eyes; sometimes you glared at them, then ripped the pages out. Striking a forbidden match you burned them until the ashes scattered into the wind.

Because there was never anyone else—only *you.* Because the scores were always in your favor, though you used to say when you got older: How can you keep score of love? Doesn't it all come out even in the end? Because you always smiled a little when you said this.

Because I was remembering that, and other injuries, as I arrived in your town last week, though I told myself I had come here just to find you, it was important to patch things up despite what I used to think, (that you were selfish—cold and forbidding as the dark side of the moon).

But that's beside the point, I reminded myself. Why think about such things anymore? What good can it possibly do? It's been years since we've seen each other. Probably you haven't been keeping track but I'm twenty-two now, much older than you were when you left home. But you were always precocious, two steps ahead of my hatred.

I'm almost as tall as you though, "like a model" Father always said of you, but that's where the resemblance ends. I could be anyone's sister as far as looks go. My hair has turned brown as Mother's and I'm still terribly skinny. "The shadow" you used to call me, remember? The "apparition". The "phantom". The "spectre". "Watch out," you'd tell Father. "Here she comes." And he'd say, "What is it, Mary? Does your mother want something? What's wrong *now*?"

It's true I'm not beautiful the way you were. Or popular either. I never learned how to charm people, what to leave out of a conversation. I never learned how to stand with my feet posed in ballet position, or how to tilt my head at a perfect angle to catch the light. *You* were the one who had the ballet lessons, and besides, I was always shy. Completely in the dark, you said.

That was in your psychoanalytic phase. You tried to tell me what things really meant, how much our parents loathed each other. You and I were just off-shoots of their discontent, you summarized. "They had nothing to do on weekends," you told me. "Look how they live. Daddy's practically an alcoholic. Mother has her phobias. I don't know which one's more miserable. *Believe* me."

But you said these things about everybody— aunts, uncles, cousins, boyfriends. Who covered up an insatiable lust with a rage for neatness. Who was most likely to deface public property with the scrawls of guilt. If a neighbor came to the door to sell Girl Scout cookies you thought you could tell she had been beaten, in a hidden place, and with what instrument of torture.

You were right about one thing though. I've always had a hard time talking to people. I prefer life in its purest state—unharmed by the spoken word, which are mostly just lies. It's simpler too. Things stay solid. I have lots more time for reading. Physics books mainly. Not just about speed and trajectory. I'm interested in drift chambers too, and black holes, and what goes on inside the atom, inside particles tinier than snowflakes, more unobtrusive. I wrote a poem about them once: "Inside the atom there is no pain . . ." That was the first line. I never went any further—that seemed to say it all.

No doubt you think that's funny.

That's how you used to be at any rate. Some of the strangest things used to make you laugh—the way Father buried the pages of your diary you threw in the trash, as if they might be sacred, the way he said, when you got older, "I *forbid* you. I absolutely forbid you," as you breezed out the door for a date. "Just try and stop me," you jeered at him. All the wrong things amused you.

You'll probably laugh when you find out I'm here, that I ever bothered to track you down. You'd certainly laugh at the old guy who's been badgering me since I checked in here. You know this place—the General Wayne Inn? You of all people know what kind of hotel this is, for older, more respectable affairs. Businessmen and professionals, especially, like it here, the ones over fifty who still care if anyone finds them out. They like the gas lamps and the red, plush carpeting. They like the thickness of the walls.

There are lots of them here this weekend, in fact. Some kind of meeting or convention. Oral surgeons— this old guy in the lobby informed me, the one who tried the pass. He was giving out brochures and schedules. He said if I was interested I could come to one of the lectures, "Controlling the Hemorrhage"; he'd try to get me in for free. Or maybe we could just have dinner. We could listen to the lilting strains of Chad Lewis and his band of renown. That's what oral surgeons find entertaining, I guess. Clichés. Indentured love.

It was sweet the way he asked me though, as if he really didn't know he was implying anything; he was simply worried about a young girl like me all by herself in a strange town.

Oh, he seemed like a very nice man. "They always do after a certain age." Isn't that what you once said of Father? "All old men are nice. That doesn't keep them from destroying you."

It's also difficult to imagine *this* man hurting anyone. Such a gentle old guy—the type who would take
his entire family out for Christmas dinner at a steak
house because he thought it was elegant. He'd wash
out his wife's stockings for her if she asked him to. He
wore that sort of cologne, (sweet, almost feminine),
and a toupée that was light brown, sleek as the coat of
an otter. I liked the way he pretended it wasn't fake,
smoothing his fingers over it from time to time as if to
call attention to what a fine crop of hair he had raised.
I liked how nervous he was when he asked me to dinner, how, after he finished speaking, his lips went on
moving, still rehearsing his lines. "Well. So how about
it?" he said after a very long pause. "Would you con-
sent to an evening with an old codger like me?"

But I'm getting ahead of myself here. What I really meant to discuss is how you've changed. You must
have changed a lot to be living in a place like this. I
mean, to tell you the truth, Ronnie, for the first few
minutes I thought I had gotten lost. Your town seemed
so much smaller than it should have been, so much
smaller than the star I'd put on the map to pinpoint
your location. What I'd imagined were white-washed
houses and dappled lawns. The evidence of autumn
brightening the hills, the rooftops. Even the driveway
that curled around your property I pictured speckled
with happy leaves—red and yellow—honored to fall
beneath the wheels of your car each night.
That's how I pictured the grounds, and the house
itself—a grand old stone building with a front porch

made of polished oak; above the door, a row of glass chimes ringing their inscrutable messages into the wind. You always said you wanted a house like that— so many rooms to hide away in—each one locked. Private as the inside of a seashell. Some say that space is like that—each universe separate—no friendly doors between. Some say it's best that way. Some say, like Mother, "I already know *everything* I want to know about that girl."

Because I want you to understand why I did what I did next, what's been happening this last week since I arrived, why I allow the dentist to knock on my door every night at eight P.M., to sit in that blue damask chair with the mahagony eagle sprouting behind his head and call up room service—champagne, or a nice rosé, a platter of cheese and crackers surrounded by a ruffle of sliced and browning apples, why I've permitted him to caress my hand as if it's a small, restless animal while he tells me his sad story—a wife who never liked him, three sons who've moved away, far west of the Mississippi, who tell him when he comes to visit, (firmly, as if he's a travelling salesman with a suitcase filled with annoyances), "Now, Dad. We *have* been looking forward to your visit. But we want things to go just right. We want to make clear some limits . . ."

I want you to understand why I listened, why I didn't say, as you surely would have, "That's pathetic!", why I've allowed him to take up so much of my time. I came here to visit you, and yet most of my hours I've spent listening to him complain. This is the form his courtship takes—leaning on sad elbows above a brimming glass of wine. Reciting his troubles: loneliness, old age. The exhaustion of the human spirit.

Maybe it's an occupational hazard—dentists are used to a captive audience. Maybe it's the wine. In any case, he corners me and I can't say no. I never learned to be as rude as you.

"Just the person I wanted to see!" he exclaims with surprise, though he has just ridden the elevator to my fourth-floor room and knocked urgently as if he brings news of a fire. "How are you this fine evening?" he continues. He seeps past me and slides himself into my chair. He arranges his gray golf sweater around his shoulders like a shawl. His fingers stray towards the telephone. "A beverage?" he inquires. Though, when the beverage arrives, dignified by a silver bucket, he cautions me, "Not *too* much now. You're just a young twig." He insures my safety by drinking very swiftly, refilling his glass as soon as it empties an inch, as if he's conducting an experiment that might fail if the level of liquid isn't kept constant.

As soon as he's had enough to make his eyes glaze over, his recitation begins: "My life has been filled with disappointments . . ."

I can't explain why I keep listening except that I feel sorry for him. He reminds me of Father, how he used to pause at your door. "Is the queen in her chamber?" And when you gave no answer: "Ah. She is. She is. She has no solace for her humble servant," then sigh, not quite sure whether he had made a joke.

Because the laws of symmetry prevail. We live in an ambidextrous universe my physics text says. Like Father, I've always been a bit frightened to see you. Maybe that's why I behaved so strangely that first night, why I shoved my way in without knocking: (*Ronnie! Ronnie! Where the hell are you?*), even though you weren't expecting me; you weren't even home, in fact. As you well know.

But you *should* have been here—that was my logic at the time. You should have felt my presence, lurking up the street the way you did when we were younger. "Get out!" you would scream, even when I was just thinking of you. "Don't you come near me!" though I stood all the way at the bottom of the stairs.

You always denied this later, ("I never said any such thing," you claimed), the way you would have denied the looming height of your door. I expected at least some kind of barricade—a dresser propped against the frame, a chair wedged under the knob.

Instead, your house caved in before me. There was nothing there to protect, at first glance. Certainly not the dusty floors and broken furniture, the torn carpet in front of the sofa, intimations of mice, maybe even worse than mice; all those despairing dishes in the sink—it would be no wonder. It looked like a hurricane had been there, maybe a comet just passing through. I kept hoping that I'd made a mistake. This wasn't your house after all. Soon you'd come bursting in and defend yourself the way you always did when you were wrong: But I wanted it like this. This is *exactly* how I planned it.

I waited a very long time for you to do just that, almost the whole night. Though I hadn't slept for two days, (I'd been driving miles and miles), I made myself stay awake. I perched in various spots and tried to look friendly, as though you were expecting me and had just run out for a minute to buy napkins and cake.

But you never came home—that's typical of you. I got tired of waiting, tired of listening to the empty throb of your room. Just for something to do I looked in your closet the way I used to when I was little. I'd hunt for that precious diary of yours, and when I couldn't find that I played with your tennis racket waving it slowly through the air like a magic wand. I used to try on your dresses too—did you know that? You had them lined up in order of color. I'm not sure why, but it seemed very important, as if this were a part of a code for living only *you* had access to. I respected this. Starting from the left I worked my way through them, first the ivory ones, then the yellow, then the reds, the greens, the royal blues. They were always yards too big and this comforted me. There was still time to learn your secret. I'd grow into them someday if I just concentrated a little harder. I used to close my eyes and say a prayer: "Please, God. Pretty please?"

Afterwards I sometimes took things just to see if

you'd notice, very tiny things like a button or a bit of thread only a truly *special* person would sense were missing. You were in junior high by then, no longer hanging around the gas station on Saturdays. You had shopping to do and girlfriends to meet for sodas and piano lessons at the conservatory. How regal that word sounded and how I envied it: "conservatory." Father left work early to drive you there because he didn't want you taking the subway where someone might grab and twist your pretty hands, where God only knew what might happen. You showed such "extraordinary promise". Everyone said so, didn't they? Father sat in the anteroom while you played and he hummed and whistled and tapped his foot until your teacher had to cry out, "Please! Stop it!"

Oh my! he'd apologize, your foolish father. "Forgive me. I guess I got carried away—she's really the nines now isn't she?" And then, as soon as you started once more, he tapped his foot again or clapped and sang a few bars in counterpoint, erupting all of a sudden as if he just couldn't contain himself. "He really *is* an embarassment," you told Mother. "Why can't I do this solo?"

That's the way you talked in junior high: "Father, I'm much too old for that." "Father, we're worlds apart."

I'm not saying that's why I did it. Maybe it got under my skin that, despite your impoverished circumstances, you still have an awful lot of clothes, a whole long rack of silks and cashmere and lace, and shoes

lined up in rows, unscuffed, aloof. I remembered all
the outfits Father used to buy you—the pleated skirts,
the ruffled blouses—how you scorned them precisely
because he bought them to make amends.

And for a while there I was sure I ought to apologize, give it back to you. It seemed so much larger
once I'd gotten it to my hotel room. I hung it in the
closet before I went to sleep and when I got up in the
morning it had grown, from a careless thought into a
deliberate misdeed, an act of malice it must have appeared to you.

I really did make an effort to return it. I covered it
back up with plastic. Very gently, so it wouldn't wrin-
kle, I draped it over the back seat of my car. I breathed
slowly, quietly, as if it were a child fast asleep after a
long, exciting day. I released the brake and eased my
way from the curb.

But on the way to your house I grew frightened. I
just couldn't seem to face you. Instead, I drove around
town looking for a place to throw the dress away, behind a high and concealing fence, or into a cluttered
dumpster. I even went so far as to drop the dress into
the river, but the current wasn't quick enough. I sat
down on a bench to wait for it to float by and disappear, but it got trapped in a flurry of weeds near the
bank and wouldn't sink. As I watched the other shapes
that drifted by in the river, the rotten logs and bundles
of leaves all sullen with winter, I felt sorry for it. I
fished it from the water. I ran back to my car. I was
almost to your house when I realized I couldn't possibly return it in such an awful, bedraggled condition.

Because the truth is, that as the dresses began to accumulate in my closet a really strange thing occurred. I began to notice some very distinct changes. Each time I put one on I felt taller, sleeker, more sophisticated. My hair, as I strode back and forth in front of the mirror, whisked against my shoulders, a heedless rhythm it had never had until I put on that black silk of yours. A joyful sheen bloomed on my skin, an eager glimmer in my eyes.

I found myself doing things I never thought I could do: tipping my head back to laugh, and knocking the ashes from cigarettes onto the carpeted floors of restaurants and bars, ordering room service at 4 o'clock in the morning, to bring me caviar and croissants, luxuries I knew I'd never eat, that of course I couldn't pay for—I'd barely had the money for the trip. "Just put it on my father's bill," I said. "He's paying for this." I pointed at the dentist who was slumped at his table at the far end of the lobby, his hand caressing a plaster demonstration mold of a perfect bite. "He's very kind."

I'm not sure why they believed me. Maybe that's the way of a backward town like yours. Maybe the dentist refused to say anything—thinking this generosity atoned for broaching my room every night, for offering to show me "the sun, the moon, and the stars."

"That's redundant," I corrected him. "You ought to know that—you're a scientist of sorts, aren't you?"

But he thought I meant the glass of brandy he had poured again, forgetting, as he made his proposal, that he had already topped it off. It spilled across the dresser, shimmering gold drops onto the floor.

"How clumsy," the dentist said, as he mopped the puddle with his handkerchief, and then I felt sorry for him. I didn't remind him that the moon was dust, the stars were dying.

Still, when I realized how easy it was, I put everything on his bill. It was a mystery you had known these many years—how to manipulate affection, but I had never learned this elementary approach. It was like a law of gravity, ever-present but rarely noticed. It was like the wind tipping over the trash cans in your front yard and spilling garbage. Or the simple law of a match touched to a frail curtain. It could burst into flame at any moment. Or be compressed into a simple column of figures: One hundred dollars. Two hundred dollars. Five hundred dollars.

Breakfast, lunch, dinner, videos. I even had your dresses dry-cleaned, and altered to fit more snugly. Why not, I thought? Didn't that make people pay attention? Shouldn't I enjoy myself like you did? I asked to be moved to a nicer room, a suite if they had one, with a king-sized bed, a view of the mountains, bigger closets.

When the hotel got boring I strolled through town admiring myself in windows as I walked, and gazing into mirrors in the stores, smiling, as if I knew a secret—they only worked for me. When the charm of that wore off, I practiced seeming impatient. I leaned on counters and frowned, shaking my head, sighing. "Could you pick up the pace a little? I don't have the whole day, you know. Are you alive back there?" though the dentist said this behavior wasn't becoming; young ladies didn't act that way.

"What do *you* know about *becoming?*" I demanded just the way you might have demanded it of Father. My words made an angry glare against his startled face. "Is it becoming to cheat on your wife?"

"I don't have a wife," he protested, though he might just as easily have said he hadn't cheated.

"*All* men cheat on their wives," I told him. "It's a law of nature."

"That isn't true," he said, but he stayed on anyway after the convention had ended. The rooms shed his compatriots, those lovers of porcelain, of the gleam of inert materials, and we went driving, many times as the dusk was settling, bringing fog like a speechless visitor. I drove right into this mood, speeding through the red light at the edge of town. "Slow down," the dentist warned me, but he really didn't mean it. This was also *his* first time to be so careless. Together we reached a lot of places, a waterfall that bound some farmer's property like an old, grumbling vein, the billowing meadow behind the Cold Springs' Tavern. At each stop he tried to convince me I was special, lovely, enchanting. This was a landmark we'd remember for years to come, if only . . .

"If only *what?*" I asked, as if I didn't know.

"If only," he said. "You know what I mean, don't you? How can you be so cruel?"

I shrugged the way you might have. "How can you be so stupid?"

But even that didn't deter him. He kept right by my side as I went reeling through the days. Wherever I stepped, he did. Wherever I paused for trouble he paused too. We actually went together to your house to pick up more dresses, though the dentist wasn't too crazy about that. "Breaking and entering," he called this. "We could be arrested."

"We already have been," I said, because this was the kind of pun you might have used. "Anyhow—this is my sister's place. You don't need to worry."

But he did worry. He worried that you and I didn't get along. He wondered what kind of a relationship you and I had that didn't require a key. "My boys, too, were full of rivalry," he said sadly, but I told him he didn't understand. He didn't have the slightest idea what had passed between us all these years; nor what hadn't. "My sister *lent* me these dresses," I said, finally, because that was a fact he could understand, a simple equation. "She owes me a great, big favor. *Believe* me."

And it was true. Each time I took another dress I felt justified, for the way I had kept a vigil after you'd left, for the way you said, "Take *you* with *me?* That's insane!" I sat on your bed and stared at the patterns in the spread, mandalas on Indian cotton that had bled until they looked like spiders. I meditated despite these blurry cues, the way you used to, because you swore that nothing in life was solid; thought could arc from one body to the next like lightning. I sent my thoughts to you, (Come back! Come back!) trying to picture where you stood—in West Virginia? in Canada, maybe? Some place where, in the fall, the flocks of geese rushing by made a sound just like the ocean. That's where I thought you were all these years, a place where only the sky remembered your features, the impress of your walk, where there was nothing to bind you. You often said that's how you wished your life could be. No more of this slavery.

That was when you got older, of course, and thought it was your right to be dramatic—everything else was so dramatic; how else could you cope? You were in high school then and Father was sick. This isn't a time of life, you insisted, when someone should have to be upset. I'm supposed to be happy now, aren't I?

Maybe you were right. That was what the doctor said after all. "The human heart is unpredictable . . ." just like that, as if he were a doctor in a movie breaking the bad news to someone who might faint. "What am I supposed to do?" you asked Mother. "Give up my life?" She wanted you to be nearby, "just in case."

"But what does that *mean?*" you asked her. And, "Why can't *Mary* watch him? She's got nothing better to do."

My pulse would quicken until Mother said, "I asked *you* to watch him, Ronnie. I want you to act like a responsible adult." You two would argue about it until Father heard you and called down from the bedroom. "I don't need to be watched! Let her go out if she wants to. Go on, Ronnie, honey," until you actually went, slamming the door with relief, as if he'd really meant what he'd said.

You always acted as if he did. Every night you prepared to go out with friends of yours to the movies or a rock concert, for a ride in a hot, new Mustang, where you would drink wine and smoke joints, and much, much worse, you implied as you glossed your lips and smiled, so that I'd have to imagine what I really didn't want to—the arms and legs all tangled together, the hazy kisses, the wispy, drugged-up sighs. Your "debut into the underworld" you once called it, as if this could soften the blow.

No smiles at dinner, however. You didn't want to be left behind with us, trapped inside the dark, humid cave of waiting. You streaked through your meal, one eye on the door the whole time until halfway through dessert you dropped your spoon into your dish, "That's it!", as if you had taken just about as much as a human being could endure. You grabbed your coat from the hook where it was poised, eager to flee.

Sometimes Mother was too tired to argue. Other times she said, "Wait just a minute, young lady—I want you to take this upstairs." She handed you a tray she'd prepared for Father, the soft, light foods to ease his heart—soup, mashed potatoes, a wan bowl of tapioca pudding.

"Oh *fine*," you snapped. "Wait until I have my foot out the door, why don't you?" You went flouncing up the stairs spilling the soup, knocking over the salt shaker, under your breath, whispering, "Damn, damn, damn . . ."

One awful night Father asked you to please play for him before you went out, just a little tune, it had been so very long . . .

"I can't *stand* this," you muttered, as you threw yourself down at the piano. "Why does everything have to be so maudlin?" You slammed back the fallboard and galloped through the song, fingers mumbling and crushing the notes, then shoved back the bench so abruptly it fell over, clattering your displeasure.

That was the one time I remember you apologized, though it wasn't that much of an apology, just a toss of your head as you dashed through the kitchen: "I'm really sorry, but why does it have to depend on *me*? I'm not the cure—I'm the disease—isn't that clear by now?"

I agreed with you on that one. And for the next few days I decided to ponder this thought without the additional problem of the dentist. To aid my deliberation I made it a point to escape him as much as I could. "You don't really know me," I told him over dinner.

Silly man. He gazed across the candlesticks and flatware and smiled broadly, as if this were an invitation, to press his thumbprints into my bare and shivering arm, to bump knees under the table as if we were two blind fish scavenging a river bottom.

"Don't you ever give up?" I asked him, but he mistook this too. "No," he reassured me. "I am an *ex-*

tremely determined person. And very patient. It's a characteristic of my profession."

In order to ditch him I had to get up before dawn and dress in the dark so that my room would stay immobile. I had to glide through the hallway and creep down the fire escape stairs to the back parking lot where my car was waiting, swallowed in the mist of early morning. I had to pump the gas quickly, hold my breath as the car coughed its way to life and I knew I had the jump on him.

All day long I stayed several towns ahead of him, though I knew he would follow in his car, at a reasonable, dental pace, pausing to reassess his direction every so often, deciphering the quest he had fallen into. I pretended I was a treasure hunt he couldn't help but follow. The landscape was mapped with clues for a man who was bright enough to read them correctly. At this mark is a girl without a leg to stand on. At that juncture is a girl without a home anymore.

That was how he read my travels, as I swerved to a halt at a jewelry store, hopped out, and in thirty seconds flat, ordered a diamond ring on his credit card. While the jeweler bent for his tray of gold settings, I called, "That's a nice one! See ya!" And, "My father will pick it up." Then I was in my car again and onto the next complication, a dealership where I test-drove a new Mercedes to a phone booth around the corner. "My father will drop this off in just a minute," I predicted. I slipped around the side of the building to my own car, left a note on a shining windshield, "Who can afford such an extravagance? Can you?"

I spent the whole day in this manner, using it up like a handful of cheap coins until night fell and it was time to take decisive action, to stop by your house and break a window, maybe start a small brush fire in your backyard, consoling my fears that it might spread unimpeded by pulling up to a bar and drinking until I forgot to stop, until the barstool beneath me melted away and the lights above the wavering bottles became the lights in someone's living room, someone's bedroom, where I had to scream, "What am I doing here? Get your goddamned paws off me! Are you crazy?" as I imagined you might have done, fed up at a certain point.

I know you often used this strategy of cursing. I remember how you rebuked him, as if, should you only act mean enough, your troubles would disappear. You used to argue with Father that way constantly, sometimes about the silliest things, whether you had the right to paint things on your bedroom walls: "Taking a trip? Call a head . . ." "In the midst of life, along comes the smiling mortician . . ."

He didn't understand it. Why was a beautiful girl like you thinking such terrible thoughts?

The dentist tried to explain it to me. Unlike you, he believes that we are all bound to earth—that's what causes problems. Of course, that's exactly what a dentist would think, a man used to drilling through bone, digging a tiny pocket of a universe through the weak sludge of decay, pushing his excavator into secret wells of pain as nonchalantly as if they were made of sand.

Of course he'd take an approach like that—against my wishes insisting it was about time; it would be good for me.

Maybe he was right. I couldn't claim for certain what might be good for me—three weeks in a sauna? A wrestling match on your kitchen floor? I had to admit I didn't feel bound to earth much lately, felt more like I was whirling through a vacuum, soundless and dizzy as an asteroid tugged by too many planets. Especially when I think of you, I feel these force fields doing battle. I hear every awful thing you ever said. "Leave me alone." "Go away." "You're disgusting!"

Just to distract myself I agreed to let him do my teeth one afternoon. Though I soliloquized about my fear of dentists, cautioned him not to get too carried away, he pretended I was only joking. "Now you know I'm not a monster," he chuckled. "Haven't I demonstrated that by now?" He borrowed a colleague's chair as professional courtesy and began burrowing through my soft spots.

"I'm not a coward," I told him, "but this *really* hurts."

In the way of dentists, he pretended he couldn't hear me. "Terribly neglected," he pronounced my teeth, as if they were a casting of my moral nature, it was engraved there in the brittle enamel.

"Open *wider*," he commanded, at ease now with these more familiar techniques of assault.

"It *hurts*," I cried, and he said, "Of course it hurts. Just try to relax." He used six vials of novocaine but none of it got me numb. My nerves twanged with silent screams: Don't . . . Don't . . . Don't . . . as he lectured me. "You've got to forget about the past," he warned above the high speed of the drill. "Believe me—it's your only alternative. It will be your salvation. *I* know."

"You don't know anything," I tried to say, but my mouth was pried open; steel was coursing in electrifying tunnels. "What do *you* know about my past? Maybe everything I told you was a lie . . ." The drill was whirring so fast I was confused. Maybe I *had* told lies. Maybe you weren't who I said you were. Maybe we had changed places. Or maybe it was just the vortex of pain swirling my thoughts. I *wished* you and I had changed places. I wished you could feel this ache, this throbbing. Your shadows were on my X-Rays. My life was suctioning through an evacuation tip. There were spluttering, choking sounds. Mine? Mine? I felt my tongue swelled huge and unwieldy, clogging up my windpipe and the dentist yelling at me, "Calm down! Calm down!" as I tried to tear the drill from his hand. "This will only take another minute . . . You're almost cleaned out . . ."

Back at the hotel I lay there on the bed with a minor constellation of holes, Orion's heavy belt, still in my teeth, unfilled because I had fainted. As I wept into my pillow, the dentist insisted, "We can't leave them like this. We should go back as soon as you've recovered. You'll be in agony by tomorrow."

"I don't care," I moaned. "I already am." I ran my tongue over each pounding tooth until the sedative he gave me took effect, a double dose of Darvon washed down with a glass of wine, enough to make my hands tingle and my veins race like humming telephone wires. The holes opened up into chasms— yawning and dark. The dentist lay down beside me and stroked my hand. "It's all right. There. There. Don't be frightened." I heard your voice through the smothering darkness, contradicting him. "It's *not* all right. It will *never* be all right . . ."

That's what you told Mother before you left. That was the explanation you put in your note. "As long as *I'm* here, he'll always be miserable."

That was the way the dentist put it too. As long as I was here he'd be sick with despair. I thought I heard him say this as he unbuttoned my shirt and arranged me on the bed. I couldn't quite believe I didn't dream it, that such a gentle, old man would take advantage of my situation. I wasn't sure afterwards if I had really felt my limbs being moved around, as if they were light as straws, folded into positions of yearning, then repose, then yearning again, like an interpretive dance of the human condition.

Because I want you to know that I, too, understand the true nature of love. I understand now that description you once gave of a French film you saw at the Theatre of the Living Arts. A perfect description, you said, and you laughed bitterly as you talked about the inevitability of passion: two lovers who are irrevocably drawn to one another despite the overwhelming odds against them, how the two try to resist but they can't; it's like parting flesh from bone, a soul from its maker. Their love is not meant to be but it persists anyway across vast distances of time and propriety until, finally, the woman sinks into a deep melancholy over her dilemma. There is the ultimate tortured scene on the floor of a living room of an empty house. The woman seduces her lover one last time, and then, in a moment of sweeping passion, shoots him through the head. That was love. At least in your version.

And I think I understand to some extent. I understand, at any rate, why the dentist confessed his guilt for *my* crimes, for example. He was arrested the other night for trying to return a heap of dresses to a house that was no longer there. Smoke was pouring from the windows, but he stumbled up the front path anyway, shrouded in the mist of a speech he had rehearsed on my behalf. He hadn't been able to persuade me to deliver it myself, in person, but he planned to argue his own rendition of my feelings, as if good intentions alone could spin straw into gold. "Your sister has made a grave mistake," was his intended overture. "And she offers her apologies. She is very, very sorry. *Desolate*—if the truth be told. . . ."

But he never had a chance to say any of this, nor to test his theory—that the truth could be extinguished by lies. On his way to your crumbling door, the bulk of all those dresses stymied him. He tripped over a treacherous sash. The whole silky jumble went sliding from his arms onto the ashes.

Only *then* did he notice—a man blinded by the nobility of his mission, no doubt. Or by the years of perfume ground into the cloth. Or the indelible shape of your body. Or possibly he just wasn't able to see over the top of the sprays of taffeta, over the prom dress he grabbed at the last minute thinking he had fooled me; he was sneaking away to redeem everyone by this daring act. As he slipped across the carpet with it, I pretended I didn't care anymore than you did. For what? A gown that Father had bought when you were a senior in high school? For the last gift you ever received from him?

You never even went to the prom. As soon as you got into the car you tore the dress right off. Your haste made the rows of pearl buttons explode against the windows of that Mustang you made your escape in. I know because I was watching. I felt every rip you made in that dress as if it were dismemberment, or stabbing.

"The world is full of contradictions," I told the dentist through the bars of his overnight cell. "I certainly don't love you for this."

Because now that he's gone, I've remembered the strangest things—you know what I'm talking about, don't you? I've tried to trace the origins of our troubles, the whole way back, but I only get so far. I remember those adventures he gave you, driving hours to Atlantic City, to the Million Dollar Pier because it was your favorite; you liked to ride the Dragon Express, a roller coaster ride as wild with color as Chinese silk, that became, as it clanked and grabbed its way along the rails, a journey into nightmares, a funhouse full of ghosts and goblins and skeletons, every so often, some fireworks: snap! bang! snap! that made you grab his arm and snuggle against him. "Daddy— I'm scared," you said, but your voice was low and unhurried as if his sunburned warmth had made you drowsy.

Mother tried her best to console me. You were so much older than I—that's how she explained it. "You just wait," she said. "When you're a little more grown up, he'll take you too."

OUT-OF-THE-BODY TRAVEL

My problems were simple: life and death, my mother and my father. What *her* problems were I didn't know, didn't *want* to know.

It was 1968 that winter Clara arrived from the mental hospital and took my father's place in our household. A very poor substitute in my opinion, but, as my mother claimed, Clara had nowhere else to go, no one else who was willing to care for her—not her parents, not the hospital where she had committed herself eight months earlier "just for the weekend." "We can no longer be therapeutically helpful except on an outpatient basis," the hospital people said. "She's thirty years old," her parents phoned in their long-distance wisdom. "*She* should be taking care of *us*." She had no husband anymore, no friends that we knew of. For some reason *we* were responsible. "We're all in the same boat now," was how my mother put it.

I didn't want to be in the same boat as Clara. *Or* my mother. I didn't want to think about the way that felt—to lie there hour after hour beneath the quilts, wrapped in a brown bathrobe, sweating. I didn't want to think about her eyes fixed on the doors, the walls, on the ceiling, on nowhere.

I had already seen nowhere the day my father drove up to New York City for a Yankees' game, then called to say he wasn't coming home. Not right then, at least. Maybe not ever. Honestly—he really didn't know. He really couldn't say for sure. "I've always had a false sense of security," was the only reason he gave for this sudden defection—unless you counted out-of-the-body travel as reason.

"Out-of-the-body, and now, out-of-the-house," my mother said. "This is an explanation?" But my father said, "*I* was the one. *I* was the one who almost died."

He claimed to have had a "transcendental" experience the spring before when he'd suffered a heart attack. As he was lying on the table in the emergency room he felt his spirit or his soul or whatever-you'd-call-it suddenly ripped away from his body—as if it were no heavier than a shadow. Then it was sucked through a long, dark tunnel quicker than an arrow, like a memo through a pneumatic tube. This wasn't the pleasant, near-death experience most people describe, the shimmering vista of fields and flowing rivers, the loved ones who have passed on sprouting like an enchanted forest to wave a wordless welcome: We missed you ... We love you ... "I was frightened," my father said. "Absolutely *terrified*. There was nothing there. Not light. Not sound. Not water. There was nothing at all—nothing at the end of the tunnel. You understand?"

"*I* understand," my mother said. "I understand that your father hates us. I understand he believes *we* caused his heart attack. I understand how these things work. People think they can just throw you away when they get tired of you. They think they can drain every drop of your life's blood and never even say so much as 'thank you.' I understand your father thinks he's making up for lost time, that he's having a great whirlwind of fun."

"What *is* he having?" I asked. And that invariably spurred on her lecture. I, too, had funny notions of right and wrong. I was getting just as bad as *he* was. I talked fresh to everyone all day long. I made a mess everywhere I went. I was always in trouble at school. I was ruining my chances for a college education, for the future.

I had to admit she was right about this. I hadn't been very cooperative, not since my father left, but what did she expect from me anyway? Of course I wasn't interested in the future. Each time I went to New York to visit my father, he told me the same story about his dying—the staring lights, the awful, chanting voices: Code! Run a CODE!

Somehow this chanting always led back to me. "You're fifteen," he told me. "You're a beautiful, young girl. You're full of energy. Zest. Life! You should be having fun. Don't make the same mistake I did."

I wasn't sure exactly what his mistake had been and he never exactly said, but I was convinced it had something to do with our curtains—the funereal, purple ones in the dining room, the heavy, gold plush that fell in a gloomy cascade behind my mother's china orchestra. It was that orchestra which she dusted and rearranged daily, as if each night they performed a different symphony and had to be curried like horses after a long, hard race. It was the way she fussed over the furniture, polishing the wood, plumping the mattresses, patting, gently, the arms of the sofa. It was the way she punctuated each sentence with a sigh. "Suzanne." (Sigh). "Would you mind doing a little homework?" "Suzanne." (Sigh). "Would you mind explaining why you flunked this test?" "Suzanne." (BIG sigh). "If you keep behaving this way you're going to end up in the streets. You're going to end up just like your father."

I didn't see what was so wrong with my father. He had his own apartment in the Village. Four new sets of tie-dyed sheets.

Maybe that was what drove me to misbehave, to cut off my own nose to spite my face, as my mother described it. Maybe it was Clara's fault. Or maybe it was just 1968 and I thought I should feel the earth move the way everyone but my mother did. I owned a drawer full of literature on the subject, all forbidden, all cherished, especially a ravaged copy of the Kama Sutra my father's girlfriend, Donna, gave me after we all went to see, "I Am Curious, Yellow," together. My father was embarassed by that movie but Donna wasn't. "Very honest," she called it. She told me about her own sexual awakening, how she had been sprung, at an early age, from the "bourgeois trap" of virginity. It had happened right there in my hometown of Philadelphia while she was visiting—a very groovy communal "pad" near Rittenhouse Square.

It wasn't just the pad though. Or the guy. (Though he had studied Zen for many years and that certainly helped). Or the drugs. It had been the combination of all these elements that had made it such a very beautiful experience for her—as if every one of her planets had suddenly snapped into perfect alignment.

While my father was out buying bagels, a Sunday New York Times, Donna gave me a fuller description of that "slow, dark evening," the "dark, murmuring room," the way this guy Geoffrey had unchained the oppressive links of society and her soul had opened just like that—had blossomed just like a flower.

I believed Donna. She wasn't that much older than I was. I wanted *my* soul to open like a flower, not shoot down a tunnel the way my father's had. Still, despite my efforts, the many afternoons I hung around the Square shivering in my miniskirt and jean jacket as

I waited for interesting people to come along and guide me through the universe, nothing ever happened. The only thing that blossomed for me that winter was more misery. The very first Sunday in January when I arrived home from a ski vacation with my father and Donna, I found Clara there living in *my* room. Without my permission all of my belongings had been moved to the attic—books, posters, scented candles, even the stars I had pasted on my ceiling that glowed in the dark, pale blue. In their place Clara had filled the room with her despair. I saw this through the door my mother cracked open with her foot, only an inch, as if to keep Clara's grief from spilling out too quickly and drowning us.

Sad things. Sick things. There were rows of pill bottles on the dresser. Crumpled tissues in heaps, like withered roses from a forgotten prom. Dresses lay slumped on the wicker rocking chair, on my ruffled bed. Where I had painted the word "LOVE" on the wall with magenta Dayglo, someone had draped a sheet.

"Why *my* room?" I asked my mother. "Why do *I* have to be the one to sleep upstairs? It's *freezing*."

"Skiing!" my mother exclaimed triumphantly, as if this were some kind of brilliant counterargument. "What sort of vacation is that? Up the hill. Down the hill. *Up* the hill. *Down* the hill. Your father has a serious heart condition. Does he want to kill himself?" Before I could say a single word in his defense she answered her own question. "*Obviously.* Obviously he cares as little for his *own* welfare as he does for anyone else's." Then she warned me to keep quiet; I was to resist the urge to tell her any more nonsense, such as what a terrific time we'd had, or how my father had confided, as we propped our legs before the ski lodge fire, that my mother was really very difficult to live with. "I don't want to hear another word," my mother scolded as if to illustrate. "I want you to go right in there this minute and say hello to your cousin. Be nice to her. She's been waiting eagerly to see you."

I doubted that my cousin had been eager to see anyone in the last twenty years, that she had even blinked during those decades. She was stationed in my bed like a zombie dedicated to the spell of the TV. It sat on the desk six inches from where she had collapsed against a mountain of pillows. The volume on the set was turned all the way down. The covers were bunched around her waist. She was wearing that brown bathrobe, twisted open so that one breast hung out, drooping to the side, and she was gazing intently at the screen, her lips moving, filling in the missing sound as if every catastrophe reported that evening were her own.

"Are you going to just stand there?" my mother demanded. She apologized to Clara. "Please forgive my daughter. It seems like lately, unfortunately, she takes after her father. If you know what I mean."

Clara didn't say a word. Apparently she didn't remember my father, nor his myriad misdemeanors.

"Clara," my mother said. "Clara, honey..." Though Clara lay there like a stone, my mother made me bend down and kiss her on the cheek. "*Tell* her," my mother ordered. Clara's castoff breast glared up at me until finally I said, "You're very welcome to use my room, Clara. I'm really glad you're here."

Of course I hated Clara instantly. I hated how unhappy she was, how much the world upset her. Wind. Noise. A bright smile. The first three bars of "Light My Fire." The last three bars. Everything unnerved Clara. She cried when a window slammed. She cried if the knife scraped across the plate when you were cutting up her meat for her. She cried because the birds in the trees outside her window chirped too loudly, or because they *stopped* chirping when the sky clouded up. She asked my mother where they had gone. Who had chased them away?

The answer seemed to be *me*. At least that was what I made of Clara's refusal to speak to anyone but my mother, how, each morning when my mother made me perform a ritual kiss before I went to school, Clara pulled her head away. Her hand rose to the spot on her cheek where my lips had touched and rubbed at it over and over, as if I'd left a threatening message there in Braille.

I hated how my mother defended her for that, ("Pay no attention—she's just a poor, frightened girl."), how often my mother defended her for just about anything. "It's the medication," she always said. "She's not 'koo-koo' as you so nicely put it!" But then she scurried through the house getting rid of lethal objects—the Clorox, the Lysol, her own prescription for a kinder existence—yellow, heart-shaped Valium. She even hid a pair of fingernail scissors that she swiped from my make-up tray, then swaddled in a bolt of corduroy.

I hated all those implications of suicide, especially because my mother tried to speak of them in fables. As we prepared dinner together she recited from a menu of thwarted dreams. There was the accountant who worked in my father's office who hanged himself at tax time. There was Marilyn Monroe. There was her Uncle Isaac who had swallowed cyanide, many years back, when he read about the Jews in Europe. "It happens," my mother said, then added a last, liberal dash of gloom, "People lose all hope."

I couldn't stand that either—how many times I came home from school and misunderstood the eerie silence. I stepped gingerly across the living room carpet as if it might be mined. A pool of blood would appear at any moment. And farther on, another pool of blood. A huddled form, arms outstretched. "Mother?" I called. "Mother? Mother!"

I hated most of all the way that felt, the moments that swelled between my question and her answer, the way I ran up the steps on trembling legs just to find her spooning applesauce into Clara's wobbly mouth, or folding up the newspaper she had just read aloud from start to finish as Clara grimly and deliberately slept.

I might have felt sorry for Clara if my mother hadn't decided to make such an issue of it. Each time I returned from New York her anger at me doubled as if

I wore the days I had just spent with my father like a new mink coat, flaunting my good fortune. Before I even stepped inside the front door I'd already been condemned. I found a piece of my own flowered note-paper pinned to the mailbox, blazing a trail to her anger. "Come upstairs *immediately*," it warned. "*No* dawdling." I found my way to the glowering look my mother had prepared, to a lecture for all seasons. "You've been getting away with murder the entire year," she said when I came home wearing a T-shirt that Donna had designed. "War kills," it declared beneath a G.I.'s grinning face. "Love heals," beneath two intertwined, naked figures. "Is that some fool's idea of a work of art?" my mother marvelled. "Is that the great 'learning experience' your father left us for?"

"I want you to understand that *other* people exist too," she said after my next visit. She ambushed me as I was sneaking past Clara's bedroom hoping to tuck myself away in the attic before another strip search. "Stop right there," she commanded, and then she shook me down, my backpack and purse emptied right onto the steps without mercy, as if she were a border patrol looking for stolen contraband, or maybe my father's secret orders to defect.

Not finding these she chose innocent items to object to. She confiscated things like peace symbols, the stained glass, dangling earrings she called "outland-ish," and "hypocritical." She threw in the trash the magazines I borrowed from my father for the train ride, "Rolling Stone," and "Village Voice," a "Play-

boy" Donna had bought him to counteract the blues
after his latest visit to the doctor. ("What do doctors
know?" Donna told him. "They're just another front
for the Pentagon. They tell them which chemicals to
put in our water. That's what makes you feel so bad—
those chemicals they make you swallow. That so-called
'medicine' . . .")

"So *what?*" I protested after every seek-
and-destroy mission was carried out. "What's wrong
with some different ideas? *I* haven't done anything."

But my mother insisted I had. As she snatched a
new piece of incriminating evidence, she interrogated
me: "Where were you all weekend? You were having
such a wonderful time you couldn't phone me? Your
father took you on another trip? Was that good-for-
nothing Donna with you?"

When I answered yes to all her questions, "*Good*
guess!" she got furious. "Where will it end?" she
seethed. "What will be the outcome?" She pressed the
box of strawberry incense, (a peace offering Donna
had sent along), to her ear, as if maybe it held Donna's
good-for-nothing philosophies. Maybe a ticking bomb.

That was where Clara came in. As punishment for
everyone's sins my mother decided I had to spend time
with her—an hour every day, longer if I felt like it. As
atonement I had to sit by her bed and pretend to hold
a conversation.

Fifteen minutes. Twenty minutes. Thirty-five
minutes.

While Clara dozed I babbled into the thin air

about clothes and boys and how institutionalized learning made me want to puke, how sometimes my mother made me want to puke.

When Clara didn't even stir, I made things up. I described the trouble I planned each day at school, the creative hours I spent in detention doodling obscenities on the bottom of my chair. SHIT. BARF. PISS. Nothing fazed Clara, certainly not the biology insurrection I told her I was going to lead on Monday. At a pre-arranged signal we would all throw our dissection pans right out the window, crayfish hurtling through space. Nor was she interested in the scenario I invented about the art supply closet, my interlude of cavorting there with four young aesthetes, the flurry of handprints that was left upon my skin.

"Red and green and blue," I added to see if Clara might be listening. "In some very touchy places." But Clara just snored on peacefully, as if I had disappeared, into another dimension, perhaps, one set aside for silly young girls, for total ingrates. She didn't even ask about the pre-arranged signal.

When my hour was up my mother came to get me. "Well!" she exclaimed, jolting Clara awake for a second. "I hate to interrupt but Suzanne has some studying to do. Did you two ladies have a nice talk?"

"No we *didn't*," I complained as soon as we got out into the hall. "I'm not doing that *ever* again—she scares me! She's so out of it she doesn't even know where she is."

"She certainly does," my mother glared. "She's in a place where people *love* her—do you understand what I'm saying?" I had to march back in there and spend another whole hour. I had to sit through Clara's moaning and sighing while I tried to read to her from some book my mother shoved at me on my way through the door: "Great Expectations," or "Gone With the Wind." Classics, but they both made Clara cry.

To console her, my mother suggested various, unpleasant strategies. Though the embarrassment alone would have killed a much heavier person than I, my mother made me sing lullabies to Clara recalled from my infant days. I had to tease Clara's hair into a "becoming" bouffant, or sponge her face with a washcloth doused with witch hazel so strong it made me gag, though my mother swore this aroma was a sure bet. "Very refreshing!"

Despite all these efforts, Clara held her ground. The one activity that seemed to give her any pleasure was her daily sojourn in the bathroom. As if it were a long-awaited voyage to Europe she stuffed her overnight case with cosmetics and hand towels.

This packing required every ounce of her concentration. She wended her way across the carpet as carefully as if it were heaped with broken glass. Half a lifetime later, when she reached her destination, the vanity table, she paused and scanned the contents of the mirrored tray as if it were a puzzle to be deciphered, as if maybe the creams and bottles of lotion and the lipsticks all added up to something. Several minutes later, her arm, bewitched by a mysterious spell, rose slowly from her side and drifted forward. Her hand hovered above the tray, dazed, uncertain, until finally it dropped onto a nail file or a barrette or a compact filled with the bleakest of beige powders she spilled along the way back to her suitcase.

During this process she never noticed anyone, not me, standing in the doorway marvelling, not my mother who tried, in her way, to be helpful: "Would you like to take this with you?" (holding up a polka-dotted shower cap), "What about this?" (a bar of scented soap), sometimes bringing offerings from her own room—ruby-colored bath oil beads. ("My! Aren't these lovely?"), a pair of slippers encrusted with rhinestones, her voice aglow like Christmas lights. "Oh, Clara. How would you like some of this perfume? Smell how nice!" But at these times Clara was oblivious even to my mother. We were ghostly detours that might lure her from her mission.

Neither of us knew the reason Clara spent so much time in the bathroom, (unless, of course, somebody had the *gall* to propose out-of-the-body travel again as a reason). "Can't you let up?" my mother asked me, but I said, "Maybe she really hates it here— did you ever think of that? Maybe she doesn't give a hoot to be with people who 'love her very much.' Maybe she can't think of anything more *boring*."

Only such "smart-aleck" remarks could have torn my mother from the keyhole where she knelt, from her endless scrutiny of Clara. ("I don't want to deny her any pleasure, but I'd still like to be on the safe side . . .") "What did you say?" my mother demanded.

"Did you dare say to me 'boring'? Is that what you think makes the world go around?"

But I thought Clara had the right idea. Once the door clicked shut behind her we never heard a sound, not the gurgle of water, not the scraping of the sliding glass cabinet door, not even the clatter of a comb against the sink. It was as if she had escaped through the bathroom mirror into the backwards, soundless world where she longed to be.

I longed to be there too—especially since it came highly recommended by Donna. "Turn on and tune out," was her slogan. When she was in town I played hookey. In exchange for a dime of pot the girl who took roll in my homeroom agreed to mark me present whenever I wanted. On these mornings I hopped on the subway and rode downtown just in time for a 'perpetual party' that was happening in that pad near Rittenhouse Square, the magic scene of Donna's flowering. I joined Donna's friends who were draped, all day long, on the couches and easy chairs, who lolled on the floor wrapped in a sweet mist of marijuana, a humming lethargy of words and music and not caring.

The minute you walked in the front door it hit you, and it kept on hitting you the entire day if you wanted—all you had to do was take a few tokes and melt into the crowd. "Perpetual high," Donna said, "equals perpetual freedom." That was the "square root" of her philosophy. "It's okay to do anything here—except be uptight." We could take off all our clothes and smear butter on our skin, if we liked that. We could sit in a closet for ten hours and stare at our knees. Not a critical word would be spoken. Only praise wafting from the four corners of the apartment, unlimited acceptance: "That's okay, Suzanne. That was a really beautiful idea, Suzanne. You're a beautiful person, Suzanne."

At home my mother said: "Keep quiet."
"Don't argue."
"Watch it!"
"Must you ruin every-
thing you touch?"

Donna's friends were just the opposite—sweet and generous. We did everything as a family—drugs, meditation, analysis of our dreams—no one was excluded. We had rituals that made the day hold together in a kind and loving net, ready to catch us if our mood showed any signs of falling.

The first thing we did each morning was drink tea together, something mysteriously Eastern in a ceramic mug where the twigs and branches floated like a miniature logjam in the eddies of hot water. Bancha tea or ginseng—to cleanse the spirit. Often there were odd pastries, brown and chewy and flavorless. I was pleased to hear these were macrobiotic, the perfect balance of "yin" and "yang," the "male component" and the "female component" according to Geoffrey, who was still studying Zen at the university and knew the most about spiritual things.

After breakfast we did yoga. Sitar music buzzed

like a hive of electric bees and we bowed down to it twisting our arms and legs to the contortions of the scales and breathing, "deeply ... deep-ly ... DEEP.... ly ..." until objects began to waver, a shimmering haze crept around the outlines of the furniture and the curtains and people's faces, as if they were about to change form.

Sometimes we enhanced this effect by smoking dope beforehand. Sometimes we held back until after we had climbed the "crystal-staircase-to-inner-peace," as Geoffrey identified it. "So very fragile ..." Then we passed around a joint or a pipe or a chunk of oily, black hash impaled on a tapestry needle. We sucked up the smoke through the end of a ballpoint pen. "More precise even than a bong," Geoffrey explained.

Getting high was my favorite time of day. I felt most at ease then as the smoke crept through my body, as if the sun were going down in my veins. I became a windowpane that warmth was pouring through. I could light up the whole room and make it glisten. I could touch the person next to me and his arm would glow.

I felt no such glow at home. If anything, Clara was more silent, my mother, even colder.

"Be more careful," she warned when I tripped and dropped a load of schoolbooks as I ran past Clara's room.

"Turn that down!" she scolded when I crouched before the mumble of my radio.

"For crying out loud!" she exclaimed when I so

much as coughed or sneezed or even shook my head, "No! No!" too vehemently.

All of my attempts to be helpful seemed to back-fire, from the cheery, red polish I spilled in Clara's lap, to the burn mark I pressed into the blouse my mother bought for Clara as a Valentine's Day surprise. "Who-ever taught you to iron silk?" my mother cried. "Are you *crazy?*"

That was the dimension I lived in. This was how it felt to be me, I told the people at Geoffrey's—as if I had shrunk to a pinpoint like the tiny dot on the TV screen once the power is turned off.

"This is what my mother does to me," I told them. I described all the weird ideas she had lately, how she made lists, in a spiral notebook I wasn't us-ing, of the many "opportunities" she and my father had "missed," the vacations they'd never taken, the plays they'd never seen, the exhibits, the operas. "Daddy *hates* opera," I reminded her, but it didn't seem to matter. "He would have loved that new pro-duction of 'Butterfly'," she said mournfully. She made me sit next to her on the couch while she played me tragic arias. I had to nod my head as if entranced while Nellie Melba sputtered and trilled, trilled and sputtered from the hi-fi. "Heavenly," my mother pro-nounced this.

"Another tragedy," my father affirmed. "Your mother always loved them."

And I agreed. On those nights she didn't sit in her

chair and monitor Clara, she monitored me. I had to sleep with her in my parents' sagging double bed, curled up in a ball on my father's side as if I were a new recruit in training to betray her. I had to listen to her talking in her sleep: "You liar . . . You murderer . . ." and wonder which one of us she meant, (though, at dawn, she often gave me clues, unveiling them as if they were answers to a Zen koan, the kind that could live forever in a state of suspended animation: "Your father doesn't miss anyone. Believe me— he cares only for himself. He doesn't care what we think of him. Or what we remember. If he had any compassion whatsoever . . .")

"What are you talking about?" I asked, still groggy from her restless nightmares, but she wouldn't repeat it. "Far be it from me," she said, "to worry you for no reason."

I thought maybe she was joking. But the next night was dead serious, often completely wordless. I had to endure her again, her smell, rank and sweating, as if she ran all night through her bad dreams, no doubt chasing my father. I was sure of this because, frequently, in the more troubled stages of her sleep, she flung her arm across my chest and clasped me so hard I couldn't breathe. When I complained about this the next day she stared at me, her eyes dark with bewilderment. "What! I hugged you? My own daughter? Is that such a crime?"

But the next minute she was screaming at me again. I was clumsy. I was inconsiderate. I had absorbed my father's reckless spirit the way a sponge soaks up water. "It's frightening," she said, and for once we both agreed.

So did the people at Geoffrey's. "Bad karma," was their diagnosis. More pot, was their prescription. Keep smoking that weed, they advised. Around the clock. Around my mother's outbursts. "Don't lose that buzz—whatever you do."

They held joints to my lips and made me sip at them like precious water in the desert. They made me lie down in the middle of the floor and try to levitate my sorrow. They gave me little presents—a chunk of hash here, a bag of pot there, three hits of acid, as innocent-looking as pieces of white confetti, I was only to use in case of "dire emergency."

They gave me other presents too—words of wisdom from their favorite authors. They used to read aloud to me from "Demian," phrases I was to repeat at home to build my confidence, to build an understanding of my condition, the HUMAN condition, the realities that were in conflict. As we lay side by side on Geoffrey's mattress, (the whole group sometimes sprawled like a pile of pick-up sticks), he quoted his favorite passages. In a flourish of wafting smoke the words drifted past: "Every man is more than just himself; he also represents the unique, very special, and always significant and remarkable point at which the world's phenomena intersect . . ."

I was usually too stoned at this point, actually, to appreciate the wisdom. I didn't quite see how it ap-

plied to my situation: I wasn't a man and I wasn't remarkable, no more than Donna whose parents
divorced when she was only nine, whose older sister
had run away and never come home again, whose
mother was an alcoholic.

I was also too stoned to object to what went along
with his words—another remedy, much more comfort-
ing—at least according to Geoffrey's theory. As the
others floated off to meditate in separate bedrooms,
Geoffrey grabbed my hand. "Don't be afraid," he
whispered, and I whispered back, "Afraid of *what?*
Why should I be?" though I could feel the music from
the stereo someone was blasting thudding through my
body like a runaway heartbeat. The sound was turned
up too high to say no; something was turned up too
high, so that the walls threatened to cave in, the glass
ornaments Geoffrey had propped on his windowsill
somersaulted to their doom; it was impossible to tell
where the music was coming from—from the speakers
that were set up all over the house, or from the ceiling,
or a violently yearning portion of my brain; it was impossible to remember how I'd gotten to Geoffrey's, to
his bed, what room I was in, how long I'd been there,
though even as I wondered I could feel his fingertips,
brushing against me light as butterflies, hovering
against my skin, his hands soothing my neck and
arms, gliding onto my hip, very gently, on my thigh,
my breast, and elsewhere, fluttering, fluttering.
"You're very sweet," Geoffrey said. He leaned over
and let his beard tickle my skin, poured words into my
ear that drenched me in beautiful colors, just as

Donna had promised. We smoked another joint and then he pressed me into the mattress, against the quilt his grandmother had sewn, many years ago, for *her* marriage bed, for marriage was *bodies,* not paper, patterns of past and present, though later he said, "Hey, Babe—that was kind of interesting . . ." as if I had just told him a little-known fact about the weather, or described a new diet for enlightenment—brown rice mixed with cauliflower, Marxism mixed with Zen.

None of it made any sense—the way sex felt, why my mother hadn't found out yet the trouble I'd gotten into, the host of crimes I had committed—just like my father. When she did, I planned to blame it on the pot which, by then, I was smoking not only at Geoffrey's but everywhere, carrying supplies of it around the way a diabetic carries insulin. Whenever I had the opportunity I pulled a joint from the leather pouch Geoffrey had given me, and lit up—in the woods when I should have been at band practice, or in the girls' bathroom as I stood on the window ledge and waved the telltale fumes towards open air.

In the attic, on nights my mother set me free, I listened to her voice rising in a crescendo of useless comfort through the heating vent: "It's not so bad," she reassured the thin air, because, by then, Clara was snoring soundly. "Things will get better if you just hang on a little while longer . . ." I lit a joint under the eaves and toasted her lies. "You don't really believe that stuff," I planned to tell her. "Look how many pills *you* take."

But she already seemed to know this, seemed to have caught whatever was bothering Clara. As if it were the proper show of sympathy, she began crying constantly. At the oddest moments—when she brought forsythia branches from the garden to decorate the dining room table, or if the phone rang unexpectedly, she suddenly burst out: "This is too much! I can't bear it!" I found her weeping in the kitchen when she was laying out the tablecloth and napkins.

"What's the matter?" I asked and, just like Clara, she wouldn't say a word, as adamant as if she'd taken a vow to confuse me. "Nothing's the matter," she finally replied, though the tears were still running down her cheeks. "Everything's the matter. I'm sorry." She took the cup of coffee she was holding and poured the contents into the sink. Then she stood there shaking her head at the grounds that seeped away into a dark and acrid ring on the white enamel. "I just don't know what to do anymore."

Neither did I. By then I thought that everything in the whole world was my fault—I couldn't see who else to blame. I was sure it was my complete lack of understanding, (what Geoffrey called "existing on a literal plane"), that had caused the mess we were in— not just my mother's incessant weeping, but Clara's breakdown too, my father's desertion, the long, downward slide my mother said we were on, (impossible given that she had already said many times we had hit "rock bottom.").

How many times can you hit, I wondered? Maybe

I didn't understand that either. Not even the simplest things, such as why I hadn't felt the earth move, not even a fraction of an inch, not even with the inevitable practice of repetition, whenever I slept with Geoffrey. I couldn't understand why I continued to sleep with him in spite of this, in spite of the way I cried the first time, how I made Geoffrey turn away and sigh, "Not *this* trip . . . *Please* not this bum trip . . ."

I couldn't understand why I didn't feel anything, though Donna said I probably just didn't notice. "It's not necessarily an earthquake," she elaborated. "It's more like a landslide, a very slow landslide, sometimes moving slower than the naked eye can see. *Or* the naked body," she added, but it still didn't make any sense.

Nor did it make any sense that she never told me she and my father were breaking up, that this was the last conversation Donna and I would ever have. From Geoffrey's she departed for points unknown. "As a driven leaf," Geoffrey commented—a much fuller analysis than the one my father gave me.

"What happened?" I asked him about two weeks later. Out of the blue, between sections of the Sunday paper, he casually announced that he and Donna were finished.

"Finished with what?" I asked. I stared around the room for new decor I hadn't noticed—curtains or bookshelves that had eluded my dizzy grasp, until it dawned on me it wasn't furnishings he meant. But I still couldn't grasp why they'd done it. "Don't you love her anymore?" I demanded. "I thought you LOVED her. Weren't you the one who said love was the only version of eternity?"

"That wasn't me," my father shook his head, and I felt that swooping sensation that had rearranged my insides lately; without any warning, making the room spin an indescribable number of RPM's. I truly couldn't remember whether he had said that or not. And if he hadn't said it, then who? Donna? Geoffrey? My mother? Surely not my mother—we all knew what she believed these days.

"Don't," my father interrupted my chaos. His voice seemed to filter through a screen before it reached me. "Be upset," I heard. He put his arms around me and hugged, as if he could squeeze the disappointment out of me. "Life is so much more complicated," he reassured me, "so much more difficult than a person can understand at your age, Suzanne."

"I *do* understand," I protested, but my father just smiled wistfully. For a "treat" he took me upstairs to see a psychic reader, an old woman Donna had introduced him to, who wore a sleeveless housedress though the living room where we waited was so cold our breath steamed like clouds in a crystal ball.

At her order we sank into the lumpy sofa and she showed us pictures of people who were supposed to be dead, though "magnetized," still attached to the living. They trailed behind them wispy as smoke. "These are the departed," she said, "who still love us." Then she told us to close our eyes, to imagine a great, white light. "This is the future," she intoned. "All you have to do is *will* it."

"What kind of a treat was that?" I asked my father after we had left our ten-dollar donation on her coffee table and retreated downstairs. "Is something the matter? I mean *really* the matter?"

"I don't know," was all my father would say. "Don't worry, Suzanne—she just cheers me up sometimes." I had to ride back through the racketing darkness of the train wondering what had gone wrong, why no one wanted to tell me anything. I had to lie there next to my mother that night, who cried that she had missed me terribly, (her little girl, her precious daughter!), and wonder what had provoked this kindness, why it seemed to make the earth fall away, leaving me in a vast and empty space, so dizzy I wasn't sure which way was up, which way was down.

I had to smoke four joints the next few mornings before I could get anywhere near that "perfect buzz," before my head seemed to swell up like a giant helium balloon. I couldn't see any other solution though, at school, it made the hours stretch forever, the way the corridors stretched from one grim classroom to the next, though, in each, I sat completely dazed by the glare of the fluorescent lights as the teacher's voice pulsed secret messages I didn't remember copying, that appeared, days later, in my notebook: "If two sides of a triangle are congruent . . ." "In the early nineteenth century the doctrine of manifest destiny . . ." I watched as other students pantomimed interest in words that dissolved into syllables as soon as they struck air.

What was the teacher saying? Why was everyone nodding? Why was *I* the only one who didn't understand?

I thought that acid might give me the answer—
that was what Geoffrey claimed—it would bring me
enlightenment. I believed him as much as I believed
anyone at the time. What's more I had the perfect opportunity for a test run a few weeks later when I came
downstairs one morning and found my mother hurling
figures from her china orchestra onto the hardwood
floor. "My God!" she kept exclaiming, "Oh, my
God!" as if some cruel, outside force had taken control
of her hands.

She had already destroyed most of her favorites
when I asked her what on earth she was doing. They
lay smashed on the shining wood my mother had just
waxed and polished the day before, frozen in awful silence like a broken army on a terrible battlefield—
arms and legs and torsos scattered everywhere.
"What's going on?" I asked again. "Are you losing
it?" But she didn't even get angry. Her only response
was to kneel down and pick the pieces up one by one
and hold them to the light—the cellist who had lost
his cello, the conductor who had been beheaded.
"How *could* you?" she demanded, and I was afraid
she had discovered everything—someone had called
from school to say I was flunking out, or I'd been followed by narcs, or she had finally realized, while
watching one of those endless documentaries she and
Clara preferred, that the smell in the attic wasn't just
that lousy incense Donna and I worshipped.

When no lecture erupted I imagined that maybe I was wrong, maybe this was a new form of therapy I hadn't heard of. It might have been that technique called "Primal Scream" that Geoffrey had sworn was almost as good as sex itself, was used to enhance sensations, in cases such as mine especially, where feelings were blocked, buried under an avalanche of ice and snow, under many layers of repressive parenting.

If that's what she was doing it seemed to be working, because, in a few minutes, my mother put down the two halves of the flute she was holding and straightened herself up. She took a deep breath and informed me that the three of us, "You and me and Cousin Clara," were all going to take a trip to the seashore.

"What for?" I asked her as we packed up the car with picnic things—paper plates and egg salad sandwiches, a plaid blanket in case it got "a little chilly." This hardly seemed like a reprieve—three hours in the car with my mother and Clara, more hours doing who knew what? probably sitting on the freezing dunes in a sandstorm. Knowing my mother we would no doubt have to pretend to frolic in a landscape as cold and windswept as the moon.

That's when I took the acid, when my mother, once again, made it a moral issue not to answer me, as if answering meant she had joined the careless new social order my father and I now belonged to. "Why do you have to ask so many questions?" my mother said, and her voice seemed unnaturally bright, like a banner shuddering in the wind. I couldn't believe the acid had worked *that* fast, but Geoffrey had refused to set a time frame. "Some people take five minutes," he said. "Some people take hours. And every once in a while," he sighed, "you get stuff that's just placebo. You just *think* that you're getting off. That's life . . ."

"I only asked ONE question," I said, just to see what my *own* voice would do.

Apparently it did nothing. My mother acted as if she hadn't heard me, as if my words just skittered away like seaweed blowing along the beach. She was more concerned with getting Clara into the car, leading her by the hand, slowly and carefully down the garden path. As if she were blind she kept prompting her, "Come on, Clara—there's a little bump here. You can get over it. Just pick your feet up a bit. Watch out for that stone there. Be careful of this patch of ice. Suzanne didn't shovel very well."

I might have protested, "Yes, I *did*," but I was still trying to decipher my mother's logic. I was concentrating very hard on noticing changes, the way it felt, for example, when my mother finally loaded Clara into the car and snapped the locks shut, as if we were all sealed in for a launch into outer space.

The way it felt as we sped along through the Pine Barrens, my mother's "shortcut," that took us through the bleakest part of the forest, no forest really, just the burned skeletons of fir trees sticking up through the sand, sad reminders of other careless people, other hard times.

Was this enlightenment I was feeling? Was this hallucination?

As if to purposely confuse me, my mother called back over her shoulder to Clara, "Isn't this lovely? This stark beauty . . ."

Of course there was nothing lovely about it, nothing lovely about going to the shore at all—forever the scene of some disaster for our family. I had broken my leg there one summer just by falling off my bike. My grandmother had died on the beach, in a deck chair, tucked away by the seawall, still squinting against the sun. My father always drank too much at the shore and ran around insulting people, especially my mother who fell into a deep depression she insisted was the fault of the ocean. ("I can't stand how it keeps repeating," she used to moan.) This was also the same beach where my father had his heart attack during another off-season visit. There was no hospital on the island so we had to drive him forty miles to Tom's River where the nurse made him lie flat across the plastic chairs in the waiting room while she hunted up a physician.

Though my mother had sworn she would never set foot on sandy soil again, here we were barreling down the highway much faster than I'd ever seen my mother drive.

Seventy. Seventy-five. Eighty. Somewhere near the Green Top Market the speedometer actually nicked one hundred—I was pretty sure I didn't imagine that. "My God!" I heard my mother exclaim once more.

She slammed on the brakes for a second and the car fish-tailed. A spray of pebbles hissed across the shoulder into the ditch, but I couldn't tell if it was our velocity that had startled her or the sight of the market.

This was the spot where she started chattering about my father. She actually turned the car around half a mile down the highway and drove back. She told both Clara and me to get out of the car so we could see better, though there was nothing to see, just the weatherbeaten stands that got painted a bilious green every summer so that the fruits and vegetables would look brighter, their glowing heaps would attract customers. That was what my mother said anyway. "Sam and I always stopped here to buy produce. It was extremely fresh," she told us. She ran her hand across the splintered wood as if it held an unspoken secret of their marriage, then herded us back into the car. "I don't know if we should be doing this," she said. "I'm not sure it's wise."

Not that this deterred her. Our ride to the shore was endless—even more so when we finally arrived. My mother seemed determined to give us a tour of her lost love. Her purpose in bringing us here was even worse than I'd suspected. She insisted on going over every inch of hallowed ground. "This is the place!" she kept crying. She aimed each word as if it were an arrow shot straight to her own unsuspecting heart. Love. Love. Love. Love. Though there wasn't an ounce of love in sight, not even the faintest, glimmering aura. She kept stopping at inscrutable landmarks to trace the outlines of invisible happiness with her pointing finger. "There! Over *there*," I heard her say, as if it were a drifting spirit that she'd sighted, an elusive ghost that kept popping up to taunt her.

"Isn't it wonderful? What a life we had!" She made Clara and I crawl out of the car at every spot and wobble across the soggy ground, on a mysterious treasure hunt for artifacts of an abruptly halcyon past. We didn't know what we were looking for but we stared anyway as intently as searchlights in the midst of a foggy storm. We reached down for pebbles or twisted branches, for shining gum wrappers, bottle caps, as if maybe one of these had caused my mother's rapture, not the bent and twisted synapses of her ruined memory.

There didn't seem to be any other clues. Only these facades of ordinary objects my mother had the sudden and amazing power to see right through to a much deeper truth. "He loved me," she chanted to Clara. "He really *was* crazy about me . . ."

"The material world is deceptive," Geoffrey had once told me, as an excuse for turning away after sex. "I *didn't* turn away." Perhaps my mother knew this too; this was something else adults shared, truth was just a matter of willpower, of desire. As we rocketed along the asphalt, from shrine to shrine, she transformed ordinary reality. Even without acid my mother was capable of seeing what wasn't there. "The beach is where Sam and I first met," she told Clara as we stumbled up a mountainous sand dune. "A big wave tumbled us into each other and we fell . . ."

"In love," she added, several carefully timed minutes later when we were back in the car again blurring towards another gap in memory, as if she had rehearsed all night for this exact moment, had rehearsed her whole life to say it the exact second we were passing the spot where he'd proposed. It was a spot so indistinguishable she could only remember it by the mile marker. "Nineteen," my mother alerted us. "Coming up on your right." She slowed down so we could honor it with our sighs, some tears, then sped towards other visions that appeared as quickly as she conjured them. We were passing the little gift shop where my father had bought her a string of seahorses . . . We were passing their favorite restaurant where they used to eat delicious lobster . . . We were passing the Seashell Inn where they had honeymooned in a room with a nautical theme, fishnets draped like delicate shawls along the walls, where shells and barnacles and starfish nested, where they didn't get out of bed for three days and three nights except for room service coming and going in a flurry of nectar and ambrosia . . .

"Some say life is a dream which never ends . . ." my mother announced an eternity later after we had swept the entire island for romantic inventions. I was hoping it was all just an interminable hallucination, that in fact I was at home safely burrowing through time, under the covers with my imagination. I hoped that I'd soon experience what Donna had described to me, the benign setting she beheld each time she tripped—the butterflies and rose gardens and rainbows

199

all whirled together, that any moment I'd wake up and I wouldn't be tripping at all, would only be dreaming the dream which never ends . . .

But the next minute we were stopping once more. We were pulling up at the drugstore to buy hats and suntan lotion, we were leaping onto a tiny inboard boat my mother raved over as if it were a cruise ship, just like the one my father used to own! that he took us fishing in every Sunday afternoon in summertime, just trawling along through the absolute joy of sunshine, the open sea! the three of us, a perfect family without cares or disagreements, that was sure to make me seasick, this tiny garvey, as flimsy as the past my mother was reconstructing, (Such a glamorous life!), or fall apart as soon as it hit a wave. "Isn't this exciting?" my mother asked. "Suzanne—do you remember? . . ." as we staggered across the deck to our seats, nothing to grip for support except the gunwales that disintegrated beneath my touch, the paint shedding flakes like gritty snow, the air shedding smells so awful they made me retch, as if the boat had been entombed since last summer in brine and beer and fish scales, worse for my mother's rendition of it all: "This is exactly the kind of outing that Sam would have loved. A fine day in the sun, a fine crew for company . . ." though there wasn't any sun, despite our sunglasses, the so-called crew consisted of three old men as scrawny as the burned up trees that lined the highway, all three of them exactly alike in horror except for the captain who had an additional blight, tattoos that swarmed across his face and arms, curling ropes that bound his wrists, a wriggling scythe on one cheek, a sheaf of arrows that rained across his forehead. Did my mother mistake him too? The way she was raving I thought she had. Or maybe she was just trying to encourage Clara. "This will be a wonderful trip. Such a lovely guide. A terrific person... *You* are a terrific person," she said to someone, as if she couldn't see clearly, the captain was so busy running back and forth, menacing us with fishing poles, "Take one. Pick one. A light one if you don't know what you're doing. Take this plastic reel... it's easier..." as he hoisted up the bait traps from the murky water, and pulled in the anchor, and wrapped the line around and around in figure eights, maybe all of this just to refute my mother, to erase the sound of her voice, the lies that were apparent maybe even to him, ("Our love was so strong... everlasting!") who had never known my father, as he gunned the engine through her recitation and we chugged slowly out of the slip, the engines thrusting against the choppy sea, against my mother's delight with everything she saw. As far as she was concerned we were riding past the same sights we'd seen only a few minutes ago, that had loomed in our path for hours, years. As we plowed through the churning whitecaps of the bay, nothing discouraged my mother, though a furious wind kicked foam into our faces, biting and salty, my mother busily retold her strange, backwards history to Clara, as if she had finally succumbed to *her* view, had entered Clara's world where everything was reversed—long became short, hate became love; my mother's voice looped, crazy as a gull in a hungry landscape: "There's the Seaside Bar . . . There's the Lucy Evelyn—a famous ship that wrecked here a hundred years ago—they made a museum of it—Sam used to take us there—he adored stories of the ocean, the dangers . . ." as Clara sat there and nodded as if she believed every single word of it, the rippling of the waves, the billowing of the truth, and my insides began to lurch up and down with the boat as we slid up one hill of water and down another, smacking the bow each time we plummeted from the swell, as we headed towards the inlet, so that I had to grab the rail with both hands to keep from falling, so that the captain yelled at me, "Don't do that! Sit down!" Or was that my mother forcing me backwards into my seat, "Sit down! I have something to tell you . . ." forcing me to listen to her discoveries rushing in like the tide: "I always loved the shore this time of year—so stately, so romantic . . . You can see the boarding house where we rented the first summer after Suzanne was born. It had gingerbread trim all around the porch . . ." And on and on, describing scenes she had imagined—the clam bakes, the games of gin rummy, the miniature golf clubs swung high above our heads from sheer exuberance, "Those were the days . . . We were blessed! . . . We were so lucky . . . Weren't we the happiest people we knew?" until I couldn't take another second of it. "Shut up, Mother!" I heard myself yelling. "Would you PLEASE just shut up? Daddy's gone—don't you get it? He *isn't* coming back—**don't you understand anything?**"

"You're right," my mother said, I don't know how much time later. It might have been just a single minute, it might have been hours according to the way her voice went flat, as if I'd pressed a scorching iron to it, burnt it up like fragile silk. "You're right," she repeated, as if she weren't sure she'd actually said it the first time; she had never said this to me. "I've been trying to tell you all morning . . . I didn't know how to tell you . . ." She put her hands on my shoulders so gently I felt my heart stop for a moment. She stroked my hair so fondly, I felt myself falling backwards into her arms.

That was the moment when I was finally convinced that the acid had kicked in. When I was small I used to dream of being electrocuted, of stumbling onto the subway tracks, onto the rail that hissed and sparked, then ignited a breathless fire up my spine. "What *is* it?" I begged my mother as she pressed a loving kiss onto my cheek. I pretended for as long as I could that I didn't understand what she had to tell me, the whole afternoon, it seemed, as the waves or the water or the panic rose through my body, as the captain cut the engines and handed around the fishing poles, admonishing Clara to keep the rod upright, the tip pointed to the sky. "You have to be able to see them bite," he told her, and he made a demon face, working his jaws so that his whole face wriggled, his tattoos jumped and squirmed. Clara didn't seem to mind this. She let him bait her hook with a real live minnow; she let him stand behind her and hold her arm. She leaned back with him as if they were both going to throw a discus, then stepped forward just as unexpectedly and hurled the line towards the sea. She clapped when it hit the water. At least I thought she clapped. Maybe she couldn't hear the news my mother kept repeating, heard only the dip of the waves, the thundering fish on the end of her line, though my mother repeated it at least twenty times: "He's gone . . . He's gone . . . He's gone . . ." as the captain trudged behind me: "Is she sick? Is she going to pass out? . . . I have medical supplies in the hold . . ." And I said, "No! . . . No! . . ." And then my mother again, "He's gone . . . We've got to accept that . . ." And Clara's line went singing towards the horizon, a thin thread I thought might be holding her in place on the deck, might be holding all three of us from floating off into the ether, or jumping into the sea, from following my mother's words, "I know it must seem like the end of the world . . ." that surged around me like waves. What happened? What happened?

Though of course I knew perfectly well what had happened, what couldn't be explained, not ever, no matter how many times my mother told me, "I'm sorry. I wanted to spare you . . . I don't know what I was thinking . . . I wasn't thinking anything . . ." I could already see what would be there for years to come, what Geoffrey told me later, as consolation? were acid flashes—what a normal person couldn't possibly see or hear, what I had imagined for months was bothering Clara as she rolled back and forth beneath the covers at night in her starless room—moaning, trembling. I could see my mother when she washed up at night, drying her face with the towel, patting it softly upward as if it might break. Smoothing away the wrinkles. Tears. And my father, I could see him as clearly as if he were still up there in New York, mixing himself a gin and tonic, stirring it with a swizzle stick made of red plastic bent like a candy cane, lighting himself a cigarette, then squashing the cigarette out and going over to the window, pressing his forehead against the glass. I could see the two of them standing in the empty streets where they first met, completely empty, and the sand that blew across in patterns that wavered and swirled like snow. And the houses with their shades pulled down and their striped canvas chairs stowed away. The driftwood and the seashells knocking in the surf, though these were miles away. Years away. I could see the room where my parents had first made love when they were young, and conceived me—the bedraggled curtains and the fishing nets, the wallpaper festooned with red and blue anchors, the sandy footprints leading to the bed like clues in a murder mystery.

CONCEPTION

There! At the window! A white face, pleading eyes. A face worn down by sorrow, worn down as smooth as stone. A cameo of sadness adrift in the darkened glass, in sighs that form and frost the windowpane though it is summer out there, a steam-filled, molten night swelled up with lightning and thunder and the heavy gloating rain that clogs the air, with these words that crackle and spark: *Let me in let me in let me in* . . .

I've always believed in ghosts, all kinds of ghosts, not just the ones who seek retribution, but ghosts drawn back to earth for other reasons: they miss their homes or they have a message to deliver or they refuse to stop mourning the living. I've heard of ghosts, as well, as mindless as butterflies. Frivolous souls with time on their hands they flutter here and there still chasing after something pretty—a bit of embroidery or a bracelet, a chip of colored glass, turquoise or amber or green—that's all it takes to bring them back. I've heard of all kinds of ghosts—frightened, desperate, lonely, evil, crazy, of ghosts who came back for no reason at all, for whom the earth is a piece of distant music behind a locked door they can't find. They draw closer, anyway—pursuing, though the music escapes down the hall, across the road, to the edge of a forest where it hovers until it turns into something else.

A bright blur of daffodils, the haunch of a deer, the horrible silence of a touch that's unreturned; no matter what it finally becomes they keep right on following. "Just like the living," somebody once told me. "They don't know when to stop."

It was in Colorado, where I lived for a while, first, with an architect, then with a carpenter, then with a man who tended bar, then back to the carpenter again, (though we both knew it couldn't possibly ever work). Before I moved on I went to see this psychic, an old woman grown huge with her years, with the enormity of souls clamoring to be revived. All day long she sat in an easy chair and spoke to them. Their misty faces swirled around her visitors, a gigantic sea fan of spirits waving back and forth through the dense water of time.

"Time," she informed me, "is very long, but even so, even if it's long and dark and wide, as it must seem to you, my dear, it shouldn't be wasted—you under-

stand?" It was this woman who explained immortality
to me, the blindness that goes beyond the grave, the
attraction that persists even after the flesh melts away,
how live souls draw the dead ones to them and the
dead souls cling like pencil shavings to a magnet until
they're freed, loosened by indifference, occasionally by
joy or miracles. "Some folks have a trail of rainbows
behind them, some have a trail of nightmares." One
day she offered her help. "It's not just a matter of
fate," she explained, as she led me out back, "nor of
intentions."

Behind her toolshed she had dug a compost
heap—ashes, leaves, and grass, bone meal, blood
meal; lodged in the humus—the bright corpses of vegetables, slick with the oils of decay. She made me kneel
beside all of this and bow my head. "Don't be afraid,"
she instructed, "it's only a ceremony." Then she took a
pruning shears and chopped off all of my hair, long
brown tails of it that she threw on top of the mulch.
She clipped me bare as a nun. "When this turns over,"
she promised, "your life will turn over too."

That was many years ago. You were *wrong*, I've
wanted to tell that old woman so many times.

"What have you done to yourself now?" asked
the carpenter when he returned home from work.

"You're crazy," said the next man I stayed with.

"Desperate," said the third.

"Impossible," said the fourth, "Absolutely impossible."

And so said the one after that, and the one after

that one, and the one after that one too. They all said the same thing, just like the carpenter: "Let's forget this whole deal, all right? What do you want from me, anyway—rubies, nirvana?"

Perhaps.

At any rate, here I am many years later, feeling hopeful once again. Expectant. Eager. Dreaming. Ardent. What other choice do I have? I'm trying, tonight, many loves later, here in my bedroom at the top of the stairs, in this mansion, in this state, (the rigid calm before a window shatters), to remain: breathless, yearning, as happy as any other bride to be. Soon, I imagine, I'll walk down these steps, across the swift river of carpet, and into his arms.

Mail-order bride. In an earlier era that's what they might have called me. A woman who travels for love. From house to house, and city to city, across eons, to arrive here, where I wait patiently for an earnest man, determined and lavish—apparently; he promises me a better life, "smooth as the sweep of a breeze across the fields," is what he has vowed. Stable. Serene.

It's true I've never met him. I haven't glimpsed his face, nor heard his voice; I've never felt his breath against my cheek, but so what? Why should these small details stop me? They never have before, that old woman would point out if she were here. And she'd be right, of course. I've always been afraid of knowing the small details: last names, first names, prison records. Insistent anchors, they'll hold you in place and drown you if you're not careful. They can stand,

too, in the way of what you want to be: an arc between two histories, a precise conjunction of words
and touch and leaning.

Besides. I've always believed in a world where
anything might happen. Is that childish? I don't care.
I've believed my way through many more strenuous
situations: through breakups and infidelities, abandon-
ments, fistfights. Once, I was shot in the leg as I ran
down an alley, and, in the mountains, after an opera-
tion, I nearly bled to death. I've also lived in an igloo
amid vast, fibrillating silence—an experiment a friend
and I performed after reading about sensory depriva-
tion. I guess it's really not all that difficult for someone with my experiences to accept a few, extravagant
letters.

Such perfect margins. The creamy white paper. So
what if he wishes to remain head-over-heels but anonymous? "With great sincerity," "Most truly and lov-
ingly yours,"—that's how he signs his messages. I'm
sure he'll show up sooner or later. Why else all these
letters—the ones he slips under my door every night,
that ambush me beneath the pillow and beside the mirror? Granted, in any other situation I might have
grown tired by now of so much mystery, despite the
showers of admiration. I might even have called the
police. But this is no ordinary situation.

Take, for example, this house, itself a strong argument for enchantment. A hall of mirrors. An architec-
tural bacchanal. A place where each corridor is an
endless sigh past rooms filled with wonders—jade and
brass and crystal, whose long-ago curves have projected

their grace into this future. In every corner, in the niches that shadow the walls, on marble pedestals veined with shining ice, the statues rise on their pedestals, pale and splendid, pleasures that have subsided into memory, then hardened into stone, exemplary and fixed as prayers. Though outside it's lush, humid summer and the green woods clatter with birds, in here it's always silent as a portrait, another century, perhaps, another universe.

"Sweetheart! Angel! O, darling, shining marvel! I'll love you, forever, my darling, until the mountains wear down to silt, until diamonds turn back into coal." Why shouldn't I trust him? Each night he promises more and more, to worship and exalt me, to love, cherish and obey, to revere, to glorify, praise, laud, extol. "Our love will be like a prism," he swears, "from every angle refracting into radiance that will dazzle the outlines of our embrace, no matter which way we turn. From every angle we'll be spellbound."

How did he know?

Was it the way I stood one morning and breathed in the lake? Did he see me, during that concert, as the piano and the violins and the flutes strained against the frescoed dome of the hall, close my eyes? Did he notice the way I ran my fingers along the edges of the mirror, the one above the mantle in the living room? Swans. Grapes. Pears. Cornets. Did he follow me to the county fair, past the pavilions and the livestock to the Ferris wheel where I rode, again and again and again, repeating that moment when the earth falls away—far, far below, the relief when your soul leaves your body as you go over the top?

"O perfect urn of my desire . . . O, my desire—embodied, personified . . ."

Never mind all of her warnings: Take your time don't rush now don't go pining after shadows . . . I've decided, as usual, to defy the frank, bland face of common sense, to array myself on this bed. According to his instructions, I've put on this wedding gown of satin and pearls and lace, yards and yards and yards of gauzy cloth in slumbering folds all around me. I've curled my hair and tugged on my gloves, powdered my skin and rouged my cheeks; I've sprayed perfume on my wrists. I've drawn, lightly but deliberately, a veil of blue across each eyelid. "Gossamer blue," as he advised, "the way the notes of a song seem in winter."

Never mind that I don't know who he is or where he lives, how tall, how thin, how dark, how blond, how wise or how insane or why he wants me, I've decided to do as he requests. I've made a garland from ribbons that he described, a green and gold and purple chain "to encircle our love", and I've tied it, as he asked, from bedpost to bedpost. I've also spent hours selecting music—Handel or Haydn? the Bach or the Brahms? and days sewing ruffles along the borders of the spread he told me to make, (a beautiful and billowing taffeta ablaze with peacocks and macaws), and so many more days, then, stitching mottos onto the pillowcases with the silk thread that I untwirled until it became fine enough to slip through the eye of a needle, to announce our future, "Till death do us part."

Never mind that he's tricked me and seduced me and disguised his true identity, eluded me always, I've collected ferns and pine boughs, willow fronds to drape along the floor to make an altar, ("We are gathered here to join . . ."); I've made up my mind to dedicate myself, as he has begged, to polish my nails, my attitude, to sit very still and dream of him, of our first, exacerbated touch, to keep my eyes fixed on the window where the lightning shimmers from tree to tree, to endure this heat, this dizziness, the awful effort it takes, sometimes, just to swing my legs over the side of the bed and sit up, the slow, sickening swoon of this creation that he's forced out of nothing, out of an emptiness so like the first knowledge of endless space.

"There you go making excuses again." If that old woman were here she'd probably frown at me. "You're just fooling yourself, honey. Space *isn't* endless. I know it must seem so to you now," she'd declare, as she did that evening when I came to say goodbye, "but no matter what's happened, you can't fill the space up by running." She'd shake her head if I protested, as I did then, "But he seemed to really mean it. It's not my fault I misunderstood . . ."

Is it?

For weeks these letters have been seeping under my door—extreme and unsigned. They arrive with all the outward hints of a miracle, nestled in envelopes that are bordered with lace, sealed up with wax, a dark red mound where the recent stamp of a flower still hisses a fine trail of smoke into my hand. "I'll love

you always," the writer swears. "I'll give you everything—love more glorious than an opera, love that's
braver than a trumpet!" It will be whatever I want it
to be: the fastest horse, the ripest fruit.

Each night these letters appear, still warm to the
touch. Feverish thoughts. Incendiary, really. He goes
on to speak more fully of these, of the endless perspec-
tives of his passion, of the vanishing point of the mind
swept over the horizon by lust. "I'll take you everywhere," he vows, "to all of the places you've ever
dreamed of."

This is not to say I've never hesitated. More than
once I've told myself this is just some joker, some cruel
person who looked into my eyes and saw, in a brief,
uncharitable glance, enough to tell him everything.

These notes began, after all, the very same night I
arrived here, sweaty, exhausted, from so many
cramped miles on the bus, from the familiar weariness
of leaving, the landscape and everything in it, speeding
backwards into dust. In a cafe near the station I saw
an ad: "Artist's model wanted. Resort location. Room
and board. Perks." It didn't mention the amount of
the salary, but I'd used up all of my money to come
here. I couldn't afford to hold out for a better situation. I was also curious. The man I had just loved had
spent a summer here casting in bronze. He'd spoken
very highly of the aura surrounding the place. "The
vibrations there are in overdrive," was how he'd put it.
"Why don't you take a chance?"

"Hey! Don't look so sad," the man who led me to
my room advised. "There's nothing worse than a

woman who's down in the dumps. Know what I mean? It doesn't translate well to canvas. It doesn't translate well to anything, actually." I wondered if that was what "perks" meant—free advice, free insights. "I'm not so sad," I told him. "I've been through this before."

"Oh, yeah?" He offered to cheer me up anyway. "You look like you could use it," he explained. I wondered if *that* was what "perks" meant.

Or perhaps it meant the fan in my room broadcasting the humid air, or the dinner chitchat about the techniques of transformation and illusion, of unblocking through self-hypnosis, self-massage, the list of places in town that offered peak experiences, (if that's what I was looking for), a good margarita, if my demands weren't quite so high.

"Nothing new here," I thought. I began making plans for my next move, (a job at the racetrack? an archaeological dig?) I figured I'd just take a quick bath before I packed my things. I'd leave in the morning, catch a ride for a while, then hike until I reached a lookout where the hills and valleys opened out with some conviction: Here, here, here, here . . .

I believed I'd really go until I opened the door to my room and found, on my bed, stacked in a pyramid of care, a towel and washcloth, scented soap, (one bar, lime, one bar, sandalwood), even a robe and slippers, just my size, cozy purple, murmuring leather, never worn, (purchased just for me?) until I waded through the dozing hallway, past the draped light of the other bedrooms, past hidden moans and crinklings, (the sounds of doves settling into sleep)—a symmetry of mood that charmed me as I finally sank into a porcelain tub, one with gold knobs and a gold spigot, more golden echoes all around—the chair legs, the handles on the vanity tables, where even my face and my body looked gold, burnished in the glow of the lamps so that I marvelled at myself, at my skin that looked so polished, so content: Could that be me? Could it be here?

Perhaps.

Someone obviously thought so. When I returned to my room the first envelope was waiting there as I opened the door, my first glimpse of that old-fashioned script, as if the writer had studied calligraphy, a design that could carry his love with perfect poise. "Oh, golden, dappled woman," it affirmed. "Oh, dappled, golden dawn of a woman . . ."

If that old woman were here she'd probably cut my hair again. She'd probably say, "Some people are born for trouble." She'd shake her head when I told her, "But I never really intended this." She'd glare at me sitting here in my wedding gown. "Good lord! Don't you know the world isn't a piece of satin? It's not a piece of lace or taffeta or gauze. Neither are *you* for that matter. How could you let this happen again?"

I don't know. I really don't. I only know that I was looking for him.

Each day I tried to figure out who he might be. Among these artists I had come to pose for, (bending when they asked me to bend, stretching when they asked me to stretch, flinging an arm above my head as if I felt exhilarated), which one? I looked for signs of longing—a gaze that adhered; in conversation—significant pauses, the non-sequiturs of desire. Chance meetings. Compliments.

"Nice dress," someone said, and my skin quickened.

"How about a beer?" someone else offered, and I nodded: (What took you so long?)

"Could you please, honey, pass the potatoes?" another suggested, (pleaded, actually); I passed him my hand instead. "What's this?" he smiled and I smiled back. "You should know," I whispered.

"Know what?"

That's how it went. Each day I said to myself: for all I know I may be posing for him right now. That's what I do here—pretend that I'm a vision—sometimes real, sometimes abstract, sometimes beautiful. Who could blame him for getting confused? Or me, for that matter? My work: to stand naked in these makeshift studios, barns converted for the sake of art, wooden cathedrals where the dizzy odor of oil paint and turpentine molders in the heat and makes me drowsy, shaky, as my head fills up with sunlight, with the burning sound of a distant mower whining through the high grass of summer.

"Can't you look more vibrant?" the artist begged. He handed me a towel to wipe the sweat from my belly, from my thighs that were sticking together, from my forehead that shone in a way that was "almost too meaningful" as he complained. "I want you to be just a *shape* in my picture," he reprimanded me. "A *bright* shape, but anonymous, a woman reduced to the concept of a woman, a rose reduced to a simple flower—you understand what I'm saying?"

The towel he gave me was rough, made of coarse cotton so convincing against my skin. I nodded: Of course I understand. I understand everything—women, roses, fantasies. I wasn't at all surprised when he strode towards me to rearrange my hair. He lifted it from my shoulder like something sticky. "Too much texture," he announced, but his hand loitered; his fingers caught my breast. White hot, they traced a path around one nipple, then closed together and dropped swiftly over the curve of my stomach and came to rest between my legs. The artist sighed, as if I were a difficult ski slope he had just traversed. "Does that feel good?" he whispered. "Would you like to take a little break?"

A little break? Is that all he wanted? Still, I forgave him. He had no idea what I'd been imagining. For him, this was just something that had happened. So many things do when the sun is hot and the day is long.

Maybe that's why, on another day, I forgave the sculptor, who, in the moist clench of sunset, exhorted me to—bear down! to sink my arms and legs into the earth, so deep! that soon I'd yearn for air; soon, I'd find myself gasping, please, please! gazing up through the layers of dirt. "*Human* dirt," he emphasized. "None of that spiritual crap, OK? Don't give me that bunch of crap—promise? No more, sweetheart. Look at me. Don't look away. I'm sorry I'm not one of your supermen, but I'm here, you know. I'm alive."

It was true, so I forgave him as I did the librettist who works in a tower in the middle of the lake, the one who asked me to lie with him in the peach orchard beneath his moon-drenched skin. A fine conceit makes a fine time, he said. I forgave, as well, the man who makes collages and the man who works with metal, (stark, steel figures stretched to the point of breaking); also, the man who carves wood. The air was so sultry, the sheets, so smooth, it had been a boring afternoon, we'd been drinking too much—I forgave them all for different reasons. From moment to moment they made time stand still. This touch, that trembling. The blare of radios. The smells of coffee percolating, somewhere, of hay that had just been cut. Bright sprays of flowers decorated the rooms— fireworks, as the sun lit them. Far away shouts sifted through the screens to merge.

Afterwards, there was always a cold beer or a tumbler of scotch. There was the embrace of a borrowed robe, and, often, words so gently spoken they sounded like proposals: "Would you like an orange?" "Have you seen my shoes?"

Forgiving was the easy part.

Each night he switched metaphors. Each night, he sent me another view of love. "It will be blind as the bottom of the ocean. It will be sharp as a splinter of glass, of flint, of ice."

For a while I tried writing back to him. "Why in

the world should I trust you? Would you mind just telling me who you are?" For two weeks I wrote the exact same thing, but he never answered, though I went to great trouble to reassure him. I whispered into the hallway: "I have something for you. Don't be afraid. Look—right there." I put my letters on the precise spot where his usually appeared. I left my door unlocked as a pledge of my confidence in his motives. Then I crawled into bed and forced myself to sleep. Maybe he's horribly shy, I thought. I closed my eyes to show that I understood—an exchange like this could only be made in a dream. Even if he doesn't wake me, I figured.

In the morning I imagined I saw proof of a visitation, in the curl of the sheets around my body, in the sweet hum of dawn outside my window. My heart leaped until I noticed, past the glare of early sunshine, the envelope I'd tried to send, still lying there on the floor, too weak and tired to transmute.

This went on for quite a while. I listened all the time for his footsteps in the hall, though the carpet soaked them up much quicker and more thoroughly than water. Timid? Eccentric? I tried to listen beneath the carpet, beneath what I understood about men. Sometimes I placed my feet on the bare floor as if it were a ouija board that could carry his tremors to me. I hoped these might translate into a foot or a wrist or the sad, longing oval of his face.

I really did everything I could think of. Certainly, I did whatever he asked. I braided my hair and sprayed it golden. I put on a brand new nightgown and stood before the window, first, this angle, then, that one. Bedazzled? I looked for him everywhere.

"Meet me in the library," he'd command.

"Meet me at the fountain."

"Beside the herb garden."

"Behind the kitchen."

Once I waited all night in the boathouse listening to the water slapping against the dock.

Often as I sat and waited I thought about where I was headed. I wondered, to tell the truth, how I'd ever gotten to this point. It wasn't what I'd intended. Of course it wasn't.

When I was small I used to believe the bits of mica that I found were really diamonds. I would walk in the woods for hours prying stones out of the ground, rubbing the soil away on my sleeve. Garnets too, I looked for. And emeralds. Elfs. Leprechauns. Witches.

As I grew older I believed I'd marry, have a family—three daughters: Jessica, Josephine and Christina, good little girls, sweet little girls, designed by intention, with care, and a husband who'd love me with the same precision. I used to imagine we'd lead an orderly life together. We'd live in a comfortable, red brick colonial situated at the end of a cul-de-sac, crisp, patterned paper on the walls, a ceramic deer on the front lawn.

Every year we'd plant a garden. After dinner we'd pore over seed catalogues until we'd decided: snap beans, lettuce, melons, asparagus, zucchini—because that freezes well . . . When the plants came up each girl would have her own row to weed or spray or thin as she saw fit. My husband would measure the growth of the plants each week and record it in a notebook. He'd be a mathematician at the local college, a gentle, careful man who'd spend hours in his study sorting his thoughts out into numbers, adding and subtracting and correlating the world. "You must learn to concentrate," he'd tell his students. "Start with something real, something solid," he'd advise, the way he'd concentrate on me, once our girls were asleep, as if I were the finest concept he'd ever hoped to grasp.

"Our wedding . . . our destined ceremony of joy— let me paint it for you . . ." In silver ink that glints and shifts he described a fairytale: bridesmaids, ushers, satin gowns, velvet suits, a coach drawn by milk-white horses with manes as fine as clouds.

I listened closely to conversations, for some hint of loyalty or infatuation:

"Be cool."

"Back off."

"Don't make more of this than it is."

"Let's just have a nice time, shall we?"

Codes of a romantic nature?

Still, I persisted, through the cocktail parties and the Sunday picnics, the outings to wineries for tasting and toasting, through the thin lines of white powder drawn from tiny mirrors. I even listened to the awful stories the composer told at dinner. Every two minutes he made an innuendo—this baritone he'd once entertained! that coloratura! the wife of a famous concert artist he'd known when he'd lived in Florence, a passionate lady in love with the "gentleman" who tuned her husband's piano. "She used to let him tune her too," the composer laughed. "In the key of C—ha! ha! In the key of *F*." He tapped a rhythm on the table with his knife.

"Oh, that old bit of gossip! Even *I* know that one," the man sitting next to me exclaimed. He rested a hand on my bare arm to make his point, a hand that felt warm and drooping like a lily left too long in the sun. "Temperament," he leaned close to confide. "The usual." And then he added: "That poor woman. Her husband neglected her, that's all. She wasn't really very passionate; just lonely. I knew her well, you see. No one in his wildest dreams would have called her passionate. A little anxious, perhaps. A little tired of waiting. After all, how many hours can you wait for a man to stop practicing?"

Who knows?

Still, I remained faithful. Why not? Who was I, anyway? A map of moments—this touch, that trembling.

The garden.

The conservatory.

I even went to that party, the one where we all tripped, because he begged me to: "Look out your window. Don't you understand? Can't you see? Every road there is leads to our love." I went downstairs to find him. I picked my way through the people who were assembled in the barn, sprawled out in postures of oblivion wherever they'd happened to fall. I searched for a guilty face, but they were too far gone for guilt.

Someone tapped me on the leg. "Have a drink?" he asked. "Have a drink and a mushroom? A mushroom and a drink? Vice versa?" I still can't remember exactly what happened that night, though I've tried, I really have, for almost a month.

A fragmented night, it comes back to me that way—an arm around my waist, a leg jutting out, a chaos of limbs, of caresses. It was a party in honor of one of the painters, that much I know. He'd completed his stay and had invited everyone to a showing of his work—huge canvases awash in color where body parts drifted around like flotsam, the way the sounds and the colors and the people began to drift as soon as I'd eaten the mushrooms, desiccated bits of sponge that left the brown, musty taste of earth on my tongue, that turned the minutes into hours and the hours back into minutes, then whirled them all around.

To keep things moving they passed the wine, little sparkling cups that glittered and flashed. White wine, red wine, wine the color of lust, someone said. The color of an orgasm, someone else said. What? What? The hell color is that? another voice asked. Purple? Magenta? They argued about it for a while: crimson, scarlet, cinnabar, hyacinth, carnelian . . .

"Pthalo green," someone kept insisting. "You know that's my favorite color."

"A confession!" someone cried. "Why don't we play 'confessions'?"

"Consequences," another suggested. "Big, bad consequences—ha, ha, ha."

Sometimes we were constellations. Sometimes we were atoms colliding. We were nucleii dividing and re-joining, clinging, twisting. Sloping bodies, sleeping bodies, bodies that grappled and writhed, that quilted the floor, bright, revolving forms that clasped and un-clasped, crawled and sank, rose and settled, settled and rose, that scattered away, rippled out beyond the re-ceding walls, dissolved through them into the dark and returned, suddenly! reformed, as the ceiling above me, the unending structure of criss-crossed beams I stared at, past the face that rose above me too, vague, featureless, blanked out, inexplicably, by something floating right in front of it—a huge, green apple, a bunch of chrysanthemums. "Look out!" someone shouted, as if there were a car veering towards me. "Look out!" Then there was a vast explosion of light—a camera, maybe? the car? the vehement jarring of my head against the cold, dirt floor?

Tonight, though, is different. Tonight, I'm pre-pared. Organized. Ready.

It's a perfect night for a wedding. It really is. Cool, for a change, and quiet. All the rain has dis-persed, and with the rain, the heat. No lightning or thunder. For once, no aftermath of a party out there on the lawn, no couples kissing beside the fountain, no heads clustered over some drug, marijuana, cocaine, a flask of whiskey, squares of acid, beer, whatever. For once, no music pounding against the trees. No laughter, no plumes of smoke, no glass cracking, no cursing: Hell. Goddamnit. Goddamnit to hell. Goddamnit to hell you son of a bitch . . .

It's completely silent out there. The moon hangs low and full above the landscape, so bright that each outline is succinct: this branch, that leaf, the curlicues of the scrollwork gates. He has to show tonight. It's just so perfect—the weather, the season, the timing, all this rehearsing.

As always, I retrieve my dress from the closet where it hangs next to my other clothes—poor cousins, these flannels and denims; I've had them with me all these years. In the round glow of the candles I remove the plastic covers, unsheathe the dress very slowly, very carefully, so that nothing will run or snag. In the still air these wrappings cling to me, soft and breathless. I have to shake my arms to get them free, make them fall, whispering, to the floor. Then I hold the dress up to the mirror and admire it. The satin and lace shiver like stars in a shattered lake until my head clears, my hands calm down, and I'm able to smooth the cloth, prim and unyielding as it is, against my body. Pale ice that may transform me. Is that really me?

I've even gotten a wedding cake. As beautiful as the dress. Extraordinary, I think. Five whole tiers. Perfect squares that grow smaller and smaller until they reach the top. Icing as deep as snow. Silver bells and glittering forests twirling along the sides.

When I've unwound the foil, I place the cake on a marble pedestal near the window. I adjust the figures that stand in the center of the topmost layer where the canopy of spun sugar rises like a temple. First, the bride. Then, the groom. Straight and solemn, full of their own importance, together, they glisten there.

Candles. Silver. Satin slippers. Lace gloves. Champagne and violets. I've tried to follow all of his instructions. If it's a spell, I don't want to ruin it.

The music box wasn't easy to find. Two county roads over in an antique store in the middle of nowhere, a junk store, actually, one of those places with stacks of chairs for sale, the kind without any seat covers, and bins full of garments that still smell of the attic or the basement, piles of shoes too twisted to fit anyone's feet. I saw it there and reached—a lacquered box, hand-painted with a scene of gazelles leaping through gnarled trees. It plays a tune I don't recognize, high and wistful, over and over.

I've gotten quite skilled with all of these preparations, deft with the buttons on the gown, (one hundred and fifty-five of them including the ones that bind the cuffs), agile with my hairdo, expert at gliding across a wooden floor in these high-heels without scuffing them or falling. He has to show tonight. He just has to.

"No one has to do anything." If that old woman were here that's what she'd say, as she might have said on so many other nights. Then again, she might take an even stronger approach as she did that other time, before I ran away from the carpenter, from the look in his eyes. That was the longest love I ever had—one year from start to finish, an arduous affair that ended in rage and accusations: "That wasn't what I meant, you bitch! What have you done? Goddamnit. What the hell have you gone and done *that* for?" that left me standing by the side of the road not knowing which way to face—north or south or nowhere. An elderly couple in an Airstream stopped. They gave me a ride up into the national park. Though there was really no need to tell them anything, I explained that I was on my way to a retreat, an ashram—to fast and meditate and be silent; I thought that by some trait of age or authority, by a tremor in my voice or the cloud of guilt I was sure must be hovering over my head like a dark angel, they'd know too, what I'd just done— everything: the staring lights and the stirrups and the sinister soothing talk of the nurse: "This will only take a few seconds. You'll feel a little pinch, then some cramping . . . It won't take long, you'll see, it won't take very long it won't hurt very much . . . that didn't hurt very much, now did it?" I spent that night in a campground, bleeding so much I was afraid my insides would turn white, so alert with despair that even the pine needles rustling made me want to scream. Even- tually, I ended up in the hospital, spent two weeks there with a terrible fever dreaming that I was giving birth to corpses and monsters and things that were even odder than that—a burlap sack of potatoes, the lint-covered lining of an old winter coat. When I'd re- covered they told me I'd probably never have children, that I was lucky, myself, just to be alive. "This happens in a small number of cases," they said, as if that were a fact that might comfort me.

"There are no simple answers." If that old woman were here I'm sure that's what she'd say. "You'd better stop and consider, for once," as she did that other time. She grabbed me by the shoulders and pushed me down into a chair. "Now look." She picked up her broom and began sweeping her floor—wide, furious circles that stirred the dust, drummed up clouds of it that settled in other places. She didn't even bother with a dustpan. I got her point but she kept right on going. From sweeping she moved on to the dirty dishes in her sink. Instead of squeezing soap into the water, she picked up a bucket of ashes from her fireplace and scattered handfuls over the plates. "I'll just let them soak," she said.

From dish-washing she moved on to polishing, with a grease-spattered rag, the cutlery. After that, she unmade the bed, upset the trash, smeared oil onto the curtains. "You don't have to ruin your whole house for me," I kept telling her. "You don't have to ruin your health," but she wouldn't stop. "Not yet," she gasped. She hauled an old ironing board from the closet, set it down—thump! on its rickety legs, and threw down a heap of brand new handkerchiefs while the iron stoked. "Watch me now," she cautioned. "Are you still paying attention?"

When the iron was searing hot she lifted it high above her head, "Like this!" then slammed it onto the pile, "Like this!" ground it into the delicate linen until the hiss of smoke announced burns, until all that was left were the jagged, charred layers sticking to the merciless board. "All through," she said brightly.

"All gone." She held out the iron to me.

"You don't have to," she said that night. "Don't even think about it."

Sound advice, so I'll try thinking, instead, that at any moment he'll appear—faithful, honest and true, all night until I can't think it anymore, until, instead, I think, as I did that other night waiting for the carpenter to come home from God knows where and change my mind, about the story they used to tell when I was a teenager, about a hitchhiker, a pregnant woman in a long, cotton skirt, big yellow daisies strewn across the cloth, who carried nothing but the weight of her own body, which was ripe, ready to burst open. She always appeared after dark, they said, at the edge of the woods, like something that had grown there in furious preparation for the arrival of this car. "Where you going?" the driver would ask, and she'd point down the hill past Blue Ridge Summit. "Do you need the hospital?" he'd try again, assuming she was in pain; that's why she wouldn't speak. She'd shake her head, stare out the window. The driver would make conversation in that stumbling South Mountain way: Been here long? You from around here? Don't you think it's a little foolish to be out on this road all alone? In your kind of shape especially . . .

Near the bottom of the hill there was a curve where the road crossed over a river, turned primitive for a stretch, and became a wooden bridge. At this point, no matter how good the driver, no matter how intimate with the gears of his truck or the heft of his automobile, he had to slow down, put both hands on the wheel and keep his eyes on the turn.

When he looked over again, she'd be gone—disappeared into the black water? escaped back into the woods? "She must have jumped out," these drivers used to say. "You have to go just about that slow back there," but they didn't really mean it. They might just as well believe the ghost—a woman could be that mysterious to them, that puzzling.

Eager.

Ardent.

Crazy.

Desperate.

PASSOVER

Sunlight and palm trees. Cancer and heart attacks. Ashes to ashes and dust to dust. From here to eternity she lay in her bed listening to the fleet of sirens complaining in the night.

They are busy—picking up their passengers, wailing at their doors: "Hurry up already, will you? Stop *dawdling* already—will you? Just get your pajamas, pack your toothbrush, say your prayers. You can leave the oven on. Someone else will watch it." They stop at a different house each night, sirens calling, engines grumbling, "Hurry up! We're waiting!" like a car pool to the beach. Every night they stop at someone else's door, (across the street, around the corner, the other side of the canal); attendants, polite and helpful, guide the chosen to the van. But they won't stop here. Not so soon. Not again. Besides—who is there left to take? Shira is too tired, and her mother? her mother would never go willingly; they'd never bring *her* in. Not her. *She* wouldn't rush towards death with arms flung open; she would face it slowly. She would sidle up to it and frown; and maybe, maybe if she found something in the face which she approved of, maybe if she found that Death had been to law school, had manners or knew how to make a girl happy, she would say, "Just a second, please!" and get her shoes.

But for now, they're safe; what more can they lose? Across the dining room, across the kitchen and the darkened living room, her mother lies sleeping. She dreams of Shira's father, dead now two years.

Shira dreams her own dreams of what's missing, of the way things used to be. She dreams the spot where a deer has just run through the woods, the snapped twigs, the branches still quivering.

Her mother wakes under a layer of sweat and disappointment as she reaches out and finds, not a warm body curled in familiar sleep, but the orange cup that goes, "Tok!" against her fingernails, and next to it, two yellow pills—Valium, five milligrams. She takes the pills. She drinks the stale water.

On her side of the house, Shira waits, as she did when she was little and frightened of the dark, as she has many nights since then, for one thin line of morning.

"Why *now*?" her mother asked when Shira called to announce she was coming down to visit for the holiday. "After all this time, suddenly you deign to come see me? Where were you when I was unpacking cartons? When I was lugging furniture and cleaning out closets? Where were you when I was crying every night? Now that all the evidence is gone—"

"The evidence isn't gone and I didn't leave you— *you* left *me*, remember? You sold the house and moved away."

"You blame me for that? I had to move. There wasn't any money. Everything went for the funeral— for the roses and the fancy box, all those gold handles and limousines. You would have thought it was a wedding."

"I don't blame you for anything," Shira said.

"Well, you can't just throw someone in the ground."

"I know, Mother, I know. Look. I just want to come visit you, that's all. I need a rest."

"From *what* I'd like to know! From sitting all day reading a book? From lying around in bed all day with that boy? From *that* you need a rest?"

"I don't lie around all day. I need a rest. I want to see you."

"You couldn't tell me sooner? Two days before you call? When will I clean?"

"Please."

And when Shira got there: "This is what you came for? To sleep twenty-four hours a day? You're a healthy girl. Why should you need so much sleep? Even bears don't hibernate in this season."

"I don't sleep twenty-four hours a day. I go to the pool. I take walks. Besides, I came here for a rest."

"A rest?" Her mother grabs at the phrase like a pin that has fallen into the carpet. "What do you need a rest from? Your life is so strenuous you need a rest? From daydreaming all day you need a rest?"

And: "What happened to you? You used to be so skinny. What happened? All those beautiful clothes you had. They don't fit?"

"I gained weight."

"I have eyes," her mother says.

And: "What degree is it now?" she demands. "Still the M.A.?"

"That's right," she says softly.

"Aren't you going to finish it?"

"I don't know."

"What do you mean you don't know? Who knows if *you* don't know? What kind of a degree is that anyway? Human biology. This is a subject for higher education—birds and bees?"

"I've told you before—it's *not* birds and bees. It's psychology, motivation, chemical processes. Anyway, I wish you'd drop it. I didn't come here to talk about my M.A."

"Then what is it you came here for? To sleep? To eat? How much sleep does a young girl need? How much food?"

"God, Mother. Pete and repeat! That's what you do. Just like that old joke," Shira says. "Pete and repeat were sitting on a fence, Pete fell off and who was left?"

"Fresser!" Her mother frowns. "That's not funny."

Shira shrugs.

Her mother wants her to go out with Molly Goodman's son. A nice boy. An accountant. "Molly says he's very handsome. He has his own condo in Tamarac. Just meet him. Couldn't you just do that?"

No. She can't meet him. "I know what he's like, Mother. *Boring.*"

"How can you say boring? You never met him."

"*Boring.* That's what he is. Polite and boring. He probably carries a handkerchief. His mother irons his shirts—the permapress."

"Miss Know-It-All! You never even met him."

"I *know*," she insists. "A creep!"

Besides, Shira has seen these "nice young men". Every day she goes to the club, sits in a lounge chair and listens to the filter churn, watches the old bodies bob slowly in the antiseptic water. Across the pool sit these "nice young men" with their dark mustaches, their pale, freckled bodies, timid eyes, ivory legs. They wear baggy swimming trunks; they play cards with each other; they coat their noses with Sea & Ski. They talk about cars and dope and lays. These are the nice young men her mother wants her to meet. Well, she doesn't want to meet anyone and besides; they aren't interested in *her*. They want the nurse, the slim one with the red hair who sits and smokes her cigarettes, languidly. Shira watches them, day by day. They spot her, bum a cigarette or some suntan lotion, take a chair nearby, make conversation: who are you visiting? where are you from? On vacation? A nurse? what hospital? what city? . . . as she reclines, one hand resting in the tentative space between her thighs, the other tips the cigarette to her mouth.

And they bend forward, glancing a hand against the girl's white calf as they reach for the oil. They smile indefinitely at the sun. Every day one of them arrives, bums a cigarette, darkens, and leaves, but the girl never changes her position, or her expression, or the station on her little black transistor radio.

And what is there to get excited about in this place after all? What is there to do?

Shira and her mother have just finished playing Scrabble again, are eating ice cream. Her mother spent the last ten minutes searching for a place to use her two remaining letters, 'm' and 't', even though she is at least one hundred points behind. She groans. Bites her lips. Fiddles with a strand of dark hair that has come loose from her bun. But it's no use. The board is closed. Completely closed up. And she looks at Shira accusingly. "The board's all closed up," she says as though it's a house nailed shut for good. And then sighing, asks again, "What's the score?"

Shira says it quietly, because she didn't want to play in the first place, but allowed herself to be persuaded as on other nights out of boredom, out of fatigue, because what else is there to do here, the two of them? because in spite of this, she has robbed her mother of her little pleasure of winning—the curve of her mother's shoulders tells her so. "I'm supposed to know a lot of words," she tries to console her. "It's part of my profession. All those heavy psych texts. If you read as much as I do—"

"You think I don't read? I read plenty. Look at this—"

She pulls a thick paperback from the mahogany bookcase, latches the glass door and places the testimonial volume on the table. "That looks good, Ma," Shira says politely.

"You didn't even look. You think I don't know what a good book is," her mother complains. "You forget I also went to college."

"I never said that," Shira reads the book jacket: *Designing Women: A Tale of Two Loves.* She nods thoughtfully. "Hmmm."

"OK. I know," her mother admits. "It was only for a year, I should have finished. I started something and I should have finished it. I always told you that, didn't I? But who else would have run the business?" she demands. "Who else would have taken care of your father. Answer me *that.* He was a sick man. We weren't rich. And you were always out gallivanting around having fun—living in strange places, using strange words—'groovy', 'uptight', 'solid'—who knew what you were talking about? Your father and I didn't like it, but we didn't say anything." Strands of hair droop from her bun and Shira says nothing. They both listen a minute to the silent house as if her father might chime in, "Who knew what you were saying?

I was a sick man. Why couldn't you speak plain English?"

"Well." Her mother puts the book on a little tray table behind her and stands up. "How about some more ice cream? There's some left, I think." She gets the carton from the refrigerator.

And Shira hears herself say, "Yes, please," even though she isn't hungry, even though the ice cream she has already eaten has swelled inside her to an ache, even though she is thinking she'd like nothing better than to go to sleep or to drive to the ocean in her mother's car, windows down, radio blaring; she'd like nothing better than to find some bar with neon flashing pink palm trees and blue water, a bar with spongy carpets, air so cold it clinks, juke box pounding like surf.

But her mother has already refilled her dish—"Eat quick before it melts!" She has already brought out the album and wet her finger with the tip of her tongue ready to turn the pages.

Here it is again. THE ALBUM. Hundreds of photographs, some with torn edges and yellow splotches of time burned into them, some in little cardboard folders, bright orange, which hold ten shots or more cascading out, all dedicated to, all memories of, the lost Camelot. Shira can't say no to this either. Her mother would say, "What. You didn't like our family? You don't care about it anymore?"

Her mother turns the pages of the album slowly, stopping heavily to consider each picture, groaning like an old bus picking up a new load of sorrow. "Look at this," her mother says. "Here's your cousin Nina at her Sweet Sixteen. Can you believe it?"

No, she admits, it's difficult. Nina in a white dress. Corsage at the wrist, hair in waves as neatly drawn as the curlicued writing beneath: *Nina's Sweet Sixteen Party: 1959.* Smiling. Nina? No, she wouldn't believe it.

Her mother sighs as they both think of Nina as she is now. Her dimples are gone, the hair, frizzy, and instead of the smooth-skinned gently rounded girl, there is a wraith who picks at her face, who dresses in black, who forgets her last sentence.

"Have you seen her lately?" her mother asks.

Shira shakes her head. "You know how she is. Whenever I call she tells me she's living in darkness, that her life is a dark little room with all the shades pulled down."

Her mother stares at the picture sorrowfully. "She's in a bad way, Shira. You should try to help her. She's your cousin."

"I can't stand her."

"Don't say that."

"It's true."

"Don't say it anyway."

She plods wearily on to the next page. Uncle Harry and Aunt Lillian. Look how young! Look how healthy! How Harry doted on her. Lilly of the Valley he used to call her. So many bouquets he used to buy her. He sent four hundred dollars worth of roses one week because she said flowers didn't mean anything, they were just flowers. So she married him. (Harry, Lillian—both dead.)

Next page. Ella and Uncle Joe. The rich side. The wealthy ones in California. "To the edge of the earth, they went. Remember them? They came to visit when you were little."

While her mother speaks, Shira looks past her through the sliding doors at the sprinklers across the street. After ten o'clock and they are still twirling away, whipping water through the stiff sawgrass into the dark. All the gardens are the same here—a hedge, a piece of transplanted lawn, a clump of tropical shrubbery lit with green and blue lights. Somewhere behind each of the screened-in porches people are watching television, snipping recipes from magazines, drinking tea, dozing in chairs. And Shira thinks for the hundredth time how much she would like to just get into her mother's car and roar off into the night, to the beach, to a bar, to anywhere; just to float through the night for a while with the radio on and the windows down and the breeze washing her arms and face clean of sweat.

But she can't borrow the car. "For what?" her mother would say. "It's late." And how could she explain? "I have to go out. I need to get out of here"— the way they used to, she and Tom, way after midnight, the speedometer past 90, roaring along, dragging cornfields and moonlight in their wake.

Her mother is still turning pages, absorbed in ancient history. "There's Kitty and Sarah!" she exclaims as though she has been waiting for them to arrive. "And there's Ada and Harry and all the rest of the group. I remember this," she says.

Shira shakes her head. Why bother? If she objects: "Of course you do! How many times have you looked at these?" her mother will say: "It's human nature to remember." Shira can't argue with that.

Her mother leans closer as if this brings her closer in time. "This was the picnic we had in Atlantic City before the war."

There is the gang. All of them. Sarah. Eli. Golda. Sam. Her mother sways back and forth above the picture, leaning closer and closer. Her fingers caress the page. She sighs. "We always had such fun together."

Shira nods.

"We always had such fun." She broods above the page another minute; then, instead of turning, she flips to the back of the album and slips, from a secret pocket, another picture, yellowed with age, but not tattered like many of the others. The picture is dated 1940 also, and shows her mother riding in a rolling chair on the boardwalk. She wears a white skirt and sailor blouse; her hair curls loosely around her shoulders, and she holds her head, as she still does now, tilted back, as if the expression "looking down one's nose at" had been coined just for her. Beside her sits a short man with a stiff, neat mustache. "Lou Balin," her mother informs her, "not your father."

"I *know*, Ma." She has already seen this picture five times. Every night her mother pulls it out and tells her the story of Lou Balin, of how handsome he was, how he spied on her in the office, found out from one of the other secretaries that she was going to the shore that weekend, how he showed up on the beach on Sunday morning with a bunch of roses and a bottle of perfume and insisted that she let him take her to lunch and dinner and dancing. "I was very popular you know. He liked me very much." Going over and over the details of the story as if, were she only to linger long enough, she would never get to the next page where Shira's father waits, ready to love her too.

"So he took me to this beautiful restaurant right on the boardwalk," her mother continues. "It was an old hotel, the Marlboro-Blenheim, (not so old then, of course). The restaurant was right in the middle between these two buildings like a dining car in a train. He insisted we have the table by the window so I could watch the ocean. Oh, it was really wonderful," she says, but her voice dies down like the tide settling back. "Really romantic."

Shira stares out through the glass at the green and blue spotlights across the street that halt the palms as if they were criminals caught in the act of growing. She would like to ask her mother for the car keys, just for a little while, to go for a short ride, to say, "Why don't we *both* go out and not think about things?" but she doesn't. Her mother would say, "What do *you* have to not think about—that boy?"

As her mother slides the picture towards her ("Here. Take a closer look"), she says, "Yeah, Ma. That's really nice." She stands up. "I'm really sleepy." Crosses to the bedroom.

"Wait!" her mother says, turns the page, and seals her fate once again. "Just look at this. Your father."

"No!"

But, the same as every other night—sirens. The same as every other night—the flashes of red wheeling across the walls. And then, a stillness like shadows steals over the floor. But the lights don't stop. They are twirling through the room. They streak the darkness red.

Shira slides from the bed, pulls aside the curtain. She rolls the heavy glass door open.

They are taking someone away. There is the ambulance parked across the street, light revolving its slow carousel. Its beam becomes red mist in the rain from sprinklers still turning, but there is no sound. Only the light moving, with the whip of the water, past the hedges.

Shira waits for the stillness to subside, for the spell to break, for the van to disappear. She breathes deep, but it remains. She shakes her head, but it remains.

And then, a door opens. A stretcher bound with sheets is carried from the house, one man on either side, a third steadying the bottle of clear liquid. And the breeze that lifts the palm leaves brings a sound. Someone groans.

Ssssshhh, the aide says. He drops the mask. Breath begins. Ssssssshhh. Fiddles with a valve and presses the mask again as the man groans. Ssssssshhhhh. They lift him to the open door, slide him in the vault.

"Wait! Wait for me!" A woman in a pink house-coat comes running from the house, running towards the van with her housecoat flying behind her, night-gown billowing too, running barefoot, carrying a painting as though her house is burning down. "Wait!" she cries. "He brought this all the way from Russia!"

The doors open. Hands reach back for her. They wrap her in grey blankets and pull her in.

They're gone.

"Last night?" her mother asks. "You must have been dreaming."

"I *heard* them. I *saw* them."

"A dream," her mother says. "There was no one. My bedroom is right there and I didn't hear a thing."

It's her mother's opinion Shira should go out somewhere. Not just anywhere. Not alone. "No wonder you're having such dreams. You've been moping around here now for a week." She should go out with Molly Goodman's son the accountant. "A girl your age should be out doing things, not moping around the house. Look!" She pulls aside the drapes. "The sun is shining. Look at that sky!" She beams back as though it is her own creation. Then she scowls at Shira. "You don't even go to the pool anymore. You used to be such a swimmer. What happened to you?"

"I got tired of it."

"You got tired of it." Her mother snatches the words up and deposits them in her satchel of evidence. "Tired. What do you mean you got tired? You haven't done a thing since you came here; that's why you're tired."

And Shira sees that she has made another mistake. She meant only to divert her mother from the purpose of Molly Goodman's son. Now she has fallen back into the quicksand of the old argument.

"I haven't seen you in ages," her mother is saying. "I made all kinds of plans so that you would enjoy yourself here and you don't want to do a thing. Just eat and sleep. You never used to be this way, Shira. It's that boy's fault, isn't it?"

"Quit calling him 'that boy'. His name is Tom and it has nothing to do with him. I had a rough semester and I'm tired and that's all there is to it."

"I don't think you should see him anymore. He's making you fat and tired and unhappy. I don't want you to see him anymore."

"I'm *not* seeing him anymore."

"Well, good. Then come to the pool. I told Molly you'd be there. She's bringing her son."

"Oh, *Mother*," she groans.

But they are sitting in lounge chairs at the pool. The sun beats fiercely against her arms, her face, her thighs.

"A m'chaya," someone says. "This weather—it's a m'chaya, a real pleasure!"

But Shira thinks, it's miserable; utterly miserable. Her arms and legs are stuck to the plastic braiding of the chair. Sweat rolls down her back, accumulates in a sticky river between her legs, but she doesn't get up.

She knows that when she stands; her thighs will cling to each other, two fat Siamese twins; and rub. Her breasts will wobble.

The women in their pleated swimsuits, their flowered caps, they have an excuse. They're old. They cross the pool breaststroke, pulling the water aside like curtains, gently. Some of them merely bob tentatively at the pool's edge, up and down, up and down. Or dangle their legs, splash water on their flesh, sparingly, as if it's a potent drug. Even her mother beside her, skin of wrinkled tissue paper, legs where veins have spread like root systems, whose blood doesn't flow, but seeps, an old woman like these others—husband gone, children grown, life rebutted; and like these others she repeats the daily motions of her life, like an old Hebrew prayer, chanting monotonously, never knowing the meaning.

But they have an excuse, these women; they're old. Shira looks across the pool at the nurse whose slim body, long ivory limbs, accuse her. She's having a field day. Three men. One on either side. One at her feet spreading suntan oil on her calves as though he's icing a cake. They're all trying to talk to her at once as she lies there yawning, stretching her arm out from time to time to donate an ash from her cigarette to the empty soda can the stubby one holds out for her. He looks like a troll crouched at her feet. His voice stands out above the other two who are also hawking their wares. He's great. He knows his stuff. Owns the hippest clothing store in New York. Fancy, he brags. Only name brands. Calvin Klein. Halston. He recites them proudly, like the names of rich relatives.

The girl nods, but doesn't speak. She gazes out over the swimming pool as though it's the ocean. Maybe she sees some tropical island through the spaces in the fence; no stucco, no condominiums; a place where the sun's gold is real, where the young men won't say as these men do: "So what are you into, anyway? What turns you on?" As though hobbies and sex and TV are all equal. Just like Molly Goodman's son, she's sure. She knows the type. No shoulders. Three hairs on the chest. Delicate fingers digging with nervous passion. An aging adolescent.

Where are they anyway? She glances at her mother furtively to see if she has noticed. No. Her mind is elsewhere. She's talking earnestly to the woman on her right, a little gnome with tufts of white hair sticking straight up from her scalp as if someone had said: "Beat rapidly to form stiff peaks." Her lips are painted wide, persimmon red. She gestures sharply as she speaks. "I've been afraid to lift," (her nose pecks the air), "afraid to strain."

Shira's mother clutches Commentary magazine like a prayer book in her lap, and for a moment, Shira thinks they must be discussing religion, metaphysics, or nutrition. Then she realizes she's wrong. It's nothing so rare and bracing. Just the usual—cancer. This woman is another chemotherapy victim. Her hair sticks up like that because it isn't her hair; it's a wig. She doesn't look as if she'll last until next week.

"You're lucky," Shira's mother says. "When I had my first one Shira was only two years old. I couldn't lift her. I couldn't do anything. They only did radicals in those days. It took me years to retrain the muscles. I couldn't wash a window, couldn't hang curtains, couldn't carry my bags from the supermarket."

The woman bobs her head again, pecks. "I know what you mean. I know it too well," she says and begins her own recital of chores left unperformed, things she can't do. Shira checks to see if they're listening, the entourage. No. They're playing a game of Hearts. The tall one nestles behind the nurse. With his arms around her waist as though he is showing her how to swing a golf club, he plays her hand for her.

What if Molly Goodman's son is like that? Opening doors for her, ordering in restaurants, urging her into bed with him? Or worse, what if he's not like that? What if he's little and pale, beard pointed like a candleflame, an intellectual who wants to hold hands, talk about Sartre and cybernetics? Or worse even than that—what if he's handsome? What then? Shira shudders. She wishes she hadn't come; and the woman who has strong-armed her, her mother, is still talking about what she can't lift.

"The vacuum cleaner. Al used to carry for me. The garbage. On Passover—the dishes from the basement to the kitchen and from the kitchen to the basement. See?" She lifts her arm to show the woman the hollow where the muscle used to be. "See? Cut to the bone like a chicken."

The woman flinches, but Shira can see her calculating. How far does the cut extend? How deep an incision? How does it look where the breast has been removed? Worse than hers? Better? Where did they tuck? Where did they sew? Why was Shira's mother lucky enough to recover?

To her right, more losses are going up on the scoreboard. "No," Shira's mother says. "No grandchildren. Not yet." She sighs the sigh of all her Russian ancestors who ever looked into the potato sack and found it empty.

Shira knows what's coming next. She leans forward to get up, but she's too late. "Not married yet?" The woman cast her question, ropes her to the chair.

"No." She tries to smile. "Not yet."

The woman reaches into a plastic sack which is slumped against her chair and digs into a pile of knitting. She pulls out an old wallet bulging with credit cards, receipts from ancient transactions, grandchildren. "Look." A string of photographs in opaque plastic cascades from the wallet. "Kinder," she croons. "Maideles."

Her mother joins the chant. "Oh, Shira look! How beautiful. Shane maideles, aren't they?" She prods Shira with her elbow. "Aren't they?" she repeats.

"Yes, beautiful," Shira says without turning her head to look.

"And *smart*!" The woman's voice rises matching pitch with IQ. "Already in accelerated class, the oldest one."

"Isn't that wonderful, Shira?" her mother prompts.

"Yes, Ma. Wonderful. Children are wonderful."

She is watching the nurse and her entourage watch her. The red hair glints in the sun, bright as zinnias, as the nurse bends her head to whisper. They all look at Shira and laugh. She can feel the beads of sweat between her thighs, between the ripples of her midriff. Is that what makes them bend their heads together, three dark, one red, in collusion?

"Not married yet," the proud grandmother says again as she folds the faces of her "maideles" back into the wallet. "Why not? A nice young girl like you, not married! You don't like boys?"

"I like boys," Shira mumbles hoping that the group across the pool isn't listening, can't read lips. Again they bend their heads together and laugh; but here, on this side of the pool, it's as if she had never spoken. The woman turns to Shira's mother, places a claw confidentially on the armrest. "Such a lovely girl. She doesn't like boys?"

The question burns inside her like a swallow of soup, too hot. She looks at her mother, rolls her eyes, pleading with her to stop the conversation, as her mother searches her bun with slim fingers, nicks a bobby pin back in place. "Of course she does," she says firmly. "She has a boyfriend up north, a composer and musician, don't you, Shira?"

Treachery, Shira thinks, treachery! as the woman exclaims, "A composer! A wonderful profession! Though not a great deal of money in it unless you're a Beethoven or a Mozart. A lovely girl like you, your boyfriend must be a real Mozart, right?"

"I don't think so."

"Shira," her mother warns.

"Well. Maybe you're right. You can never tell."

"And soon," the woman goes on building on this one small ray of hope, "soon you'll marry. Give your mother some nice grandchildren just like mine? She could use a little nachas, you know." She waits to see if Shira knows her lessons.

"Certainly, she'll marry," Shira's mother says, stepping around the question like a ladder she mustn't walk under. Her words are a magic spell to assure the future. "Certainly, she'll marry," she says again, "won't you?"

Shira thinks of Tom, the last in a long line of prospects, loves that were never quite "true loves." Even with Tom, after everything that had happened, they had worked their way backwards into nothing. They had parted politely, subdued, as if they had just met. "Marry?" she says wearily. "Children? I doubt it, Mother. At the rate I'm going, I really and truly doubt it."

"How could you embarrass me like that?" her mother demands.

"It was none of her business. She was being nosy."

"You were being rude," her mother says.

"I was telling the truth."

"Well," her mother sighs, "what *did* happen with him?"

They're washing dishes. Her mother sponges

plates with a sudsy rag as gently as she'd bathe an infant. Shira has a terry towel; wipes steam from the rims haphazardly. She sets the saucers down hard, one on top of the other, clacking.

"Shira!"

"What?"

"I *asked* you."

Shira pretends to think. She wipes a fork carefully, rubbing it and rubbing it dry; then tosses it with a clank into the drawer. "Nothing."

"So." Her mother turns the syllable over slowly. She peers into the soapy water looking for an answer. "So you just got tired of each other?"

"Yes." Shira takes a glass from the dishrack, stuffs the towel inside.

Her mother didn't expect this answer. She plunges her hands deep into the water rumbling cups and china. Her hands erupt with a splash clutching a serving platter that earlier held chicken. She turns it over. Considers. "I think I'll let it soak some more," her voice apologizes. "The Shake 'N Bake gets stuck." But she isn't concerned with the Shake 'N Bake. She's wondering what went wrong. Why is it so hard to ask a question, to get a reasonable answer? "Shira," she says through the running tap water, "can't you tell me the truth? I only want what's good for you."

"I know that, Mother."

"Well?"

"What do you want me to say? I don't *know* what happened. Things don't always turn out for the best."

Her mother turns to her, water flowing from her fingertips, over her wrists, into the satin cuffs of her Sabbath blouse. "Why don't you ever tell me anything anymore?"

"There's nothing to tell."

"There *must* be. I know there's something wrong, I can see how you're acting. I worry about you. About why you're so unhappy. I think the worst." Her mother touches Shira's cheek with her wet hand, leaves tiny soap bubbles. "When you were little you always told. *Tell* me."

But she shakes her head, wipes away the soap. "I can't."

Her mother shuts the spigot. She lowers her voice to match the sudden quiet of the room. "I read a book, Shira. It's called: *How To Fall Out of Love.* Maybe it will help."

"Oh, for God's sake!"

"Well, maybe it will. Why do you have to be so smart?" Her hands hang suspended above the soapy water like fish that took the leap of faith. "Maybe it will," she says. "You'd be surprised at the things that helped me after your father died."

"That's not the same. It wasn't *your* fault he died, he just died. You couldn't help it. And you can't help me. It's too late, OK?"

Her mother's eyebrows rise suddenly. She looks at Shira shrewdly as her hands dive through the soapy water to snare another plate. She asks carefully; she measures the syllables, as if doing so will divide the impact of her question. "You're not pregnant, are you,

Shira? Is that what this is all about—this dragging around? this down in the mouth all the time? Is that what's wrong?" The thought of such a thing frays her voice, unravels all the edges. "You can tell me," she whispers, "I'm your mother. I would help you."

There is steam everywhere, suddenly, and mist on the window. Her mother's round face shimmers. Shira wipes the dish she has just wiped dry. "Please," she says, "stop prying, Mother. I'm *not* pregnant. I swear to you I'm not. I swear to you there's nothing you can help me with. There's nothing to tell."

But her mother, now her mother would tell any stranger her story, any stranger willing to pause a minute, to lift an eyebrow, nod. "I wake up at night, too," she is telling a thickset woman she's trapped on her way to the water. "I wake up at night and reach for him and—nothing." Her hands reach out, grasp air. "Like when you're falling and you grab for a rail that isn't there." Her hands drop.

"Exactly," the woman exclaims. "Exactly!" She nods her head so vigorously her whole body wobbles in assent. She is wearing a pleated suit, kelly green; gold spangles dripping from the hem shake too.

"And the bed is empty," her mother continues embroidering her complaint as carefully as the tablecloth she made for Sabbath, twenty roses in a cluster, blue and gold. "They say you get used to it after time passes. That's what they say—the experts." She waits for the woman to nod again so that she can continue. "What do *they* know? Of course you forget. In the daytime you can't remember how he looked precisely at breakfast or what he would have said at the door when he left, but at night it all comes back to you."

She pauses for a moment to let her complaint sink in, and the woman nods. *She* understands. But the nurse; now she knows nothing about empty beds. She's sitting only two chairs away listening to everything. Someone is rubbing oil on her, on her arms, her calves, her belly. She yawns and stretches in the sun.

"In fact," Shira's mother continues, drawing her train, clackety-clack, clackety-clack, along the rusted roadbed of her grief, "in fact, sometimes I feel like a traitor there's so much I can't remember. I can't remember the jokes he used to make or which year he graduated from high school or what he used to sing in the shower. Did he sing in the shower at all? I can't remember what we did in restaurants; did we talk or watch the other diners? I can't remember which nephew he liked best, or why, which hat he wore to concerts . . ."

The nurse and her companion tense to listen. He stops rubbing; she stops receiving, as her mother gains momentum.

"I forget what aftershave he used, what his nose looked like, what he liked to do on Sunday afternoons. Where did he have moles? Where did the wrinkles first show? I can't remember anything. I could be blind for everything I can't remember; and still I know there were so many things that seemed important when they happened. I know I thought, 'I'll remember this as long as I live', but I can't." Her voice rises. "I can't remember what his office looked like, what he wore at our anniversary party. Did he like baseball more than football or football more than baseball?"

She's practically shouting and the nurse and her companion are watching her as if she's one of those people in the subway who suddenly come up to you and start screaming.

"I don't even remember what he sounded like. Just yesterday, I took the record we made when he went into the army, the record of his farewell party, and I sat and listened to him two full minutes before I recognized his voice, for two full minutes before I said, 'That's my Al!' But at night," she leans forward in the chaise and her voice leaps ahead, rounds the bend of her lament, "at night when I want to sleep, *then* I remember; then I hear everything." She shakes her head.

The nurse rolls her eyes. Her companion smiles back. They hold hands. And Shira wants to say, "Mind your own business. You're the ones who are fools. You're the ones who missed the point. It's true. Everything *does* come back at night, everything you've pushed away in the daytime." Of course she doesn't say this. They would laugh at her too, and roll their eyes. The nurse would stretch her queenly legs, raise a fashioned eyebrow.

"Do you have to yell?" she asks her mother. "Does everyone in the whole world have to know your business?"

The nurse and her friend laugh anyway; they stare anyway at the idiot, and now, the daughter of the idiot.

"Don't be so fresh," her mother says. She lowers her voice.

But not for long. Not long before she's rolling again. "*My* fault?" she asks. "*My* fault you're unhappy? *My* fault you're so rude?" She looks behind her as if there's a bin where she can throw her guilt. "How can you say such a thing? Look how cute you were!" She shuffles the packets of photos as if it were a card trick and whichever one Shira chooses will prove her correct. "Remember this outfit?" She holds up a picture of Shira, age five, in a black satin dress with sleeves of velvet and fur buttons. Her hat is trimmed with white silk roses and tied with an elastic under the chin. "What a beautiful child you were," her mother murmurs. "We had great dreams for you, your father and I. Remember how you could read so young? We thought you'd be a lawyer."

"A lawyer!" She's astounded.

"Yes. A lawyer. We bought those books about Clarence Darrow, remember?"

"A lawyer!"

"*Yes.* Why are you so surprised? You think we didn't dream for you? Look at this." Her hands scramble through the folders. Shira, age five. Shira, age nine. Eleven, twelve, sixteen; it's true. She looks happy in all those photos, her smile, the unfocused smile of a baby. She *was* happy then, she remembers. Life had an order. It was neat and bright like the flower beds they used to plant together, rows of color they measured out with a yardstick: zinnias, marigolds, four-o'clocks, sweet alyssum. Everything came up wild and bushy. They had to thin and separate. They had to transplant. They would go away for the month of August and when they came back they couldn't find a path through all the flowers.

"How is it *my* fault?" her mother asks again. "I'd like to know."

Shira shrugs. What can she say after all? Where can she begin? And yet she knows it must be true; someone must be to blame. She knows that somewhere in the chain of this and that; somewhere in the tangled line of all that has happened, all that has not happened, there must be a moment, a knot she could cut out. Her mind skims the map of memory, but none of it's clear.

"So." Shira's mother presses her advantage. "It's *my* fault you're unhappy. *My* fault you're lazy. Show me how. I never raised you this way."

"I'm not lazy," is all she can think to say. "I'm just tired." She folds her arms across her chest, stares out the window.

But her mother won't let her go. "You won't tell me what's wrong, but I can tell *you* a few things. You don't know what 'tired' is. I'll show you 'tired'." She points across the street. "Mr. Greenstein. And *that's* no dream."

It's true. He's alive after all; at least he's upright. They watch him, a very old man in Bermuda shorts. Bare-legged and trembling he drags the length of plastic hose, bending forward with his burden as though he's pulling the whole house. Every now and then the hose catches on a bush or spiky leaf; and he turns to it, lifts his arms high above his head like Atlas pressing the weight of the world. Then he lets it fall. He pulls a handkerchief from his pocket, and fans his chest. And while he fans he contemplates the hose which he dropped, peering down at it like a river coiled deep below him in the valley. Then he begins the long trek back across the vast desert of lawn. With halting steps, scanning the ground as though each inch holds treachery; mopping his brow, cursing the heat, pleading with heaven. Forty years his arid steps have taken him to cross this lawn. Forty years, his long-suffering shuffle. And for what? In his last days to soak this tiny patch of green, to water palms and croton leaves he may not see next year.

"So," her mother calls her back. "Don't tell me *you're* tired, Miss Know-It-All."

"And furthermore," her mother says, "had it not been for me you wouldn't be here. Had it not been for me, you wouldn't know 'too tired' from 'not too tired'. Had it not been for me, you wouldn't have a life to feel sorry for or the leisure to do it in. Therefore, you can do this one little favor for me and cooperate. Is that so much?"

"I don't want to go out with him. I don't want to meet him!" Her hands scoop walnuts into a bowl. Her mother chops. Spread before them on the table: apples, nuts and cinnamon, wine and honey. Her mother rocks the chopper in the bowl, crunches walnuts against wood, making sweet mortar for the Seder. She chops them fine, pushes a mound of grayish crumbs up the slope. "More," she says.

Shira throws in a handful and then another handful. The blades of the chopper are swift and constant, shaking the glass table as her mother pounds. "Did you hear me?" Shira asks.

"I heard you," her mother says, "but I don't see why you're making such a fuss. There will be lots of other people there. Molly said if we wanted she'd make a little get-together and that way it won't look so planned."

"Oh, sure. It'll look like mere coincidence that he's the only man there with hair. She'll probably make us sit at a card table in the corner—the young people. She's probably bugged him to death about me too. 'A fine young girl! An intelligent girl! A lovely young person!' He probably hates my guts."

"What are you getting so worked up for? You don't have to fall in love with him."

"You bet I don't." Shira waves a walnut in frustration. "Will you please listen? I don't want to meet him. I don't want to go out with him. I don't even want to meet his mother. Or his pocket calculators. You act like he's my last chance."

Her mother sighs. She begins chopping again, pounding the paste in the same spot, over and over. "Why are you being so obstinate? I only want what's best for you, what every parent wants for her child."

"I'm not a child."

"You're certainly acting like one. Worse than a

child. Stubborn unto death. I had an aunt like you. She also thought she was too good for everyone. She had a sharp tongue just like yours, just like a little knife. She knew how to set your teeth on edge as they say." She places her hand on the rim of the bowl and revolves it slowly as she chops, looking for the memory, turning until she finds it. "Not beautiful," she says, "but a great wit. She married late in life, a nice steady man named Herbie, when she finally got it through her head no one could please her; she was too smart ever to be pleased. When I was ten we went to her funeral. She died in childbirth. She was already more than forty when she finally got married, almost forty-five and then she decided God owed it to her to give her a baby. If she couldn't have a man to make her happy, at least she could have a baby. Oh, she had modern ideas too. That's what killed her."

"I don't think I'm too smart," Shira tries to interrupt her. "I'm not like that at all," she protests, but her mother isn't listening; she keeps on chopping.

"Everyone told her not to have a baby, but she wasn't one to listen." She wags her head, remembering this foolishness. Her hands close on the rim of the bowl, to steady her place. "I still remember how her father cried, for this grown woman—more than forty when she passed away; and he sat on the floor in his stocking feet and rocked back and forth, crying. A 'zweigele' he called her. A 'zweigele'—a little branch." She bends her head and stares into the bowl as if the scene is printed there in the paste of walnuts. "We all loved her, my aunt. She made us laugh. But she was too smart for her own good. *We* were the ones who were happy."

Shira tries to decipher what her mother is saying. If she marries too late, she'll die? Even accountants can provide happiness? Life isn't fair so don't be so hard-headed? Shira knows that she's stubborn. Her mother has been telling her so for years. But she's also been telling her for years: "Stubborn is good. Stubborn is what kept me alive through all those operations. Stubborn is how I survived that last time with the chemotherapy." And Shira believed her. She knew that God was a sensible type who must have figured he'd never have a single minute's peace until he agreed to make her well again.

Small wonder, Shira thinks later that afternoon, small wonder the poor aunt died. They probably hounded her to death, her family, with what was best for her. If they were anything like her mother, they never gave up. She's at it again, matchmaking, arranging, working out solutions for Shira's life. "Of course, Molly. I understand. It's tax season." She shouts into the phone, because, as everyone knows, phones are inanimate objects; they can't talk back. Even if they could the effort would be wasted. "Why not bring him over one evening?" her mother is saying. "We're always home. Just for a cup of tea," she adds.

Shira is sitting on the porch reading a book. At least the thumb that holds the page might be reading. The rest of her is sprawled in the lounge chair staring through the screen at the man who is mowing the lawn. He looks a lot like Tom. At least through the screen he does. He isn't handsome. Dark. Lank hair. Heavy-waisted. Heavy in the thighs and shoulders like a man who wrestles alligators. When he leans forward on the mower the white line of his underwear shows above his belt.

As Shira's mother negotiates their future, Shira watches his shoulders heave the mower forward, then rein it back and heave it forward again, pressing his knee against the grip of the wiry grass that sticks in the rusted blades. He bends to pry a clump loose and his haunches rise against the tug of his belt; and when this happens Shira can feel her own haunches tense in sympathy.

Then he straightens again and she straightens too. She feels herself stretch.

She watches him for a while forcing his way through the grass, up one side of the yard and down the other, darkening the lawn where he cuts it in ever-tightening circles. An odd way to cut grass, Shira thinks. Maybe he's bored. Maybe this is his version of proletarian revenge. If her mother catches him she'll scream.

As he closes in on the center of the lawn, huge and darkly proud against the dwindling light, she thinks of a poem she once read for an English class she took back in high school. She doesn't remember the title, something about a mower, but she remembers the refrain, "For Juliana comes and she, what I do to the grass, does to my thoughts and me."

She thinks she understands it now, watching the man as he mows, coming closer and closer, mowing in straight lines now, back and forth, back and forth, grinding up the grass.

He moves forward relentlessly, past the black olive trees and the fan palms, alongside the house and the hibiscus, knocking blossoms down with his shoulder. They drop easily, rain-soaked from the night before. He mows a path beside the porch, deep and clean, wedging the wheels hard against the l-shaped corner where the screens meet, making them rattle. He's so close she can feel his chest heaving when he stops for breath; she can see the devotion in his arms and shoulders when he bends to his work. It's late afternoon and his skin glistens. He is broad and full as a statue. If her mother weren't home, she would speak to him, invite him to come inside for a cold drink. "It's so hot," she would say. "You have no business working in all this heat." They could make love in the guest room, on the taffeta spread, the roses rustling.

She feels a wave of love, then sadness. This will never happen. Nothing like this will ever happen, no matter what her mother says. In the distance she can hear her, stubborn unto death, still pleading into the phone. "So just bring him by. Just for ten minutes, Molly. Just let them get a look at each other. What has he got to lose?"

Shira covers her ears. She stands up and walks to the far side of the porch. She stares across the rooftops at the bleak orange light of sunset and repeats to herself over and over, "For Juliana comes and she, what I do to the grass . . ." but she can still hear her. As the mower turns away towards uncut lands, as he disappears behind the house trailing green, her mother shouts hopefully, the lilt of determination in her voice, "Of course, Molly. Of course! I understand perfectly. I understand so well! Young people are *all* like that! So shy. So reluctant!"

For once she is right. When they arrive at Molly's later that evening, shy Jonathan isn't waiting; in fact, he isn't even there yet.

"He only said he *might* stop by, Rose." Molly offers them a sofa. "It's his busiest season. I told you before. If he finishes the Brownsteins he'll come over." She turns to Shira. "Why don't you sit down?" points to the sofa. Under the halo of the lamp, her hair flashes like a shiny kettle as she settles into a brocade chair.

Everything is gold here: gold sofas, gold chairs, gold drapes, gold around the mirrors. No doubt the toilets are gold too, Shira thinks, as Molly stretches a slender hand to the gold candy dish, offers her a mint. "I'll put the gas on in a minute," she says. "We'll have a cup of tea."

"Oh, no. Don't bother. Don't fuss!" Her mother shakes her head, renounces any claim whatsoever on hospitality. "After all, we just stopped by."

But Molly gets up. "No, no," she insists. "No trouble at all." She goes into the kitchen, skinny legs in high-heeled shoes sticking into the shag of the gold carpet. "Do you like tea, dear?" she calls to Shira as the gas explodes to life with a soft boom.

"Yes, please."

"And cake?" She bends to the refrigerator. "You look like a girl who enjoys a healthy piece of cake." China clinks on metal as she slides a plate from the rack. "Rose?"

"Yes, please," her mother says. She glares at Shira.

"Dear?"

"No thank you." She pulls at the jacket of the white suit her mother has made her wear, Dacron, good for office wear, good for this marriage of unwilling flesh. Wriggling into it Shira broadened the definitions of "stretch", "tug", "fasten", "grip", and "stretch-some-more." The patience of the material astounded her. "It's very flattering," her mother told her. Shira smooths the skirt over her knees, folds her hands there. "I'm not very hungry," she says.

Molly cuts her a piece anyway. "Here," she says. "Just a little. I baked it yesterday myself."

She seats them at the dining room table, removes the crocheted cloth, puts plastic placemats, cups and saucers, white with gold rims, china creamer, china sugar bowl, cheese, jelly, crackers, little gold spoons in everything.

"So," Shira's mother says. "So your son—Jonathan—"

"Jonathan." Molly cradles his name agreeably.

"So, Jonathan—he's very busy?"

"All the time," Molly nods. Her hands agree. They grasp each other comfortably. Her gold rings glitter. "You wouldn't believe how devoted he is—he never stops!"

"Never?" her mother wonders. "When does he sleep?"

Molly laughs as Shira thinks: no, *never.* He writes numbers on the shower curtain; he looks for loopholes while he shaves. She imagines a tiny man worn down by figures—always crouching, always counting.

"I think I'll just go give him a call," Molly says. "He tends to lose track of the time. I'll just see if he's coming. Please, *start,*" she adds. She pushes the plate of cheese and crackers towards them, the jelly and the cake.

In the kitchen she whispers softly, urgently into the phone. She holds it under her arm like a lap dog, cord dragging after her.

Every once in a while, she forgets herself and raises her voice. "They're *waiting,*" she says once. "Do it for *me,* darling," she says a minute later. "I'll never ask another thing. That's my good boy."

Shira pictures Jonathan, on the other end of the line, rolling his eyes, protesting, sighing, giving in. The words sink inside her like stones. "OK," he says. "But just this once, just for a few minutes." "*Great,*" Shira says to her mother. "He didn't even know we were coming."

"Of course he did. She's just reminding him."

"He had *no* idea!"

"Hush!"

No more time for debate, Molly returns from the kitchen bearing another tray with hot water, little packets of tea and instant coffee. "All ready," she says brightly. "Now doesn't this look nice?"

It's lovely, her mother tells her. "You shouldn't have made such a fuss."

"It was my pleasure," Molly says.

Jonathan, when he finally arrives, is nothing like Shira imagined. Not tiny. Not bearded. Not pale or hairless. He doesn't talk of Sartre or cybernetics or cars or lays. In fact he's slender. His eyes are dark, his mustache droops; he won't speak at all.

"What took you so long?" his mother asks. She reaches up to touch his cheek as if to convince herself that this boy, this wonderful boy is real. "Shira has been waiting for you."

He nods, eyes her thoroughly; his mustache droops even further.

"Pleased to meet you, Jonathan!" Shira's mother resounds, trying to fill the disappointment of his appraisal. "I've looked forward so much."

He nods at her too, smooths the ruffled feathers of his mustache, sniffs. "I have a cold," he says at last, his voice flat, hard, like the spatulate fingers of his left hand still stroking his mustache possessively. "I've been working too hard. I'm not really up for a party. So how are ya' doing?" His eyes brush Shira, barely, like the tipping of a bored hat.

"Sit down, Jonathan." His mother indicates the chair beside Shira. "Have a piece of cake."

He sits down reluctantly, temporarily, one leg outstretched as if to run. He isn't hungry either. "Just a
cup of tea," he says. "I'll have to go soon. Get some
rest." He tosses a lump of sugar in the cup his mother
hands him, stirs it hard, lifts the cup and swallows its
contents neat, like whiskey. From time to time he stud-
ies Shira, picking over parts of her as if he's trying to
put her altogether, make some sense of the description
he has gotten, the girl who sits before him.

His mother hands her cake. "And *you*—" she
glints at her. "What do *you* do, dear?"

Shira feels the focus of the question, the hard ring
of the voice, the expectant stare. Jonathan looks at
her, brushes a crumb from his mustache, sniffs again.

"I'm a student," she mumbles. She slides the fork
beneath the piece of cake, wide as a mattress, which
Molly has cut for her.

"A *graduate* student," her mother corrects.

"Ah," Molly says kindly. "Graduate school.
That's very nice. And what is it you study?" she asks.

"Well," Shira says softly. "You've probably never
heard of this field before. It's pretty new," she apologizes. "It's called human biology."

"I've got to admit," Molly says sadly, "I haven't
heard."

Shira tries to explain. It's interdisciplinary; it
combines several different subjects under the same the-
oretical aegis; it relates human chemistry with human
behavior. Beside her, Jonathan wriggles. He flexes his
outstretched leg, plucks at the knee of his pants. Her

mother too grows impatient. "Tell them who you study with, Shira. A famous man," she assures them. "A real celebrity."

"Who?" Molly asks, all gleaming, all hopeful, as if the answer will transform Shira, make her beautiful and good enough for her son.

"You probably haven't heard of him," Shira says. "He's only famous among academic circles, not the general public. His writing is a bit esoteric." *Esoteric.* The word sounds brittle, even as she says it. Pompous. Just the kind of word that would make a man like Jonathan laugh, laugh and tell his friends. She can just see him laughing with the nurse. "*Esoteric,*" he says as his palms part her thighs. "*Esoteric!* she said." They laugh and laugh.

"Not heard?" Her mother's voice grabs her, shakes her, tries to knock sense into her. Don't be such a fresser it says. "A famous man like that—of course they've heard!"

But *she* hasn't heard and *he* couldn't care less. He yawns as Shira's mother prods her again. "Tell Jonathan what he writes."

"Books."

Jonathan cuts himself a piece of cake, drops it onto the plate, begins eating it with his fingers, dropping crumbs onto his vest. He nods. "Interesting."

"Books." Molly rings up the information. "Like Margery Montalto? That kind?"

No. Not like Margery Montalto, Shira tries to explain. Like Freud. Like Adler. Like Jung.

"Jung." Jonathan scoops the last bits of cake into

his mouth. He grooms his mustache, brushing the crumbs back onto the tablecloth. "Jung," she can hear him telling the nurse. "She reads Juunnnng." He nuzzles her neck. "How esoteric!"

"He's a psychologist," her mother explains.

Jonathan yawns.

Shira wishes she could get up and leave. She wishes she could take her mother's car and drive to the beach. Better yet, she could walk. She could step out into the humid Florida night, into the deep enclosure of perfumed air, gardenias, camellias, the smells of sleep and oblivion; she could find an empty road where no one has built yet, where no one will bother her. She will take off her shoes and walk all night until her feet bleed, until she finds a place where she's never been before. She will walk all night.

"More cake?" Molly asks, and Shira hears herself say, "Yes, please, thank you," just to fill the silence, just to fill the empty clink of spoons and cups, the reluctance of Jonathan.

"Don't give me 'tired'! Don't give me 'dreams'!"

It's midnight. They're searching the house for chametz, for crumbs of leavened bread. They're already in their nightgowns, but her mother has tied a white kerchief around her head to indicate that this is a holy occasion. Shira is holding a prayer book. "This is ridiculous," she mutters. "Why do we have to do this?"

"Because it says so." Her mother takes a candle from the drawer and holds it to the gas flame until it sputters gold. Then she snaps off the kitchen light.

"But why at midnight?" Shira asks.

"Because it says so." Candle aloft her mother parts the darkness, bobs into the living room, as her voice washes back. "It's written in the Hagaddah: 'And it came to pass at midnight', so don't give me a hard time, alright?"

Shira follows her, clasping the prayer book like the hot palm of a child she's been forced to watch. "We never did this before," she complains and her mother shakes her head. "We *always* did. You just don't remember."

"We never did. I know we didn't."

"You know wrong," her mother grumbles.

"I *know*."

Her mother whirls towards her; she threatens with her candle. "Will you stop already?"

So now they're creeping through the house with their candle like two frightened women searching for a prowler. The problem is they cleaned today. Her mother vacuumed every inch and Shira followed with the bag of dustcloths, polishing and wiping. "Isn't this clean enough, yet? It looks pretty clean to me."

"Pretty clean is not enough."

They packed the regular dishes in cartons and brought the Passover dishes from the garage, washed each one and dried them all by hand. Then they dismantled the cupboards. They loaded paper bags with crackers and cereals and noodles to give to the neighbors. Then it began all over again—lining the shelves with paper, washing the dusty table linen, taking the tarnish off the tea set. They scrubbed and waxed and swept.

"Where will we find a crumb?" Shira asks. "You didn't leave a molecule untouched."

"We'll find. Don't worry." Her mother shines the candle in a corner, but there is nothing, not even a piece of lint. "It doesn't have to be a crumb," her mother says. "If worst comes to worst, we'll take a cracker from the garage and burn that. Then we can say the prayer: 'May all leaven in my possession which I have not seen or removed be annulled and considered as dust of the earth.' If we can't find anything we'll get a crumb from the garage," she repeats.

"Why bother then?" She pleads for logic.

"Because first you bother, *then* you give up."

So they wander single file through the house like two sisters in a fairytale, looking under bookcases, behind chairs, beneath the piano, in cabinets. "This is ridiculous," Shira mutters again, but her mother ignores her. "Don't be so fresh," she says. Better to keep quiet, Shira thinks. They're getting nowhere. At this rate, dawn will find them in a corner with their burnt out candle stub.

They wander silently, on tiptoe, lighter than air, looking under bookcases, behind chairs, beneath the piano, in cabinets. Every so often her mother thinks she's found something. She swoops down triumphantly, then comes up empty-handed, complaining, "A piece of dust—nothing more." They continue on to the next way station—an end table, a love seat; she ducks again—no crumbs there either; they continue on.

Shira begins to think this is another strange

dream—the silence, the absurdity of their mission, as if when they find the magic crumbs the spell will be broken, all of their sadness will be gone. She stares at her mother who is bending to look behind the sofa, crouched on her hands and knees. How small she seems huddled there in her nightgown, like a child hunting for a lost toy. Her braid has come undone. The nightgown droops empty from her chest; and Shira wants to tell her to get up, the floor is cold, she'll catch a chill. "This is crazy," she says, but her mother has spied something. "I told you we should have vacuumed back here."

She holds the candle close to the sofa, so close the rayon hisses, ducks again, and thrusts one arm beneath the sofa as far as it will reach. Then she starts dusting something towards her grumbling, "What on earth! What *is* this?" She holds the candle nearer. In a moment, her voice rises, apocalyptic. "How did *these* get here?"

Oh no! Shira thinks as her mother plunges her arm into the darkness beneath the sofa and draws out several yellow packets. She holds them gingerly as if they have materialized from another dimension and might be radioactive. "How did these get here? Were you looking at these?"

"I don't know," she says, stalling. How will she explain this?

"What do you mean you don't know? Who else could have been? Look." Her mother holds one up to the candle. "These are your baby pictures. What're they doing here?"

"I don't know," Shira repeats. It's useless to try to explain why she took them from the album late last night after she'd woken again drenched with sweat from her dreams, how she'd looked for a clue in the blurred map of her early features, useless to say, "I thought they'd tell me something." She had stared and stared at the remnants of herself until all the faces looked different, like pictures of lost children who might have been hers.

"So you thought you played a good trick on me?" her mother says. "Don't move the sofa, Mother, you'll hurt yourself. It's not good for your arm, Mother. Well thank you very much for thinking of me. Someday I hope you'll have a daughter who cares as much."

"I *do* care," Shira says, but she knows it's useless.

"Liar," her mother says. "I can see how much you care." She sits down on the sofa, holds up the photographs, then spreads the whole sheaf of them before her on the table like stolen money. Her voice sweeps the room. "Why did you take them?" she demands.

Shira knows she should plead guilty, plead anything; perhaps her mother will still let her off with just a warning—"Be more careful next time!" but she's sick of bargaining. She's sick of being nagged, sick of carrying the dead weight of all she is, all she is not. "I didn't," Shira says. "I did *not* take those pictures."

And now her mother has had it. Her face sags with fury. "How can you lie to me this way? Who else would do it? How would you like it if these were *your* pictures and I dumped them in the trash?" She crouches over the evidence, her nightgown is a V between her thighs.

"For God's sake, Mother! will you cut it out?"

But her mother won't cut it out. "Not a bit of truth, not a word do you tell me that isn't a lie."

"They're only pictures," Shira says, but the argument has slipped away, spread like a blaze that began in one tree, now burns in another. And Shira shakes her head as her mother repeats, "A liar I raised. A liar who can't do anything but stay in bed all day and moan, who wants everyone to run for her, to make things nice so she can stay in bed and moan—'I'm tired! I'm tired!' Well I don't believe for a second you're too tired."

"They're only pictures," Shira insists, still trying to press the quarrel back into neatness. "I didn't hurt them." But her mother cares nothing for neatness now, nothing for excuses. "Only pictures?" She snatches a handful and waves them furiously. "Don't you care about anything?" Don't you care what happens to you? You think everything's a big joke—love, marriage, children; they're all a big joke aren't they?"

"That's right," she says bitterly. "It's a joke. I don't care. That's why I came all the way down here just to see you. That's why I let you drag me to the pool and drag me to Molly's and tell me all day long what's wrong with me. *You're* the one who doesn't care." She points a shaking finger at the litter of faces her mother is holding. "You don't care about *me*, you care about *those*, about everything that's old and rotten, everything that you can't let go."

"Liar." Her mother drops the pictures as if they scorch her fingertips. "Liar." She blows out the candle. Her nightgown crackles as she rises. "Take them then. Be sorry." And as she marches toward the bedroom her back is rigid; the nightgown sticks between her thighs, rubs sparks into the air. "Go right ahead and be miserable—see if I care!" She slams the door.

But she isn't a liar. She simply can't explain. For how can she explain the dream that woke her, the dream that made her take the pictures and throw them behind the couch? How can she tell her mother about something like that? about the ward of pregnant women, all of them ready to give birth that very night, to someone's child, someone's grandchild, someone's 'shane maidele'; how she'd watched them lying full and ready, swelling happily under the white linens groaning with love; how explain why she'd taken the knife that was suddenly in her hand and stabbed them in their bellies, turning water to blood, groans to shrieks. How could she explain that? "You're sick," her mother would say. "You should be ashamed."

And she is sick. Sick and tired. She can feel it everywhere. Her tiredness fills her. Too tired to think. Too tired to protest. Too tired to run through the slow twirl of the sprinkler. Much too tired.

All she has to do is leap through the water to the other side, through the hedge, to the dark canal, and she'll be there; they told her so. They're waiting for her there. All she has to do is leap; all waiting with arms outstretched across the stiffened grass.

It wasn't hard for them. They crossed the lawn like shadows and were gone before she realized. Uncle Harry. Aunt Lillian. Uncle Joe. Her father. No good-byes. No reasons. As if they thought she didn't care enough to know. As if they thought she didn't care about *them* either. They crossed the hedge without saying goodbye, without saying why or where.

And now they've come back to stand here sighing feebly, persistently, like the lapping of the water against the concrete banks of the canal. "Come with us. Why not come with us? Why not? Come on. Give us one good reason. Just one. Just one good reason. One good one." They lift their arms. "Look. We've made it easy for you. We made a path, broke through the hedge. We left our footprints in the grass. You didn't have to do anything, you lazy girl."

It's true. She only has to jump and she'll be there, across the canal where it's quiet and she can rest. No one will ask her questions there. No one will accuse her. They will welcome her with open arms.

They're all standing together in rows beyond the hedge, swaying in unison. And now she sees that they're praying, swaying back and forth in the darkness as though the night is a huge prayer shawl. Swaying and chanting, waiting for her to join them. "All one in the great chain of love. All linked—the generations . . ."

There are hundreds of them, not just her father, her aunts and uncles and cousins, but faces she doesn't recognize, melted beyond recognition, melting backwards beyond time. They're chanting the mourner's prayer, a strange version of the prelude, one she has never heard before. "We are all one in the great chain of love. We are all linked, the generations. We are all magnified and sanctified. All of us together in the great chain of love, amen, amen, amen . . ."

Once more, just once more, she tries to lift, to tear herself from earth, leap weightless through the water, into night, into peace, but she can't move her legs, though they ache with the desire to spring.

"Shira!" Someone is rapping on her door. "Shira! Are you awake? What's wrong?"

She struggles to shift blankets wound around her body. Who wrapped her like that? Who covered her?

"Shira! Open the door! It's *locked*. Why did you lock it?"

Who covered me? She throws off the blankets, stumbles from the bed.

"Shira. Let me in!"

She unlocks the door.

Her mother is standing there, cotton nightgown flattened to her chest, face wrinkled with sleep. Her breath is warm and sour like the bedclothes. "What's wrong?" she asks. "You were crying. I heard you all the way in *my* room. You woke me up."

It's true. She lifts her hand to feel the wetness on her face. Not water from sprinklers. Tears.

"What's wrong?" her mother asks again. She looks at the twisted bedclothes as if they hold the secret of Shira's stubbornness, the shape of her sorrow. "I couldn't sleep," she says. "I heard you crying." She touches Shira's forehead as if for fever, but Shira backs away.

"Who covered me?" she demands. "When?" She shrinks from her mother's sour breath, her crumpled nightgown. "Who covered me?" She retreats from her wrinkled arms, the skinny hand that grasps for her. "It's hot in here. I couldn't breathe." She goes to the window, slides it open hard, so hard the glass rumbles. A hot wind sweeps into the room. "Did *you* put those covers on me?"

But her mother doesn't answer. She sits down on the bed, heavily, without looking behind her, heavily, like an old woman who has been waiting for a seat on a train. "What did I do?" she asks, head in her hands, shoulders hunching forward, dropping tears into the lap of her nightgown. "What did I do? Why do you hate me so?"

And Shira wants to say, "I don't hate you, Mother, I don't!" She wants to say, "It isn't *your* fault, Mother, the way things are. It isn't *my* fault. It doesn't matter whose fault it is." But the words won't come. Her lips won't move.

And still, her mother can't stop weeping. Sadness bends her like a rainstorm. "A little branch!" she cries. "What every parent wants. A little branch— that's all I wanted. I don't care what you've done— you're my daughter. How long do I have to wait?" Tears drop into her lap. Her bare neck is soft and white as powder.

Shira goes to her then. She touches her on the neck where the skin is white like a cat's beneath its fur, touches her on the neck where the skin is wrinkled as a glove, touches the spot of angry red where the hair is pulled too tight as if all the strain of her living has been hidden in that place beneath her hair. She touches the old veins that tremble for her touch. "Oh, Mother!" she says.